Three Round Towers

Three Round Towers

BEVERLEY ELPHICK

Matador
9 Priory Business Park
Kibworth Beauchamp
Leicestershire LE8 0RX, UK
Tel: (+44) 116 279 2299
Fax: (+44) 116 279 2277
Email: books@troubador.co.uk
Web: www.troubador.co.uk/matador

ISBN 978 1783064 205

British Library Cataloguing in Publication Data.
A catalogue record for this book is available from the British Library.

Typeset by Troubador Publishing Ltd

Matador is an imprint of Troubador Publishing Ltd

For Martin, Elle and Alex

Part One

Chapter One

Take a quantity of rushes during the season, and strip off the skin from two sides thereof, leaving the pith bare. These, being quite dry, dip them in melted grease repeatedly, and a good light for all purposes of a family may therefore be obtained.

MacKenzie's Five Thousand Receipts in All the Useful and Domestic Arts

When Becca arrived at Coad Farm my life changed for the better. I was a Coad by name but that brought me no advantage. The missus had taken me in when I was left destitute after the great sickness took my mother, father and younger brother. I was that grateful to be given a room and board in exchange for some light housework, I thought I was the luckiest of survivors. My lipsy leg prevented me from doing the heavy work but Missus Coad made sure she benefited from her charity. I cleaned, scoured and scalded all the pans and kept the fires burning from dawn to bedtime. When I wasn't seen to be doing those things she got me mending. The cleaning was hard and painful on my leg and feet but I was paid a small wage and not dependent on the parish poor fund.

Becca brought sunshine into the house. I swear the rain would fly before her; she radiated good nature and warmth. We shared a cot up in the attic and were far enough away from the missus and her three sly boys to be able to giggle, swap stories and do our hair together. Becca had beautiful hair, a bright corn colour and long – right down to her bottom. She always kept it plaited and sometimes looped the plaits into a big bun on her neck; when it was twisted up it looked much darker in colour. I learnt how to do it for her and she helped me make mine less unruly. My hair was wiry but with her quick fingers and a few pins she managed to make it look quite pretty. She had a comb, she said she stole it from her father's new wife. How we laughed when she described the way she had outwitted her stepmother – a come-to-God convert who swore against all adornment but hid her fancy comb away from disapproving eyes. When the comb disappeared, she'd been unable to openly blame Becca, but she knew who had it and it wasn't long before Becca was pushed out of the family home into a position as the missus' scullery maid. We didn't care, Becca had the comb and we had each other. I had never had a friend before.

Coad Farm was a darkly damp place set between two branches of the river Ouse in the tiny village of Hamsey. The nearby church was fortunate enough to have been built on higher ground. The Reverend Skillen serviced our small community with tales of hellfire – we thought that he arrived with a bear on his shoulders. He would threaten us all with dire happenings if we did not obey the Church's teachings; we had to attend services twice on Sundays and we quaked in our boots if he looked our way. Missus Coad liked to think that she was the principal person in our village and it soured her day when the Reverend rebuffed all her offers of hospitality; every Sunday we prepared a feast and by the time he declined she would be in a foul mood.

Becca usually managed to get a few bites of meat from the

family's leftovers and hid them in her pockets. She nearly got caught when the master brought his dogs in one bitter night, they made straight for Becca and were sniffing all around her. Fortunately, the missus decided she couldn't abide his stinking dogs in her newly swept kitchen and she threw them out into the night. They at least had warm hay to burrow into; the ill-fitting window in our attic room was frequently frosted hard on the inside. Yet, in the summer, the heat could be suffocating.

Becca thought herself to be thirteen years old, her mother having died of the bloody flux two years before. Her father had set about improving his lot almost immediately and soon began courting and married the widow Skarrow of Lewes, a town to the south of Hamsey.

The widow had two small daughters and complained that Becca was too big a lump to be hanging about at home when she could be set to work in service and put some much needed wages into the family pot.

I, Esther Coad, was much older than Becca at twenty-one and likely to be a spinster for the rest of my life, I had no illusions about myself, pockmarked, lame and plain, that was me. My family had some education and I was happy to read to Becca from my few books. I pretended to the missus that I was as uneducated as her sons; it wouldn't do for her to think I was putting on airs and graces. The Coads had been related to my father through several distant cousins but, as I said before, I dared not be seen to claim any advantage. She told me when I first arrived that I was to be a maid of all work and help her look after the three boys and their father, the master.

Becca arrived at the farm in the spring – the land was wet

and in flood more often than not but the lush grass provided good grazing for the beasts. During the flood they were moved up to the churchyard, which was on higher ground. The Reverend was happy with this arrangement as he didn't have to pay to have the grass scythed. In church he called all the animals dumb beasts and I didn't know whether he meant that they weren't able to speak or that they were stupid. I thought they were more sensible than we humans, finding their way to the higher ground before ever the rain began to fall.

Missus had three boys – Jacob, Josiah and Job and before Becca arrived they treated me sly. Jacob, the eldest, was mean as a bull and would deliberately trip me up just to laugh at my clumsy attempts to get back up. Joseph and Job laughed fit to burst when my efforts were knocked back again and again with the bull stick. Becca, for all her slight frame, soon sorted them out and I know the boys grew to be wary of her, she was a clever girl and saucy with it. The master laughed when she made fun of the boys; they didn't like it.

The year marched on and it was the happiest of my recent life. The farm was settled and the missus didn't hound us, she even smiled occasionally. On Midsummer's day she gave us both a half day's holiday so that we could go to the fair at Lewes. We asked the stockman if we could go down river in the master's small boat with him and, he agreed as long as we returned within four hours before the tide got out of sorts. We were not to be late or he would leave without us and we agreed with much giggling and excitement as we helped each other onto the tiny craft. The Ouse was a big sullen stretch of water with a fearsome reputation; at times it looked so quiet and placid but it had a great pull under the surface. There was only one bridge nearby and that was at Lewes, the river eventually made its way down to the sea and often the sea made its way up the river to add to the floods. For all its deep grey waters it was bountiful, with fish and fowl aplenty and many a family looked to it as a source of food. Its banks could be treacherous but fishermen were a canny lot and knew the river's ways; we wouldn't want to get stuck in Lewes and have to negotiate the walk home.

On Midsummer's day there is a hiring fair and tents to buy potions for every ill – the evil eye, love spells and drops to blight a rival in love. There were even pots of lotion to make skin heal from the pox scars. I persuaded Becca that this lotion was going to help me get a beautiful skin. We paid a half penny for this foul smelling ointment and I couldn't wait to get home to try it. We wandered round the fairground and Becca saw her father with his new wife and girls – she handed over her wages obediently when her stepmother demanded. I knew she had kept a bit back so I didn't dare look above everybody's feet in case I betrayed her. I expect they thought I was witless.

As soon as we could we escaped to the tent where you could find tinkers' finery. Becca bought a beautiful length of material, which she draped over her shoulders. It suited her bright shining hair, which she had carefully washed in nettle water for this special day. It was the first time she had worn her hair loose in all the time I had known her and it was a sight to see it ripple down her back. She told me it had never ever been cut, I looked at her in awe: she was young, pretty and happy as we linked arms and paraded round the fairground and stalls. I couldn't help but notice that people turned and watched us as we passed and one gentleman doffed his cap, Becca giggled and we hurried on.

The master and his sons were in the beer tent whilst the missus made her purchases. We went in to get a cordial and as I paid I saw the whole family staring at us or, as I later realised, at Becca. When the missus saw us she was cross and made her tie her hair up. We had a wonderful afternoon and met some friendly people that Becca knew; they all joined in the races and games put on for young people. I couldn't join in but they made me welcome and I didn't mind.

Things were never to be the same after that fateful Midsummer's day. The missus took to watching us and found fault with Becca at every opportunity and the boys, particularly Jacob, followed her every move with their mean little eyes. I warned her to stay out of their way but she just laughed and said, 'I can handle them.'

On the night of Becca's fourteenth birthday we served supper to the family. It was a light meal of meat pasty served with vegetables followed by some milk pudding. As I stepped forward to clear the table the master pushed his chair out and spoke. He rarely spoke and I stopped in my tracks. He was looking at Becca.

'Get your basket girl,' he said. 'You can come and help me with the chickens.'

I dropped my fork in astonishment as Becca followed him out into the night.

The missus jumped up from the table and slapped it violently with the flat of her hand but master had gone and the door slammed. The boys were muttering to each other whilst casting sidelong looks at their mother; she silenced them with a look. They all sat there until their father came back – he was gone for some time.

Eventually, I was dismissed and I flew up the stairs to our little attic room. Becca was crumpled on the floor and sobbing piteously. He had taken her hair out of its knot and played with it she said before forcing himself on her in the hay.

How the tables had turned, now it was my turn to comfort the poor child and I held her shivering body in my arms through the whole of the night. I tried to soothe her bruises with the cream I had bought at the fair, I even begged the missus for some of her lavender water. She hissed at me, 'You want me to treat his whore? She's a slut and I won't help him in his wenching.'

Month after month he took her out to the barn to help him with the chickens, telling her to wear her pretty wrap and loosen her hair; each time she cringed away, each time he raped her.

One night when Becca was back in our room I crept down the backstairs to get her some chicken broth. The boys were huddled together whispering – they didn't see me but I heard Jacob's reedy voice telling his brothers that his father shouldn't be having all the fun and threatening to tup the slut at the first opportunity. Horrified, I kept myself hidden until I heard them leaving. I took a ladle of broth and made my way as quietly as I could up the stairs. I tried not to spill a drop as my uneven steps made me extra clumsy and my hands were shaking like giant leaves. I told Becca what I had heard and her eyes dulled with pain; she gripped my hand and whispered that she knew their intentions from the way they looked at her.

No one had ever told me precisely what men did to women but I lived on a farm and guessed the way of it. When Becca began to fill out I guessed she was with child, and, by combining our knowledge, when, roughly it was due. As her belly filled she picked up her spirits and I thought things would be all right; the missus was bound to take the child as her own and no one would dare say otherwise; an extra pair of hands round the farm would benefit them, especially as they wouldn't need paying.

Becca stopped going to the church because she felt everyone looking at her and the Reverend's sermons were spat from the pulpit directly at us, or so it seemed. Missus no longer invited him to sup, nor anyone else for that matter. The atmosphere at the farm was frightening and we crept around not daring to look above anyone's feet.

One of our many tasks around the house was to make rush lights and thus save on the cost of candles. It was a simple task involving picking the rushes from the riverside and dipping them in tallow; Becca seemed to like this job so I left her to it. It was easy, soothing work and I got on with the heavier scullery pans. One day I was surprised to find a pile of the dipped rushes up in our room, they were hidden – pushed behind the bed. As her time progressed she began to fashion the waxed strips into a little basket. I watched dubiously, I couldn't see a baby being put in a waxed box for a cradle. I held my tongue, as she seemed quite content.

One stormy night when the river was riding high I heard the missus talking angrily to the master. I heard her scream at him that she would not bring up his whore's bastard, nor would she let it stay in the house. She didn't want them both out, Becca was too valuable a worker for that; she just wanted the child gone as soon as it was born. Becca's baby would suffer the fate of many bastard children – drowned or suffocated at birth, anything to preserve the family honour.

Becca seemed oblivious to the emotions raging round her, she dreamed her way through each day and fortunately the master stopped calling her out. The boys were not so bad that they would force a pregnant girl but we knew that the minute the child was born it would all start again. I went over and over in my mind what we could do to escape and make a new life elsewhere but I knew that no village would take us in to be a burden on the parish. The women would hound us and the men would be no different from what we had here. All I knew was that wherever Becca went I would go with her. The more I worried the less Becca seemed to notice; she did her work in a dream and her eyes and mind focused inwards. The little cradle she had made was finished and hidden under our cot; I tried to get her to talk but she just smiled her gentle smile and cradled her arms round her belly which looked fit to burst.

Early one evening we were in the scullery scrubbing the pots when she wet herself. I looked at her in horror, 'Becca – what is it – is it time?' I did not know that babies were carried in the womb within a sac of water, which would burst just before birth.

The missus was in there like a shot and she grabbed Becca by the arm yanking her out into the yard. I heard her hiss 'Get rid of it! Don't dare come back until it's gone.' She came back into the house, her face contorted with rage. Slamming the door she threw the bolts. 'You, get upstairs and stay there.' She pushed me and I fled, terrified. I curled up on our bed as I heard her tramping up behind me. She dragged the door shut and bolted it on the outside. I was trapped and Becca was alone. The baby was coming and she was all alone.

Chapter Two

And there went a man of the house of Levi, and took to wife a daughter of Levi. And the woman conceived, and bare a son: and when she saw him that he was a goodly child, she hid him three months. And when she could not longer hide him, she took for him an ark of bulrushes, and daubed it with slime and with pitch, and put the child therein; and she laid it in the flags by the river's brink.

Exodus ii, 1-10.

Becca

The air was dense and wet as I picked myself up from the cobbles and I heard the heavy bolts slide shut. I made my way along the wall towards the church, my progress was slow and I ended up crawling on my hands and knees. I had made plans, I wasn't unprepared; the rush basket was hidden in the reeds. The river was murmuring quietly, reassuring and the sounds of the evening calmed me. There was no pain, just pressure on my back, I knew what was to come and I dragged myself up, I knew where the great key was and had taken it after Sunday service. If the baby had not arrived I was going to put it back and take it again, until my time.

The night was deep and still as I shut and locked the church door from the inside. At last I felt safe as I was in the house of God: He would protect my baby. I had hidden some hay under the altar cloth and I pulled it out and bunched it behind one of the pews, one that was a long way from the altar and the crucifix. I sat waiting as bands of tightness swept my belly. I prayed, gripped the rails, prayed and must have passed out. When I woke it was dark; I knew my baby would come soon. I braced my knees against the pew and when the pain ripped through me I pushed and pushed. I had taken a strip of hard leather from the horses' tack to bite down on and I pushed some more. No one would hear my cries – St Peter's was very old and its walls were thicker than the span of six hands.

The pressure in my back was forcing my baby down and my insides felt as if they were tearing apart as it came. I tasted the blood in my mouth and must have passed out again as when I woke I could see a bloody pile between my legs on the hay. I pulled myself upright, wiping the little body with clean hay and saw that I had a daughter. A tiny little sigh came from her mouth as I squeezed her awake. She cried, a thin wail, which rose into a lusty cry as I cradled her into my body after I had cut her loose from me. My eyes streamed, as I was overcome with love for her. We lay on the hay together, I suckled her to my breast and thanked God for her safe deliverance.

A pale light was creeping through the windows signalling the approach of dawn; it was time to go. I cradled my sweet babe into my wrap, the one and only bright thing I possessed, and placed her carefully on the altar. I scraped the bloody mess up and unlocked the door before burying everything deep under a bush. I crept back to the altar, got down onto my torn knees and asked for help in what I had to do. I knew my prayers would be answered – hadn't God spoken to me? Master read the bible to us every Sunday and hadn't he told the story of Moses when I was praying for guidance? Yes, my prayers had been answered; all I had to do was take my babe to the river and give her up to the tide and a better future. I had made her cradle myself and it would be found by the time it got to Lewes, by far the busiest place around. She would be gathered up and given to a wet-nurse and later perhaps to a barren woman who would love her for me.

The sun was peeping through the clouds and I thought I heard someone whisper my name, I looked round but it was only the wind sighing in the rushes; they and the river were calling me and I hurried to where I had hidden the basket. I laid her inside it, kissing her little fingers as they caught at me. The water crept round my ankles, then my knees as we moved deeper. I had woven a bulrush to the head of the basket like a flag. I straightened it carefully, making it stand proud and then I let her go. The little craft bobbed and swirled at first then picked up speed as it got into the current and moved slowly downstream. She was gone, beyond my care and reach; I stood and watched until my eyes filled and I could no longer see through my tears. I was stiff with cold but I had one last thing to do. I unbound my plaits and pulled the comb from my pocket before tugging it through my hair until it was soft and beautiful. I waded back to the bank of the river and left the comb for Esther to find when she came looking for me.

Moving slowly now, my legs refusing to lift, my skirts billowed out as I went towards the centre of the fast moving water. I lay down in the water on my back and felt my hair float around me. I was washed clean and I closed my eyes giving myself to the river and God in exchange for the life of my baby.

Chapter Three

Esther

The missus let me out of our room to tend the fire and as soon as I could I left the house to search for Becca. I looked through all the outhouses and anywhere that there might be some shelter. I was bewildered by the silence that greeted me, even the birds were quiet. Eventually I went to the church, the door was unlocked and the key was on the inside. I felt immediately that she had been there and I soon found evidence of her birthing deep in the body of the nave; anxiety rippled through me and a tear tracked down my cheek as I stumbled from the door locking it and returning the key to the barn where it was normally kept.

'Stupid, stupid girl,' I whispered to myself as the implication of the wax cradle came to me. Becca must have hidden her baby in the bulrushes and she was probably looking for me so that we could all run away together. Spurred on by this likely thought I hurried along the path towards the river as I searched for any sign of her presence and came at last upon her precious comb.

'Oh Becca,' I cried, 'what have you done?' I thrashed up and down the bank searching, searching until at last I found her trapped in the reeds. Her face looked peaceful though her poor, limp body was shrouded by her hair. Somehow, I dragged her from the water before I began my search for the cradle. I might never have found it but for a tiny plaintiff cry somewhere to my right. I pushed my way through the shallows, deep into the reed beds until, at last, I came upon the cradle. The babe lay in her basket swathed in Becca's wrap with no more than a little dampness to show for her ordeal.

The sun was high in the sky before I had dried myself and laid the poor little scrap down on the sun-warmed bank. I had made my plan: my path was clear. I would return to the farm without the child in case the missus vented her anger on it. I would seek out the master and tell him that Becca had died and it was his responsibility, as was the welfare of the babe. I would remind him that his behaviour would bring down retribution from his neighbours and the Reverend Skillen; I would force him to give me money, enough to enable me to leave this wicked place and raise the child as my own in some village away from Hamsey. If I had money I might be welcomed into some hamlet, particularly if I sought out kindly relatives of my mother's kin. She had told me that she had family in a village called Southease, way downriver. With money I would pretend to be a widow and my looks and disabilities would not bring jealousy in my wake. I was clear in my mind that this was the way forward, now I just had to put it into practice. I tucked the baby, now back in her cradle, between two tussocks of grass, being careful to draw the long vegetation across her face so that no one should hear her if she cried. I wouldn't be long; I blew her a kiss.

The house was silent when I entered and I went straight up to our room to fetch my belongings. Missus was in the kitchen, angrily muttering to herself and slamming pots and pans around. The boys were nowhere to be seen. I found the master in the big barn surrounded by his dogs who growled menacingly as I entered. He silenced the dogs and looked warily at me as I grabbed the nearest beam and forced myself towards him.

'Becca?' he said.

'Drowned,' I croaked, not mentioning the child.

He nodded and dropped his head into his hands. For a moment I thought he was weeping but when he looked up all I could see was relief in his piggy eyes. My anger at his callousness gave me the courage to go on.

'You must have her buried,' I said. 'A good, decent funeral and you must give me some money so that I can leave here and never have to tell the Reverend Skillen what I know.' He nodded, thankful, no doubt, to be given a way out of the mess. I was surprised that he didn't argue, perhaps there was a grain of humanity in him after all.

'The child?' he looked back at me from the door.

'A girl,' I said. 'She needs feeding.' He nodded and went out of the barn shutting the door behind him.

I left Coad Farm on the master's wagon. He drove me himself so that no one else need be involved in this sorry tale. The cart carried our few belongings, goat's milk for the child and in my purse I had all my savings and the few pounds left to me after my parents died.

I asked to be dropped off in Lewes where I would find Becca's father and tell him there had been a terrible accident. I would not mention the babe. Then, I would travel downriver to seek lodgings for myself before I tried to find my mother's family. Overnight I became a young widow with a child. I had plenty of time to create a new history for us.

Chapter Four

I wanted to call the babe after her mother but as I jolted along in the cart I thought it better not to draw attention to us both, particularly if someone raised questions on the manner of Becca's death. My name was common so I had no fears there but Esther and Rebecca together would link us to Hamsey and the half dozen families who would remember us.

All the jolting had lulled the little one into a peaceful dose. There were traces of milk round her rosebud mouth so I was sure that she had been nursed before being placed into the rush-cradle. Even so, she would need feeding very soon and all I had was some cold goat's milk. I could see the master looking at me and the child out of the corner of his eye and as we approached the town walls just below the church and castle, he spoke.

'You mun keep quiet 'bout all this. I could be had up by the Justice for what I done, tho' I shall say that she led me on with her wicked ways.'

'You're a devil and your whole family are wicked through and through but I will keep your secret, as long as you give me enough money to set us up. My papa told me about men like you having to pay bastardy bonds – well, give me the same amount and I won't be telling on you. I heard talk of one such – he had to pay fifty guineas – and that is what I want.' I swallowed hard as the bile rose in my throat, amazed at my daring.

He grunted and nodded to the purse which lay between us, 'Don't ye ever come back this way again,' he threatened, 'or I will see you put in the market gaol as having murdered young Becca in order to steal her babe.' He spat the words at me defiantly, spittle collecting at the corners of his mouth before hawking over the side of the cart.

I tried not to show my fear but my stomach rolled in panic as I wondered if he could do such a thing and people believe him. He pulled the horse up under some great trees and I scrambled out clutching the babe and purse in one hand as I yanked our box of belongings with the other. Tears of relief washed over me as he clicked his tongue to the docile old horse, never once looking at his child or me. He was good with his animals but not, it would seem, his own kind.

I sat on my box and hid the purse inside my clothing before gathering the baby into my chest and tying my shawl tightly round her and my back. I now had two hands free to carry my belongings comfortably. I moved purposefully up the hill towards the gallows mound, stopping some lads to ask the way to Becca's stepmother's home. As I approached their small cottage I saw her father coming towards me. He looked up with a glint of recognition.

I blurted out, all my calm reasoning forgotten, 'Becca is dead, Master Coad is taking care of the burying.' I swallowed before rushing on, 'You must help me find a lodging place for tonight and a wet-nurse.' The poor man looked so shocked with my bald statement, I had given him no explanation or reason for his daughter's death.

He pulled me away from the front of the house before hissing, 'Is the child hers?'

'Yes, but no one must know that. You must keep her a secret, please,' I begged.

He glanced back towards the cottage, nodding. 'Aye, 'twon't do no good to tell on ye. Becca were a goodly lass and I know'd she were fond of thee. Go down Keere Street and there be a widow Makepiece near the bottom; she lets out rooms on occasion. She might know where there be a wet-nurse. She's a good woman – say I sent you. Say Ben Franklin sent you.'

I turned away, but he pulled me back urgently. 'Did he do this? Coad, I mean.'

I nodded, tears filling my eyes, 'She had the child and put herself in the river. I will bring the babe up as my own, I will say I am a widow. I have some money and no one need know.'

He looked troubled as he said, 'these things have a habit of getting out girl, 'tis not easy to hide a death and a birthing. One or t'other maybe, but both?' He shook his head. 'Where will you go?' He reached out and touched the child's face as she burped a fat contented sigh.

'My mother had kin nearby, perhaps, a little ways downstream towards Southease, I hope I can find them and they take me in for a while.'

He drew his hand across his eyes 'God be with you girl, and I thank 'ee for all the help you gave my Becca. I'm sorry I can't take you in but my wife won't be having it and it would cause too much trouble for ye and the babe. What be her name?'

'Beth,' I whispered as the name just came to me. 'Short for Elizabeth.'

'Becca would have liked that,' he nodded. 'Good luck, Esther, you are going to need it, I will try and help where I can.' He turned away and I watched him walk towards his home, he looked smaller somehow. He turned and waved and though the light wasn't good I thought I saw tears on his lined cheek. There was a light in the window and it looked comfortable and safe. How I wished we had somewhere or someone to welcome us.

Night was clipping the overhanging trees as I skirted the main streets and instinctively crept through the passages and twittens towards Keere Street. I felt cold and lonely as I hurried along, not raising my eyes to anyone. As I struggled down the slippery cobbles of Keere Street the babe began to whimper. At last I stopped outside a tiny well-kept cottage on the steepest part of the hill. I knocked tentatively, and, as the door opened I was struck dumb – I hadn't prepared myself for what I would say.

'Um, can you help me, us – have you lodgings for the night Mistress? I am sorely pressed and my baby is needing her feed.' I gabbled, 'I can pay you.'

She drew her chin into her neck as if questioning my right to have a baby at all but I gathered my wits and pulled myself up tall and firm. 'A man up town suggested you were a good kind woman who let rooms out betimes. His name is Ben Franklin.'

She raised an eyebrow but I felt her warm a little. 'Aye, I do that, if people take my fancy I can let them abide a-whiles.'

I relaxed and smiled encouragingly, 'I have no one else to turn to and the night draws in. I could go to the alehouses but I would worry for the babe.'

She was shocked, 'Oh, no, my lovey, you can't take a baby there, landsakes, 'twouldn't do. Come you in and we will see what you's made of.' She led me into a tiny sitting room with a warm jolly fire quickly dispelling my anxiety. I unwrapped the scarf that bound Beth to me and Missus Makepiece took her into her arms. 'Tch, tch, you're a bonny babe but your ma looks a bit too frail to be carting you round the town.' She looked at me as I sank exhausted and uninvited into a deep chair placed by the grate.

'I can pay for our lodgings until I find my mother's kin. Please can we stay?'

'Aye, lass you can stay. Now, what about summat warming for you and the babe?' I reached into my box and pulled out the goat's milk. I held it out to her for warming. I had no idea how to give it, I had no bottles or teats but I needn't have worried my kind hostess dripped the drops from her little finger into Beth's waiting mouth.

'She don't like it much, do she?'

She didn't ask why I wasn't able to feed her myself.

Mrs Makepiece shared her rich meaty soup with me and for the first time that day I began to warm. I could see her looking at my worker's hands and the clumsy way I tried to hold Beth.

'Your first be it?'

'Aye, my husband was a fisherman and he died in an accident some months gone,' I lied. She just looked at me and nodded.

'Well, I've brought up three strapping lads and they've all gone out into the world to make their way so I am glad of your company child.'

'D'you know of a wet-nurse for hire hereabouts? I have been unwell and have no milk to give the babe.'

'You could go to the workhouse and ask,' she said. I think little Beth will take the milk if we put some honey in it and you look a mite weary lass, why not rest up tonight and we will try and find someone tomorrow.' I blinked back grateful tears as Mrs Makepiece showed me to a small but comfortable room. It had a deep chest in one corner and we made a little nest for Beth inside it. I sank into the bed and fell into a fitful sleep.

I kept waking, listening for Beth's tiny breaths and snuffles. I couldn't escape the sight of Becca's poor, limp body lying amongst the reeds in the dirty cold grey water. My tears soaked the sheets that held me in a deathly shroud as I struggled to escape from drowning. The night was so very long and my leg ached badly and the child needed more of the goat's milk and honey – I couldn't sleep without dreaming so stayed awake and watched the dawn break quietly as the same painful thoughts kept running through my mind. How would I manage, would people believe me? Mrs Makepiece clearly hadn't in spite of her kindness. Would I be taken by the Justices as a vagrant or a tramper? Would I have to go into the workhouse? If Becca's story came out would I have to give up my little Beth? When I left Coad Farm it had all seemed so simple – just put as much distance as possible between us and them. I hadn't given a thought to the Justices or the the constable. If my as yet unknown family didn't want me I would never be able to settle down. My little pile of money would not go far. I got up and opened the bag the master had given me. I'd asked for fifty guineas, so I wept as I counted out only thirty-five pounds. I was so bitter that I spent the next few hours plotting my revenge before realising that I wouldn't be able to stand against him or his family; I would have to be a bit cleverer.

There was a knock on the door as Mrs Makepiece

brought a bowl with some hot water and clean rags. 'I'm thinking you will want to wash the little mite and give her a bit of a clean, like. I've made some thin gruel with the milk and a spot of honey, it will keep her happy while you take care of your business,' she said kindly. 'I've a mind to look out some of my boys' baby clothes – I was keeping them for any grandchildren but I don't reckon they're coming yet awhile.' Tears streamed down my face as I thanked her. She didn't ask any questions just took over the washing and tidying. As she worked she talked to little Beth who was trying to grasp my finger.

Chapter Five

The workhouse was a dark, foreboding building with lots of little square windows facing onto the busy street. I stood opposite watching for a few minutes. I determined that I would speak firmly, not cry, and I would make them think I was a young woman of respectable habit. I thought of my poor pa and ma – they were respectable folk before they died. Pa was an apothecary's assistant and knew so much more about life than most who came knocking on our door – even the quality. He could read and write and had taught my ma her letters when they first met.

After they died I wished I'd asked them about their young lives but I never had. We were so busy in our little home over the shop, we lived in the present not the past. Ma did all her own baking and making and we sold quite a lot of produce with the creams and unguents that pa made up. We had a garden out back and we grew herbs as well as some foodstuff. I shook myself out of my reverie. I had problems enough now without looking backwards.

I banged on the door. A slovenly woman appeared, wiping her hands on a dirty cloth.

'Aye?'

'I'm here to see the overseer, can you direct me?' My voice sounded high and unnatural but I faced her bold look down.

'He's out back,' she jabbed her thumb in the direction of the yard.

'Thank you.'

A well-built man shambled into sight, his shoulders stooped over an enormous belly.

'Are you in charge?'

'Aye, what can I do for 'ee?'

'I've urgent need of a wet-nurse. Have you anyone suitable here?'

He scratched his heavily-veined and bulbous nose with a dirty finger nail. 'Well, not 'ere but Mary-Jane Turvey was taken on by Missus Elwood, out at Southover and I heard that the baby 'twere born dead, like.'

I looked at his dirty clothes, 'Is she clean?'

'Aye, she is now m'dear otherwise she wouldn't have been let in,' he laughed. 'But she weren't before that. We had to shave her head to get rid of the crawlers.'

I gasped, but wasn't too surprised. 'Can you direct me please, my need is urgent.'

He looked at me carefully, speculating. 'Who sent you here missus, where you from?'

I could feel my knees quake. 'Missus Makepiece, of Keere Street.'

'Oh aye,' he seemed to make up his mind at her name. 'I'll send a young lad to shows you the way then.'

He shouted at the woman who'd opened the door, 'Alice! Call Billy-alone.'

A skinny boy trotted round the corner, pulling up in front of me but keeping his eyes to the ground.

'Take this young… um… lady to South Farm and then come straight back, mind you, no hanging about.' The overseer cuffed the boy round the side of his head as he spoke.

I thanked him and followed the lad.

Chapter Six

Billy-alone skipped in front of me, waiting impatiently when I couldn't keep up.

'Wait,' I gasped. 'I can't go so fast'

'Wa's s'matter with 'ee foot?'

'There's naught wrong with my foot. It's my leg, I was born with it crooked like.'

'Do it hurt?'

I fell into his way of speaking as I replied, 'aye, it do betimes, usually when I have been stood awhiles.'

He grunted and slowed into step with me.

'What do you want with them at South Farm?'

'I need a wet-nurse for my baby.'

'Wa's a wet-nurse?'

'Someone who can feed the babe for me. Do you know the family there?'

'No, but I heared that t'missus was a bit younger than Farmer Elwood, she be quality too.'

We struggled along the rutted track, he keeping pace with me, for which I was grateful.

'Why do they call you Billy-alone?' I asked curiously.

'Me ma and sisters was all took with the pox and I was left all alone – Billy-alone, see?'

'Do you live at the workhouse then?'

'Na, I live all over,' he said airily 'but I help out sometimes when the old man wants errands run. He's too fat and lazy to run around. I get me food and sometimes a bed – depends how full they are. I don' want to live in one place, they thinks they owns you. I'm alright as I am.' He looked sideways at me and grinned. 'Where d'you live?'

I told him I was lodging with Missus Makepiece until I could find my family and then, suddenly we rounded a bend in the lane and South Farm came into sight. I turned to Billy and thanked him for showing me the way.

'I'll wait for ye.'

'You mustn't get into trouble for me.'

'I's me own man. I'll wait.'

I smiled. 'See you awhiles then.'

I walked up the track towards an orchard. I could see the upper floors of an imposing house. A brick pathway channelled me towards the front door but as I followed it I heard a noise – I thought it was a sob so I turned aside into a small, enclosed garden. A young woman was standing staring into a well. She was sobbing piteously and jumped as she saw me approach.

'Who are you?'

'I'm sorry to intrude ma'am but I am sorely in need of help and I understand you have a young woman here – a wet-nurse?'

The young woman burst into a fresh bout of sobbing; she wailed and I reached for her. 'Hush, hush, what is it, can I help? Let me help you.'

'No one can help me' she sobbed. 'My baby died in my arms, she was so little. I can't bear it, I want to die too. I was going to throw myself down the well but I didn't have the courage.'

I held her tight, hoping to calm her down. She was very

hot and flushed. 'Is there anyone here with you?' I asked. 'You need to be resting. When?'

'Yesterday,' she whispered.

'Come, let's get you inside… hold on to me, just a little way.'

I thumped on the door whilst trying to hold the girl up.

'Help!' I called, but there was no response from inside the gloomy building.

'Can we get in round the back?' I queried.

'Yes, they will be in the pot room and probably can't hear. My husband's gone for the doctor.'

I couldn't understand how anyone could leave such a young girl alone after birthing but she said she had slipped out to get cool and no one had missed her. We stumbled to a stable door at the back of the house where a group of servants looked up as we made our way inside.

I raised my voice, 'I need cool water and towels, quickly!'

They stared at me open-mouthed. One said, 'Who are you?'

'Never mind who I am; your mistress needs help, now.'

'Where is your room?' I asked the girl.

A coarse featured woman pushed in front of me. 'I'll take her.'

'No, show me where it is, hurry, and bring the water and towels.'

Eventually, we got the girl onto her bed and I stripped her nightwear off her. She was burning hot and I washed her down as gently as I could with the cooling water.

Gradually, she calmed and allowed me to soothe her face with a wet flannel.

'Have you some cordial, something sweet, perhaps with

honey?' I asked the women who were now crowding into the room.

'Aye, Cilla, go fetch the blackcurrant cordial,' the woman who seemed to be in charge instructed a girl who was trying to peer round the door.

I hadn't forgotten my purpose in coming to this house and addressing myself to the woman I asked if the wet-nurse was nearby.

'I sent her out to bring the vegetables from the kitchen garden. What do you want with she? She'm no help to the missus.'

'I came here to ask if I can make use of her services for my baby as I heard that her charge had died.' I turned away from young Mrs Elwood as I said this, not wanting to cause her further distress.

'My master has contracted her to stay for a month.' The woman's manner was surly. 'She will be used in the kitchens for that time.'

She clearly resented my presence and I realised I wasn't going to get any other response from her. I turned back to the bed and continued swabbing the young girl and holding the drink to her lips.

She clung to me and whispered 'Do you have a baby?'

'Yes, a little girl, she is only a day old and I have no milk to give her.'

'Where is she?'

'I have left her with Missus Makepiece in Keere Street. She is feeding her with goat's milk and honey.'

At that moment I heard heavy running footsteps and a large florid man charged into the room closely followed by someone I took to be the physician who spoke loudly. For a little man he had a large voice: 'Stand aside, stand aside, let me see my patient.'

We all fell back.

'What has happened here?' shouted Farmer Elwood, clearly distressed. 'Who the devil are you?'

The unfriendly housekeeper barged in front of me and I tripped, falling on to the edge of the bed. My young charge held onto my hand and gripped me tighter. 'John, she helped me. I wanted to die, I went to the well and came over all faint. She fetched me back and helped me. Oh, John, my baby… Where is she? Can I see her again, before it's too late?'

The poor man knelt down on the floor at her side and wept. 'She is downstairs my darling. We will bury her soon, probably tomorrow, you can see her anytime you like.'

Mrs Elwood looked at me. 'What is your name?' She touched my face gently as she asked.

'Esther, my name is Esther.'

'John, Esther needs the wet-nurse, we must help her with her little girl – she is only a day old. My baby has died but we must help this one live. John, I want this, you must help.'

The doctor nodded discretely to the farmer. He looked at me saying, 'sensible young lady you are, getting her temperature down, dangerous fever after childbirth, can be fatal.'

The farmer rounded on the servants who were still clustered round the door. 'And where were you when your mistress needed you? Gossiping, I bet. Aye I've seen you all supping in the kitchen when you should be doing your work. Get out, all of you, get out.'

They all scurried away, except the housekeeper, who

tilted her head up and asked what instructions the doctor had for her to help Madam.

'He'll give you no instructions Mrs Fisher – you will not be needed in this room. Get back to the kitchen and see about a good light meal for my lady – and her – what's your name girl?'

'Esther, sir.'

I am indebted to you Esther, these fools couldn't be trusted to care for my girl, I was only gone an hour.' He covered his face with his big strong hands and began to shake.

'John,' the doctor placed his hand on the farmer's shoulder. 'The immediate danger is passed, but your wife needs to be kept calm and peaceful. A gentle light diet,' he patted the girl's hand. 'Plenty of time for you to have others m'dear.'

The poor young woman buried her face in the pillow sobbing piteously. I could have cried with her at his bluntness but it wasn't unkindly said. The farmer turned to his wife and said as gently as a man ever could, 'what if we ask Esther and her baby to stay here with you? She can look after you and get you back to fitness and the baby can suckle with the wet-nurse. Have you family Esther, could you stay with us for a while 'til my lady recovers?'

I gasped 'But master, you know nothing about me, I am that grateful but I only have one person who can speak for me: Missus Makepiece.'

'I have seen enough girl, you were a Godsend to me and mine this day. Stay with us and care for my girl. Besides, if Mrs Makepiece has the care of your child now it is as good as a character reference.'

Chapter Seven

Puerperal fever commonly begins with a rigor or chilliness on the first, second, or third day after delivery, followed by a violent pain and soreness over the belly. There is much thirst; pain in the head, chiefly in the forehead and parts about the eyebrows; a flushing in the face; anxiety; a hot dry skin; quick and weak pulse, though sometimes it will resist the finger pretty strongly; a shortness in breathing; high coloured urine, and a suppression of the natural discharge. Sometimes a vomiting and purging attend from the first, but, in general, in the beginning, the belly is costive: however, when the disease proves fatal, a diarrhoea generally supervenes, and the stools at last involuntary. The case of this fever has been commonly ascribed either to a suppression of the natural discharge, an inflammation in the womb or a retention of the milk.

MacKenzie's Five Thousand Receipts in All the Useful and Domestic Arts

I can't tell you what a surge of relief I felt – my troubles were over for the time being and my baby would thrive with a regular supply of food. I knew I could help Mrs Elwood, she was but a child herself and she wanted for nothing but a bit of love and tender care.

As the doctor took his leave he turned to me and asked curiously, 'where did you learn to lower the temperature girl? Most people think it best to sweat out the bad humors.'

'My pa, sir, he was an apothecary's assistant and he had his own views on how to treat people.'

'Your pa was a sensible man, Esther, and you are a sensible young lady.' He left the room with Farmer Elwood.

The young woman, Mrs Elwood, tugged at my hand. 'Esther, send for your baby now, we must get her fed.'

'I must get her myself,' I said. 'Then I can explain. There is a young boy with me – I will send him on ahead to tell Missus Makepiece to expect me.'

'No, no, tell Mrs Fisher to have the trap brought round. You must hurry, your baby needs you.' She began to cry again, but gently now, her body not wracked by the sobbing.

'I will be as quick as maybe, don't fret. Try and drink some more cordial, I will be back soon.'

Chapter Eight

'Well, Esther, my girl I wasn't expecting you to come home by carriage!'

I laughed and for the first time in two days had the sense that things were easing. 'How has Beth been, is she feeding?'

'Well enough to get by but we need the wet-nurse girl, did you find one?'

'Aye, I did that and I am to move into South Farm for the next month where she is fixed.'

'Landsakes lass, how did that come about?'

After I had explained Mrs Makepiece threw her pinny over her face and laughed until tears came. ''Ee I am that sorry for the poor lass but you couldn't have made a better bargain if you'd tried. And, as for that Mrs Fisher, she has got such airs and graces you'd think she was quality herself instead of a plain cook who 'as taken her mistress's status to herself.'

I ran upstairs and threw my belongings back into their box before flinging my arms round my good friend. 'I can't thank you enough for what you have done for me – can we come back to visit when we are settled?'

'I will depend on it Esther, and you can come back and stay if things don't work out.'

I climbed back into the trap with the baby cradled in my arms.

Chapter Nine

A receipt for nourishment: Boil in three pints of water, till half wasted, one ounce each, of eringo root, pearl-barley, sago, and rice; strain, and put a table-spoonful of the mixture into a coffee cup of boiling milk so as to render it of the consistence of cream. Sweeten with loaf or Lisbon sugar according to taste.

MacKenzie's Five Thousand Receipts in All the Useful and Domestic Arts

As we set off for South Farm, Billy-alone ran alongside the trap. 'Can I see the lass, Esther, can I see her?'

I asked our driver to stop a moment. He tipped his cap with a whip and called 'whoa' to the horse. Billy jumped up beside me and we set off again.

''Ee she's bonny ain't she? Not much like you though.'

Beth opened her eyes and looked at us before burping loudly.

'When you are out and about miss, I'll come and help you look for your ma's people. I know lots of places downriver; you'll need someone experienced to guide you.'

He was so cheery and hopeful I had to smile and say yes.

As he jumped off the trap he waved and shouted, 'I'll come and see how you get on.'

He'd called me miss. I hadn't corrected him.

I was shown to the room next to young Mrs Elwood. It

was beautiful, with tall glazed windows and lovely heavy drapes. There was a single high bed with a pretty yellow counterpane and a mirror with a little table and chair in front of it.

A cradle had been put next to the bed and I lost no time in settling Beth in it. As I stood gazing round me in awe there was a light tap on the door.

A small, timid-looking girl peered into the room.

'I's Mary-Jane missus. You be needing me for the baby.'

I gestured for her to come in and sit down.

'Where is your own baby, Mary-Jane?'

'He be down in the kitchen missus. He'm a lot older than this little tacker but I carry on feeding him so as I can earn some money nursin'.'

'I don't know much about your job Mary but I would be grateful if you would wash yourself before you feed Beth.'

She looked at me askance. 'But I 'ad a wash last month. And I don't know what you do mean about me job ma'am, I's just a wet-nurse.'

I soaked a piece of flannel in a prettily decorated pitcher and feeling a bit embarrassed I left the room while she undid her bodice. When I came back a few moments later the baby was latched greedily onto her generous breast.

'She'm 'appy now missus.'

'Aye, and so am I. Thank heavens for you Mary-Jane. I'll leave you now and go and see how Mrs Elwood is getting on.'

Mrs Elwood was looking much more relaxed though very pale. A tray of food, meats, sweet things and fruit lay at her bedside but she didn't appear to have eaten anything. I picked up some fruit and put it into her hand gently.

'How are you now ma'am, shall we try some of these?'

'I don't want anything Esther, but your baby, is she feeding?'

'Aye, she is that, and very happily too. Mary-Jane seems to have lots of experience.'

'She has that, certainly, I've heard said that she has too much experience but it is to our favour. Esther, may I hold little Beth when she has finished, just for a minute?'

'Of, course you can ma'am, if it wasn't for you I don't know where we would be.'

'My name is Cecilia, will you call me that?'

'If you wish, but first, before I bring Beth in I think we need to eat a little something. I'm that hungry and you need to get your strength back – if only to be able to sit up and hold her properly.'

For the first time I saw a little smile. She was such a pretty thing and her name suited her perfectly – I tried it.

'Cecilia. What a beautiful name.'

'It runs in our family, my grandmother was Cecilia. What was your grandmother's name?'

I had no answer for I didn't know.

To avoid the question I pretended I heard a cough next door and went to see how the feed was going. Beth was detached and looking content in Mary Jane's arms.

'I think she'm done missus, she be falling asleep.'

I picked her up and sniffed her wonderful contented smell. 'Wait here Mary-Jane, I'll just let Missus Elwood hold her awhiles before we change her.'

'Aye missus. I've got the clouts and I can shows you how I do it in case you have to change her in the night.'

I nodded my thanks and took Beth through to Cecilia, placing her gently in her waiting arms.

I found my way downstairs to the pot room and asked the girl, Cilla, for some small ale to take upstairs.

'I'll take it up for you miss. Is it for Mary-Jane? She be that fond of the ale.'

'Yes, all that feeding needs replacing.'

'Beg pardon miss, can I get you something else?'

'No, I'm fine, I am just going to sit with Missus Elwood awhiles.'

'The master likes his supper at six miss, will you be joining him?'

Mrs Fisher appeared, scowling. 'Of course she won't Cilla, she can have a tray in her room,' she said scornfully before adding, 'or she can come down here with the other servants.'

'That will be perfect,' I replied, and tried to muster some dignity as I made for the stairs.

Cecilia was dozing with Beth at her side. I carried her into Mary-Jane and between us we changed and settled her in the cradle. Exhausted from the events of recent days, I collapsed on the bed.

I must have dozed for some time as it was dusk when I awoke. Beth was awake and crowing. I carried her into Cecilia and we lay on the huge bed laughing at the baby's expressions. Every now and then I tried to tempt Cecilia with some cordial or sweetmeat but she took little. The light was fading rapidly and Cilla came in to light the candles. 'Mrs Fisher do want to know if you could eat a bit of fish for your supper?'

Cecilia grimaced and I laughed at her funny face.

'Perhaps you could ask for just a little egg custard with some cream,' I suggested. 'Fish tomorrow, maybe.'

'Aye miss, I'll go and see.'

It was a strange night, my first at South Farm. I was so tired, even having had an afternoon nap, I could hardly think of anything other than trying to get food into both Beth and Cecilia. I know Farmer Elwood came up and sat with his wife for a long time; he had called me in and asked to see Beth. I took him to the cradle, which was undoubtedly meant for his own baby and he gently stroked her forehead. 'I am glad to have you in my house Esther, you will be company for my wife. I hope your baby thrives.'

He looked so sad as I wished him goodnight. Mary-Jane came up before the household retired and it was quite late by the time I clambered into the wonderful soft bed. I tried to think back over the events of the last three days. So much had happened but I still kept seeing Becca in my mind. She must have believed her baby would be safe otherwise she wouldn't have done what she did. I tried to picture the Coad family – what would they be doing now, saying now? Would the master have arranged a decent funeral for Becca? Was she already in the ground? I realised I had little idea of the way of things. I would have to learn fast if I was to keep our child safe. I had seen Mrs Fisher looking at me suspiciously out of the corner of her eye. I am sure she didn't believe I was the mother of a newborn.

Chapter Ten

Cleanliness and Bathing
The child's skin is to be kept perfectly clean by washing its limbs morning and evening, and likewise its neck and ears; beginning with warm water, till by degrees he will not only bear, but like to be washed with cold. After a month if he has no cough, fever nor eruption, the bath should be colder and colder, and gradually it may be used as it comes from the fountain.
MacKenzie's Five Thousand Receipts in All the Useful and Domestic Arts

The next few days passed dreamily, I was in a joy of comfort and warmth, such as I had never experienced before. Beth, when she wasn't swaddled tight, would wriggle and punch the air. I had to resist telling Mary-Jane to leave her to kick; after all, she was a lot more experienced than I. Beth loved the milk she got from the wet-nurse and I only had to call her during the night and she would appear from the kitchen region of the great house and Beth would latch on to her greedily. I became quite adept at keeping her dry and clean and felt myself to be her mother.

Cecilia was visited again by the doctor who told me to watch for signs of puerperal fever and milk fever both of which can lay a weak mother low; at no time did he recollect that I was supposedly a new mother too and liable to such conditions.

I remembered my pa going to help some of the poorer people who came to the apothecary's shop. They had not the money to pay for medicines but he said that a few basic things could improve their lot if they did just know it.

I looked in my box and found his notebooks, written over many years of practising. His writing was tiny and cramped and for a few moments I felt quite overwhelmed seeing his dear hand again. I looked up his notes on complaints or diseases peculiar to females. The regimen he counselled was: 'the patient's drink should consist of pure water with a toast in it; barley water, either by itself or with the addition of a little nitre; whey made with rennet or vinegar; milk and water; lemonade; a slight infusion of malt and mint or sage tea.'

I asked Mrs Fisher to make some of the teas and to have barley water available should Mrs Elwood fancy it. After a few days she looked much stronger and I believe having Beth at her side did help her greatly. She was not able to attend the funeral of her baby but the house was full of local people who had heard of their sadness. I agreed to go to the service so that I could tell her all about it, from a feminine point of view. Cecilia's own family lived at some distance and were not able to attend. Master Elwood dressed in his best clothes, quite different from his farming attire, stood tall and straight at the site of the little mite's resting place. He looked straight ahead and didn't for a minute relax his guard. The man who officiated was nothing like Rev. Skillen and I am not sure what connexion he belonged to but death is death and whatever form the prayers took they must give comfort to those left behind. For a moment I wished I had been present at Becca's funeral to hear the prayers and take some comfort.

Mrs Fisher had laid out some cold collation for the mourners and friends and the taking of brandy and other strong drinks lightened the misery of the day. I kept upstairs with Cecilia, and described who was there. She thought my descriptions funny and we did manage to giggle despite the occasion. It was a very long day and I think the family breathed a sigh of relief once it was passed.

Beth slept in her cradle for most of the time except in the night when I took her into my bed and cuddled her. I had become quite adept at changing and cleaning her; I loved the milky sweet smell of her head and many times when young Cilla came to wake me she found the babe lying awake alongside me. Mary-Jane drew off some of her milk for the night-time and I was able to feed Beth myself. It was the most wonderful experience of my life.

Many days passed and at last Cecilia was able to get up and about. She showed me round the house and even found some of her old clothes for me to wear; my simple black dress was very ugly and dishevelled and I was grateful to discard it for something pretty. I took Becca's comb and did my hair as I looked in the mirror. It seemed very strange to be able to see myself so clearly and though I could never look as pretty as Becca or Cecilia I did try to improve my appearance, even standing differently so my crooked leg wasn't as obvious. Living as Cecilia's companion was a lot easier on me than all the hard scullery work at Coad Farm. I thought it was all too good to be true.

I had a visit from Mrs Makepiece and Cecilia promised to return her call as soon as she was feeling better and I would of course accompany her with Beth. Billy-alone also found his way into the kitchen of South Farm and I was pleased to see him. We walked together round the orchard on a fine autumn day. The windfalls smelled sweet as they awaited collection. South Farm was so different to Coad Farm. Apart from Mrs Fisher, everyone was friendly; there were no bad atmospheres and the place felt full of light as opposed to the gloom and bad temper at Hamsey.

I was beginning to feel safe and wanted but I knew that I was only staying as long as the wet-nurse and that sooner rather than later I would have to start weaning Beth. I didn't want to think about it. Billy found a few fallen apples and we sat in the lazy sunshine munching our way through them.

'Beth looks right bonny.'

'She does that, she is thriving and very content. We love it here Billy.'

'I wouldn't mind a job here; any chance you think?'

'I thought you didn't want to stay in one place?'

'Well, this is a bit different ain't it?'

'Yes, it certainly is. Farmer Elwood is a good man and very kind. Why don't you ask him?'

'Will you ask him for me?'

'No, but I will tell him that you are a good, kind boy and probably hard working.'

'What d'ya mean, 'probably'?'

I laughed at his indignation as I eased myself up and then pulled him to his feet. 'Come along, I want to pick some herbs. I've a mind to make some of my ma's receipts. Mrs Fisher is away for a few days so I can use the kitchen.'

We were foraging along the hedgerow when he said, 'There was a body found in the river yesterday.'

A hand clutched at my heart, squeezing.

'Do you know what happened?'

‘Na, it might be a suicide.’

A chill swept across me.

‘Do you know who it was?’

‘A maid, ’pparently.’

Was it Becca? Had old man Coad gone back on his promise to bury her fittingly?

‘Let’s finish here now Billy, I’ve got enough.’ I tried to keep my voice from trembling. When we got back to the house I asked him to find out a bit more about the girl. I made it sound casual, but to me it felt like I was guilty of something, and I knew I wasn’t.

Chapter Eleven

To Make Apple Cakes
Take half a quarter of dough, roll it out thin; spread equally over it 5 ounces each of coffee and sugar, a little nutmeg or all-spice, and 2 ounces of butter; then fold and roll it again two or three times, to mix well the ingredients. Afterwards, roll it out thin, and spread over it 4 rather large apples, pared, cored and chopped small; fold it up, and roll until mixed. Let it stand to rise after. Half a pound of butter may be added.
MacKenzie's Five Thousand Receipts in All the Useful and Domestic Arts

I was in an agony of worry and fear. Surely, I said to myself, the master would have buried Becca like he promised. I went over and over the words we had exchanged: I had asked him to bury her proper but he had cheated me over the money and I realised I had no reason to expect him to keep his word. I made myself as busy as possible and took over Mrs Fisher's kitchen to make some apple cakes for the family. I used my mother's receipts and was able to lose myself in the slapping of the dough, part of which I used for bread. I loved cooking and it was helpful to have something to occupy my mind. I propped Beth up in a washing tub and padded her with towels so she could see the activity and Cecilia even came in to chat. It was clear she had never done any cooking so after I had shown her round her own kitchen we began preparing to make the dough.

Farmer Elwood surprised us and at first he didn't look too pleased to see his fragile young wife covered in flour and learning how to knead. Somehow, we all ended up laughing and I made a large pot of tea for us all to sit with while I chopped the apples.

Beth crowed in delight and for a few hours I managed to put Becca to the back of my mind.

'Perhaps tomorrow we could do some preserving,' I suggested. 'I have found lots of my favourite herbs in your garden and it would be good to make use of them. I could preserve rosemary in oil.'

'Where did you learn all this Esther?' Mr Elwood asked.

'My ma was a good cook and she grew a lot of herbs and vegetables to use in the kitchen and the house. We lived over the apothecary's shop and had quite a big plot of land for the growing. My pa used some of her herbs for his own preparations. Mr Fuller, the apothecary, didn't mind, as long as we didn't copy any of the prescriptions that were for sale. Ma used to love to make soap and would press the herbs inside to give it a lovely smell. We sold quite a lot of things like that come Christmas and holidays.'

'You had a very busy childhood Esther. I wish I knew all the things that you do,' said Cecilia.

'I can teach you,' I offered.

Farmer Elwood rose and laughed as he wondered why his wife would want to turn herself into a kitchen maid. We all ended up laughing at the thought of Cecilia with her sleeves rolled up and eyes streaming from chopping onions.

My cakes were all prepared and I left the cooking to Cilla

while I walked towards the town hoping that Billy-alone would come. I think he realised that I was anxious about this young woman who had been found and I was sure he would come back as soon as he had news.

I looked towards Southover and stood awhile. Once again it was a beautiful mellow day. The sun had a reddish tone and though there were heavy clouds in the distance it didn't smell or look like rain. The fields to the right of the farm track were all a lush green except where the plough and horses had been at work. I could see the path of the river and I wondered again about the family I believed to be in the area. I would have to make enquiries of Farmer Elwood. He owned property all the way downriver and my family might even be his tenants. It was an uneasy thought as I didn't know what they would be like. I had recently wondered why my ma had left her family and hadn't stayed in touch.

What had happened to occasion such a rift; to marry and move household was one thing but to depart the district and never seek to return or want to talk of family was strange.

Billy-alone was nowhere in sight so I returned to the warm kitchen to see how my bread and apple cakes were progressing. Cilla was a good and willing girl and I felt quite at home with her; we chatted together as the fire was encouraged to burn up and bake the bread wholesome and crispy with its enticing smell.

Chapter Twelve

Medicinal Tea

This country affords herbs much more wholesome than either tea or coffee, and if they were all imported from a distant region, and sold at a high price, they would, no doubt, be held in great estimation. The following composition is very superior to coffee or tea, inasmuch as the infusion is very agreeable, will strengthen the stomach and invigorate, instead of debilitate, the nervous system.

Take of rosemary leaves dried 2 oz

Sage 4 oz

Rose 4 oz

Peach 3 oz

Hyssop 4 oz

Balm 4 oz

Male speedwell 4 oz (veronica)

A wineglass of these mixed herbs is sufficient to make 3 pints of infusion, which is made in the same manner as tea, sugar and milk being added. The ingredients above may be diminished or augmented at pleasure. If too bitter lessen the quantity of hyssop and add dried mint leaves. In France and Germany the male speedwell is termed European tea and is by many preferred to the Asiatic teas. As a medicine it has also a considerable share of fame, being stomachic and diuretic. It is also considered very salubrious in many affections of the lungs, as asthma, consumption etc., and to possess the power of healing internal ulceration.

MacKenzie's Five Thousand Receipts in All the Useful and Domestic Arts

Cecilia was well on her way to a full recovery and it gave me great pleasure to prepare tasty drinks and morsels to tempt her. The doctor had been back to the house to check on her and I found him to be a kindly man beneath the booming voice. He greatly approved my herbal tea when he took a cup himself. Farmer Elwood invited him to supper one night when he had called late in the afternoon and he seemed pleased to sit with him in the study before Cecilia joined them. I was walking by the open door when I heard them talking about the body that had been dragged from the Ouse.

'What makes you think it was murder?' Master Elwood was asking.

I breathed a sigh of relief: they couldn't be talking about Becca.

'There was a massive gash in her head, poor thing. She was local, you know. A comely wench with lovely hair, or it must once have been so.'

Cecilia had entered the room and asked, 'Who was she?'

'Well, her father identified her as a daughter from his first marriage. Rebecca Franklin. He has recently taken up with the widow Skarrow and I gather the girl was put out to work at a farm near Hamsey some eighteen months ago.'

My soul fainted within me as I heard Becca's name. Murdered. Wicked lies, I fled up the stairs to my room and flung myself on the bed. Why would anyone think that? I had seen Becca with my own eyes; I had dragged her limp body from the clutches of the freezing cold water, seen the mud, reeds and vegetation caught in her clothes and her open mouth. I dragged the chamber pot from beneath the bed and vomited into it as the cold fear of the master's threat came back to me. He had threatened me if I talked about him but I hadn't said a word to anyone except Becca's pa.

I barely slept that night and when I ventured downstairs the next day everyone commented how pale I was. Dear Cecilia wanted me to return to bed for the day and offered to help Mary-Jane with Beth. Gladly I accepted and returned to my room where I tried to calm myself. Should I go to Becca's father and find out what was happening? Had Master Coad done what he threatened and blamed me for Becca's death?

I tossed and turned in my bed and when I wasn't doing that I paced up and down – seeing myself in that all-revealing mirror, tormented.

Cecilia knocked lightly on my door and entered with Cilla and a tray of my own concoction of tea. 'How are you feeling now, Esther? We thought you would like some refreshment.'

I struggled to compose myself and smiled weakly. 'I am well enough now. How has Beth been?'

'Oh, she has been chirping and waving her little hands at anyone who will stop and play. Your young friend Billy-alone has been entertaining her in the kitchen. Mrs Fisher has returned so everything is back to normal. I don't think she approved of your cooking lessons – there has been a great deal of noise and slamming of pans. Cilla says she was very put out at you taking over her kitchen.'

I tried to laugh but my heart wasn't in it. 'Is Billy still here?' I asked.

'Yes, he doesn't seem to want to leave,' Cilla replied, her face pinking up.

I'll come down and take a walk in the fresh air, perhaps it will revive me.'

Once Billy and I were alone I pushed him for details. He told me that the body had been removed to the coroner's and the constable was 'investigating a most tragic crime'.

'Why do they think she was murdered?' I pressed.

'She had a big hole in her head and… she had recently had a baby. 'Tis all I know, honest, Esther. Did you know her?'

'I might have,' I whispered. 'But she didn't have a hole in her head when I last saw her and she was already dead.'

'Beth is her baby then is it? I guessed as much.'

'Billy, I don't know what to do. Beth was her baby and she killed herself just after birthing her. It was Master Coad's baby and Missus Coad wanted rid of it. I ran away from the farm to save the child. I never killed Becca, I loved her; she was my only friend,' I wailed.

Poor Billy, he looked so bewildered to be the recipient of such an outpouring, but I was all used up with keeping things inside me.

He patted me gingerly on the back. 'Don't 'ee fret miss, it'll all get sorted and little Beth will be taken care of.' I loved how Billy cared so much for Beth.

I got up and gathered myself. 'I must go to the town and find the coroner and tell him what happened,' I told Billy – but it was too late.

Mrs Fisher was coming towards us with Cecilia, smirking as she shouted, 'The constable has come for you! You'm wanted in connection with a murder and theft of a baby girl.' She was so pleased to be able to say all this she didn't even notice that she had interrupted and pushed her mistress to one side.

Cecilia spoke angrily: 'Mrs Fisher, kindly leave us this instant.'

When she had gone she turned to me, 'Esther, the constable is indeed here and I am afraid it is very bad news but surely you have some explanation. John will be home later but in the meantime you will have to go to town with Constable Wicks.'

I grasped her hand and pulled it to my breast. 'I have not killed anyone and I have not stolen Beth. She is dearer than life to me. Please believe me…'

Her clear blue eyes searched mine and she squeezed my hand.

'I will send for my husband, he is some way away today but as soon as he returns we will try and make sense of it.'

Billy butted in. 'What about Beth ma'am? You mun let 'em take her to the parish, it is a bad place for a little tacker like her.'

Cecilia looked round at Billy in surprise before saying, 'Beth will stay with us until everything is resolved. No one will be taking her away, I promise.'

I rode behind the silent Constable Wicks and felt myself to be a feeble and pathetic creature unable to defend myself, even thinking that I might be to blame for all this. Hot tears coursed down my face and I felt everyone looking at me, a suspected murderess and child-napper. I was taken to the new house of correction at the market tower and put into a tiny room with naught but a bench to furnish it. The constable looked at me, judgingly it seemed, as he left. 'The coroner will talk to you as soon as he returns,' he said gruffly. The door slammed and I was alone with my thoughts.

What seemed like hours later I could hear a commotion outside and I went to peep through the grill in the door. I could see nothing but I heard Mrs Makepiece's angry voice upbraiding the constable.

'Now see here young Wicks, you'm a fool to think that young scrap of a girl a murderer. You let me in to see her or I'll take it up with the coroner himself. Has she been charged? Has she admitted fault? Does she even know what she is s'posed to have done? No? No. I didn't think so. Did the coroner say she was a murderer? No. You just want to look important – going and dragging her in here behind you and letting people think what they liked. That crowd gathering outside will have her strung up if you're not careful and then where will you be when she is shown to be innocent of God knows what. Open that door and let me in to sit with the girl.' I heard hurried steps and the key turned in the lock to admit a very red-faced Mrs Makepiece who pulled me straight into her strong rounded arms. I wept.

Chapter Thirteen

Billy-alone had called on Mrs Makepiece as soon as he left South Farm and had poured out his worries at my being taken up by the constable. How could I ever thank him for enlisting this formidable woman to my cause? I took heart as I told her my story and by the time we had sat and talked it all out I was able to get my spirit back and I knew I had to fight Farmer Coad. I had to do it for myself, for Becca and her reputation and most of all for Beth. Mrs Makepiece said to me that unless I got myself together Beth might be taken by the parish and then God only knows what would happen to her.

She was curious. 'What makes you so certain that Becca's injuries were caused by Farmer Coad?'

'He threatened me with blame for her death and kidnap of the child if I told on him. He must have struck out at her poor body to make it look like someone had killed her. Me. And the child was to have been my motive.'

Her advice to me was that I tell the coroner exactly what I remembered and trust that he would investigate fairly and that is what I did. He came to the house of correction later that day and I was taken to him. Mrs Makepiece insisted on being present as I had no one else to speak for me. He had his back towards me as we entered but I recognised him immediately. It was the loud physician who had treated Cecilia.

He sat at his desk and put his fingers together like a steeple before starting to speak.

'Well, Esther, we meet again. Let me tell you why I have asked to speak to you.'

Mrs Makepiece interrupted indignantly. 'She was arrested and hauled through the town like a common criminal!'

'Aye, so I heard, and I am sorry that Constable Wicks overstepped his authority. Feelings are running high in the town with the supposed murder of a popular young girl. He got a bit in advance of himself. I have spoken to him.'

'Well it's a bit late, this poor girl's reputation has been most grievously injured and…'

'Mrs Makepiece, can we just get on with the business in hand and then all talk of reputations and arrests can be put under the scrutiny of the facts. Esther, you are not under arrest. A body has been found and identified as your work colleague at Coad Farm: a young girl, of fifteen years, known to you as Becca. She was the daughter of Mr Franklin and has been identified by him. Becca's father has also made allegations as to why she died and suggested that you knew the facts of it before running away from Coad Farm. I have examined Becca and found that she recently, very recently, gave birth to a child. I also would tell you that Becca died from drowning but she had some injuries to her body that are suspicious and it is those injuries that concern me: how and where she came by them.'

Mrs Makepiece was about to interrupt again but I stilled her with a gesture of my hand. 'I will tell you everything I know. I have never had to keep secrets before and I don't want to, ever again.'

'Before you begin Esther, can you confirm that the child

currently living at South Farm was Becca's and not, in fact, yours?'

'Yes, she is, was, Becca's baby.'

I told my tale from the moment that Becca had arrived at Coad Farm and he only stopped me occasionally with a question.

'Thank you Esther. I would like you to remain in the town until I have made some further inquiries but I am happy to let you stay with Mrs Makepiece if that is alright with her?' he raised his eyebrows enquiringly.

'Aye, I'll be happy to give the maid a bed for the time it takes you to get the man who is responsible.'

'I will do my best to get justice for the deceased,' was all he said.

Mrs Makepiece and I made our way back to Keere Street. The crowd outside the goal had dispersed and no one did more than glance at me as we hurried through the streets.

'I think we deserve a tot of brandy child. I will warm it up and dip some sugar and cinnamon in it to warm us through.' Later, as we sat in front of a cosy fire I told Mrs Makepiece about my family and the scourge of the great sickness. It was a relief to be able to talk freely once more. As we talked there was a loud knock at the door, my heart surged in my breast as fear clutched at me.

A dark figure with a hat pulled down round his ears turned out to be poor Becca's pa. He came in and put out his hand to me, a gesture of sympathy. 'I be that sorry lass that I had to tell on thee but I didn't know they would take thee up to blame.'

'You warned me that there would be no covering up of

such a thing,' I said. 'I should have been prepared to tell on Coad at the outset.'

Mrs Makepiece poured a tot of brandy for him as she asked whether he, as grandfather, would be taking the baby into his care. I was horrified at her words, I couldn't give Beth up now. He swirled his drink and stared into it as he said, 'I know Becca would want the nipper to be loved and cared for by her friend rather than be taken on by the parish or my wife, who would not care for her as she should. I would try and help with the odd bit of money, if I had some of my own that wasn't spoken for by my wife.'

I was flooded with relief as I thanked him. 'If everything works out and the coroner releases me I promise to care for Beth as if she were my own flesh and blood.'

'There's a long way to go yet,' warned Mrs Makepiece. 'You might be called upon to stake your claim as a grandfather whether you will or no.' And, on this worrying note I withdrew up to my old room hoping to find some peace and sleep.

Chapter Fourteen

The wheels of justice turn slowly and I was in an agony of worry for more than a week before I heard from the coroner again. I did not feel completely isolated as I had a visit from Cecilia, Beth and Farmer Elwood. They arrived during late morning and I was awash with tears and laughter at Beth's antics, and gratitude at their support. Whilst they were taking a glass of Mrs Makepiece's cowslip wine we had another visit from Becca's pa. He could hardly take his eyes off the baby as she chortled and waved her little fingers at everyone. I took the child and unwrapped the restricting blankets before depositing her in his arms. 'Take her,' I said. 'She is your flesh and blood and it is good for you to know her and God willing she will come to love you as she grows.' Beth responded to this kindly man and touched his stubbly chin with her little fingers, blowing bubbles into his ear as he held her tightly to him. I think if Farmer Elwood had any doubts about me and my role in the events for which I had been taken they were dispelled in that moment. He left Cecilia with us and walked up to the town with Mr Franklin.

Billy-alone had visited us every day of my stay in Lewes and it was from his ability to get himself into the kitchens of all and sundry that I learned what was going on.

Chapter Fifteen

Billy-alone

The overseer of the workhouse was a regular tyrant and I avoided the place when he was in his cups. Alice, his woman was nearly as bad and many's the nipper I knew to have suffered at their hands or more'n likely feet. It was one such day when I thought to avoid such a punishment by disappearing. I had told Miss Esther that I lived all over but in truth it was mainly the workhouse, or when I was really pushed and the weather fine I would settle under a haystack even on occasion moving in with the pigs at Miss Wardle's place. She was a funny one, she cared more for her poultry and sows than ever she did people. If she knew that I was nestled in with her prize beasts she never let on but I would occasionally find a few scraps of good bread and ham in with their feed. I loved Sally best – she were a fine piggy, she never tried to bite me and many's the time we cuddled up together. I was always a bit careful when she had a litter as she became a bit ornery then but generally we mucked in good.

Anyway, on this day I washed myself under the water pipe down in t'Cliffe. I wanted to look spruce for a trip I had planned to Coad Farm upstream at Hamsey. I walked along the river leaping the streams and boggy bits. I made a meal of some watercress plundered from still water off the main river. I had a few scrumped apples and felt myself to be well set up for the day. I knew Miss Esther to be innocent of all that was being laid at her door but I also knew that unless she had some help she would fall under the weight of stronger folks be they good or bad. Seemed to me that a little exploring round Hamsey might turn up some help.

I waited below the hamlet for any delivery carts and afore long one such came by.

I volunteered myself to the carter in exchange for a drink of ale to help unload his delivery of chalk to Coad Farm. We fell into talking and he told me that he regularly delivered to Coad, bringing his load from Piddinghoe way down river and near the sea. I have never seen the sea and we got right pally with all my questions and his pride in knowing stuff.

The entrance to Coad Farm was guarded by some mean looking dogs setting up 'nuf noise to wake the dead in the nearby churchyard. A young lad came and pulled aside the hurdles that were barring our way into their yard. I guessed him to be one of the sons by his surly but belonging look. The carter got down off the cart to stretch his legs and take a draught from his flask. I stayed put behind the horse; I could see and hear plenty. Old man Coad appeared a few minutes later and I knew him for a mean ole son of a bitch just by his swagger. He seemed to know the carter well and offered him a morsel in the kitchen as refreshment so I rushed round and tagged myself to their ankles. A big buxom woman who must 'ave been Missus Coad was in the kitchen sweating over a big pot of stew. It smelled good and I was hopeful I might get some but not a bit of it – we were given a crust of yesterday's bread with a smear of dripping lathered over it. A young lass came into the room carrying a pot nearly as big as 'erself. She plonked it down on the table and proceeded to chop turnips and carrots into it. I moved near to her as the old-uns grumbled to each other about too much rain, too little rain and the price of barley.

The lass were called Mary and she had been at the farm for just a couple of days but already she was a bit disheartened by the sourness of the place. No one ever spoke to her except to issue orders or threats; the missus was a real hard taskmaster and seemed very edgy anytime the master came in. 'See that bruise on her face?' she whispered to me. 'She got that when he came in t'other night and she raised her voice at 'im – he swiped her one.'

The carter broke into our talk. 'Hey lad, time to set-to.' I whispered to the girl to stay out of everyone's way, specially the old man and the sons. She nodded, as if knowing why. I didna think any young maid would be safe at that place even tho' Mary was awful plain, but I had to leave and pulling on some leathers that the carter gave me I began a long labour unloading. Truth t'tell I quite enjoyed doing summat physical and the carter gave me a drink and an offer of work anytimes he was up this way. We made our way slowly back to Lewes and though I hadn't seen much I had got the feel of the place and I had been able to warn young Mary. One thing I did notice was that all the sacks and carriers I saw in the barn were marked by the brand C. Fm. Most farmers used branding tools for their animals and I s'pose it were a simple job to mark the sacks and leather carriers as well. Next time I went to South Farm to see Cilla in the kitchen I would see if they branded their stuff as well.

I were mortal tired that night and joined Sally in her sty.

It were getting a mite cold and she was always warm if a bit wriggly. The carter had given me a few pennies and I was able to feast on a hot pie from the baker in Market Street and a pot of small ale.

My next trip out on Esther's cause was to Dr Grieve. He were the coroner as well as the physician and although I didna really know what a coroner did it were clearly important and it seemed sensible to find out. I knew the potboy in his kitchen and it were a small matter to invite myself in. Pot were a real carrot top and didn't really get know'd by his given name, everyone just called him Pot. He were blowing a fire up and puttin' some jars in boiling water when I arrived.

''Lo Pot, what yer doin' that for?'

'Mrs Jenkins be doing her bottlin' and she wants clean jars. If they have even a speck of dirt in them the food goes bad and missus will bellyache and then I'll get a tannin'.'

'Got anything to eat then?'

'Go see Judith, she'll find you summat.'

Later, we sat in friendly silence as we munched on cake washed down with a drop of ale. Good it were.

I decided to ask direct. 'D'you know if his nibs has found out about young Becca yet?'

'Dunno, but Missus Jenkins said he was planning on visiting Farmer Coad today. Quietly, like.'

'What's that mean, quietly, like?'

'Dunno, Missus Jenkins said he wouldn't be making accusations without some good reason.'

'Do 'ee know what caused the hole in 'er head?'

'Dunno, Missus Jenkins says 'twere a piece of wood wi' a sharp end.'

'Ow'd 'ee know that?'

'Dunno, Missus Jenkins don't know neither but says that's 'is job to know.'

'Ta, Pot... Sees ya.'

It was still early in the day so I ventured round to the workhouse to see the lie of the land. I needn't 'ave bovvered, they was all spark out and the place stank of brandy. I reckoned the tub-runners had been around. There was plenty of day left so I went down to Southover and made me way to South Farm. Cilla was alone in the kitchen and I settled down for a natter. She seemed glad to see me but then was all fingers and thumbs and cross. I told her what I had found out and she went to check the door was shut before whispering that Mrs Fisher was badmouthing Esther to anyone who'd listen. They'd been to market and she told everyone they met that Esther was a bad-un. She also said that Cecilia would keep Beth for her own.

'She can't do that.'

'It's better than the parish workhouse ain't it?'

'Aye, put like that, I s'pose it is but Esther will be free soon and she'll come and get Beth. Cilla, will you do summat for me?'

'Depends, what?'

'Can you look at Esther's things and see if there be a purse with letters stamped on it?' I drew the outlines of what I had seen at Coad Farm on the table with a bit of chalk.

'I dunno, s'pose I get caught?'

'Just say Esther needed some money and that I'm going to take it to her.'

'They won't believe that. Why would Esther ask you to bring her money when Missus Elwood has been visiting her in Lewes?'

‘Well, just try, ta. Is there anything to eat?’

I left South Farm without seeing anyone else and with a parcel of leftovers that I shared with Sally that night.

Next day I was hauled back to the workhouse to run some errands so I couldn’t see Esther and little Beth but a young lad called round to give me a message from Cilla.

‘She said to tell you that there be a purse with lettering on it but she don’t know what it do say and Mrs Fisher rubbed the letters off the table.’

‘Stop that yakking Billy, you’m s’posed to be swabbing down the floor, not yakking, get on with ye.’ The overseer kicked out but I was too nimble for the lazy owld sot.

‘Ta, mate – obliged to ’ee. Here, have an apple. I gave him one from my pocket, scrumped from a nearby garden.

Chapter Sixteen

To Cure Rheumatism
Take cucumbers, when full grown and put them into a pot with a little salt; then put the pot over a slow fire, where it should remain for about an hour; then take the cucumbers and press them, the juice from which must be put into bottles, corked up tight, and placed in the cellar, where they should remain for about a week; then wet a flannel or rag with the liquid and apply it to the parts affected.
MacKenzie's Five Thousand Receipts in All the Useful and Domestic Arts

I was able to use one of my mother's receipts to bring about a cooling liquid to ease Mrs Makepiece's rheumatism as the pain caused her great misery. My time in Lewes was very unhappy despite being in a warm house with an agreeable companion. I missed little Beth and worried that Cecilia, who was very much younger than me, would not be able to care properly for her. Even the thought that Mary-Jane was still at South Farm didn't satisfy me. She was an experienced mother but not very reliable. Her own little tacker, as she called him, was forever suffering from something or other, he had a permanent runny nose and sores round his mouth. I wouldn't be surprised if he harboured the crawlers! I wondered if the coroner would allow Beth to live with me at Mrs Makepiece's until he had finished his enquiries. I put this idea to my companion, she was less than enthusiastic.

'Course he won't girl. Beth is safe and well at South Farm and she hasn't been weaned yet. How could we feed her if she were here?'

I had no sensible answer but the thought just kept going round and round in my head.

The coroner had told Mrs Makepiece not to let me out and about in case some hotheads abused me but I was so restless we did venture out after dark just for a little walk.

Lewes was a fine old town and I could see the many advantages of living there.

There was a small poor-looking hamlet over the other side of the river called Cliffe. The two places were joined by the only bridge for miles. A great deal of trade was conducted by water and recently much work had been done on the navigable way. The marshes on either side of the river were being drained and the waterway straightened in places. Great banks were being built to prevent damaging floods. Mrs Makepiece told me about a time when the sea and wind had roared up the river, bringing devastation and destroying all the crops in the low lying areas; the salt wind burning all the greenery for miles around. That same year there had been a terrible snowfall and the beasts in the fields had died. A few were lucky but no one would buy them later because they thought there was something peculiar in their being found alive after twenty three days buried completely by snow. The farmer ended up selling them at a distance to a butcher who didn't know about their lucky escape.

I noticed that there were a great many places of worship in the town on both sides of the river. One of the churches near

Keere Street had a round tower and, apparently, there were three like that – all the rest having the usual square tower. As we walked we wondered why but the only explanation Mrs Makepiece had heard was that they were all built before the Normans came.

'There be one at Southease and t'other is further downstream at Piddinghoe where the river surrounds the church at high tide,' she told me.

I thought this very romantic and spent a while musing at the likely history.

'I think my mother's folk came from Southease.'

'Oh aye, be they smugglers then?'

'No, surely not, why would you think that?' I was alarmed by this suggestion.

'Most folk downriver be smugglers of one sort or other. Southease, Telscombe and Piddinghoe are known for the trade.'

'That's shocking!'

'Well, I don't see you turning down a spot of my brandy young lady. Where do you think it comes from?'

Under cover of darkness we talked about the smugglers and how most people subscribed to getting their brandy, wines, salt, spices and tea via middlemen. The smugglers were a rough lot and it didn't do to try and trade directly with them, not if you were respectable folk. I was amazed when Mrs Makepiece described some of the crimes committed in the pursuit of cheap brandy. Drink thinned down with cheaper strong drinks or even cold tea. But the worst and most shocking was the murder of anyone who got in their way: they had even been known to kill their own men if they were suspected of turning. There was not much that they wouldn't do to further their business and that trade extended for miles inland through a network of tinkers and travellers; most of the excise were in their pay as well as the constabulary.

I couldn't make out if Mrs Makepiece was for or against them but she seemed to be willing to buy as long as she didn't see the nasty side of things. I wondered if that might be why my mother had left the area. I still wanted to go and find my family but Southease had taken on a sinister air.

The next day Billy-alone called round to see me and asked what had happened to the little cradle Becca had made.

'I left it in the reeds where I found Beth.'

'If we found it we could show that it was in Becca's mind all along to give herself up for the baby,' he explained.

Mrs Makepiece was listening and butted in. 'I think the constable and his men have searched the whole area – they would have been looking for the wooden stave...'

'Did they find it then?' said Billy.

'What, the stave?'

'No, the cradle.'

'They won't know nowt about the cradle, I didn't mention it,' I said, realising my mistake.

Billy was gone in a flash and I cursed myself for a fool in not mentioning the cradle to the coroner. Billy was right in that it showed what Becca was planning. It still didn't show who had hurt her body afterwards though.

Chapter Seventeen

The very next day I was summoned to the coroner's office again. Farmer Elwood appeared at our door and said he would accompany me. I was very anxious but glad to have such a man at my side. I kissed Mrs Makepiece goodbye outside the clock tower. I knew she was worried sick but I tried to settle her spirits by being calm myself. She pushed her hankie into my hands and whispered to be brave, upright and remember I had good friends nearby.

The coroner was sitting at his desk and after a formal greeting with Farmer Elwood he addressed himself to me.

'Esther, I am sorry to have to tell you that Farmer Coad has made a statement to the constables that you did kill Becca in order to take her baby for your own.'

I gasped and started to protest but he silenced me with a raised hand.

'He accepts that the child was a result of his union with Becca and declares that she was a known trollop. He has called on his sons to bear witness that Becca conducted herself lewdly and he also called on various people who were at the Midsummer Fair where, he said, she was seen to flaunt herself to all and sundry.'

I was robbed of my voice by this shameful slur on Becca and by the knowledge that my voice against Farmer Coad and his sons was unlikely to be heard. Farmer Elwood, at my side, spoke.

'Have they any proof that Esther might have killed Becca?'

'No, it is her word against Coad's. But it is not my place to decide who is or is not, guilty. My role is to ascertain how she died and I am clear that she drowned, either by her own hand or someone else's. However, as a personal friend John, I would suggest that Esther think through everything that happened and bring to bear any fact that might shake Coad's story. He and his sons think they are – to coin the phrase – home and dry. There is the matter as to who violated the body, which might shed some light. The stave that was used to batter her has been found near the riverbank and very near to the farm. There is nothing remarkable about it other than it has been sharpened at one end and this was used to inflict deep wounds in the corpse. The level of malice is striking. The best outcome for Esther is that a witness can be found to augment aspects of her story. She can bring witnesses as to her character and demonstrate that she is not a likely candidate to inflict death or such vicious post mortem wounds.'

I was rooted to the spot in fear of what would become of me.

'What happens to me now?' I croaked.

'You must remain at Mrs Makepiece's until such time as the constable has enough evidence to prove or disprove your situation.'

'Am I under arrest?'

'No. This investigation has a way to go before the constable will move against you. In the meantime, I will release the body for burial.'

Chapter Eighteen

It is almost everywhere too common to have churchyards in the middle of populous towns. This is not only reprehensible in point of taste, but, considering how near to the surface of the earth the dead bodies in many places are deposited, there must necessarily arise putrid vapours, which, however imperceptible, cannot fail to contaminate the air. The practice of burying in churches is still more liable to censure; and not many years ago, the pernicious effects of this custom were so severely felt in France, as to occasion a positive edict against it.

MacKenzie's Five Thousand Receipts in All the Useful and Domestic Arts

Becca's funeral was a poor affair. No one wanted to have her buried on hallowed ground. I was shocked at the many pious people of Lewes, who needed so many places of worship, yet, not one of them would show any charity towards this young and badly used girl. In the end, Farmer Elwood took it on himself to allow the burial on part of his land where there was a family chapel, the same chapel where his own child had been laid to rest. Even without much faith myself it was a relief that she was buried on hallowed ground. I wore Cecilia's thickest veil in case anyone objected to my presence but we were only a few: the Elwoods, Mrs Makepiece, Becca's pa and I took the body to the tiny chapel. It was surrounded by light airy woodland and had a quiet, peaceful atmosphere. Small birds chirruped amongst the autumn leaves with a gentle wind speaking in shallow sighs and whispers. I felt the chapel to be welcoming Becca.

The hole was dug deep and proper, not like some recent burials where bones had escaped their bindings and appeared above ground mere months after the committal. This disturbing bit of information came from Mrs Makepiece who was scathing about the standard of burials in the town. She said the stink was scandalous and good people deserved better.

Becca had been popular, her father said, but none of her childhood friends had come to pay their last respects. I felt for her. To commit herself to such a death was bad enough but to have people believe the wicked lies was monstrous.

As Mrs Elwood laid a little posy of autumn leaves and bright berries on the earth I wept for Becca and for Beth who would never know what a fine mother she had. It was difficult not to feel a sense of bitterness against the people of Lewes who had shut their minds to our innocence, believing instead the malice of a wicked man and his family.

Chapter Nineteen

Later that evening we were surprised by a sharp rap on the door. It was Miss Wardle, the lady who loved her pigs more than her neighbours.

'There is a young man in my Sally's sty and I think he needs some medical attention. He says you are his friend and might help.' Her voice was irritable but I detected a kindness beneath.

'It must be Billy,' I said. I reached for my wrap and with Mrs Makepiece followed the elderly lady into the dark.

The sty was dark and I could barely make out Billy who was sweating profusely and covered in scratches and small wounds. He was wet, dirty and worryingly hot. I struggled out backwards and reported to the ladies that he was in need of a doctor. I volunteered the thought that he had been attacked.

'Well, as long as he has nothing infectious,' Miss Wardle, barked. 'You'd best bring him into my kitchen while one of you fetches someone.'

I struggled back in and eventually managed to drag Billy out of the sty. He wasn't objecting, he just seemed unable to understand what I was trying to do. I managed eventually and half carried, half dragged him to Miss Wardle's house.

Luckily it was a good-sized place with a cooking range burning contentedly so I laid Billy on the floor in front of it. Miss Wardle produced some cloths and I gently tried to clean him without opening all the cuts. His clothes were so thin they had given him no protection at all and I was fearful that an infection was setting in. As I took the scraps of clothing from him I wondered briefly why I seemed to be drawn to undress sickly people who I barely knew. Gradually he responded to the warmth and dry towels and his shivering lessened.

'What happened, Billy, where have you been?'

I couldn't get any sense out of him at all and we sat there waiting for the physician. I cleaned some of the cuts with water and for one particularly deep one I pulled the skin together and bound it with thin cotton. Miss Wardle, tutted and worried all around us but was unable to help – I asked her for some clean water for Billy to drink.

She made a hot drink as well and we were all quite comfortable waiting.

'Well, Esther, you seem to attract lost souls to you,' Dr Grieve said as he strode into the kitchen his voice booming over us three women and Billy.

He raised the patient on his pitifully thin legs and inspected the damage before opening his bag and choosing medicants and bindings.

'Who did this to you, lad?' he asked.

Billy was still unable to answer and the physician finally gave up trying to get any information from him. Miss Wardle said that he could stay the night on her kitchen floor and she produced a blanket. I made him as comfortable as I could before Mrs Makepiece and I went back home much disturbed by Billy's misfortune. Dr Grieve had said he wanted to see Billy as soon as he had recovered enough to travel. I promised to get him there and hoped he would be able to answer some questions.

The next day I hurried to Miss Wardle's. I kept my shawl

across my face so no one would question who I was and link me to Becca. Billy-alone was sitting at the kitchen table and looking a great deal better than he had last night. Next to him and propped against the table were two items, one I had never seen and the other made my heart soar. The first was a stave, sharpened cruelly to a point. The second was Becca's cradle. I picked it up and smelled it, there was a faint baby smell – how could that be possible after such a time out in the open?

I rushed to hug him but was speedily repelled. 'Get orff, mind me bruises...'

We thanked Miss Wardle for her care and she seemed quite softened by the time we left, making our way to the physician's house as quickly as we could. Billy was concerned as to how he was going to pay the doctor.

'Don't let's worry about it until he gives us a bill,' I said glibly. 'First we have to get you better.'

We had brought the stave and cradle with us and the doctor was mightily interested in them after he had redressed some of Billy's hurts.

'Tell me lad, how you came to be up near Coad Farm?'

Billy yawned, tired of this repeated questioning. 'I went up to find the cradle.'

I had to explain how Becca had made the cradle in readiness for the birth and so she could float the baby down to find new parents much as in the story she heard Farmer Coad, in all his hypocrisy, read from the bible. The physician shook his head in wonderment and spent the next few minutes inspecting it minutely. I asked him to sniff the cradle and he would be able to smell baby. 'I don't think my sense of smell is that finely tuned Esther but I accept that this was indeed a cradle, if only for a short while.' He turned to Billy.

'Where did you find it boy?'

'It was caught up in some reeds. I had to go into the river a long way down from Coad's in case I missed it.'

'Can you swim?'

'No. Leastways, I think I can now, but I couldn't then.'

'So, you stepped into the shallows and waded upriver searching the reeds for this little basket. Then what happened?'

'I was quite near Coad's when I heard some lads laughing and messing about. Reckon they were the sons, they started throwing stones at me and I kept falling into the deeper water. I tried hiding in the reeds but they knew where I was and kept at me. One of them ran off and came back with sticks and a dog. The sticks were tied to their wrists with long cords so they couldn't lose them.'

'Did they know you Billy?'

'Nah, I was just an easy target for a bit of fun, like.'

'How long did this skirmish go on?' asked the doctor, 'You have a lot of cuts and bruises.'

'I dunno, it seemed like most of the morning,' Billy said. 'I was losing ground and couldn't keep meself up no more. If one of the fishermen hadn't come down the river in his little boat I would have been a goner. He shouted at the lads and they ran off but not before losing this spear. It broke at the strap and fell into the water. He hauled me into his boat and we collected the spear and the cradle before coming back to the town.'

'Did he know who the boys were?'

'Oh, aye,' he said. 'They were the Coad brothers.'

'Who was the fisherman Billy?'

'Dunno 'is name but I knows where he lives.'

The physician looked grave and studied the spear closely before comparing it to the one that was already in his room. They were the same, except for the remnants of binding.

'Well, lad, you'll live, but you must keep clean and come back to see me if you feel at all feverish, by that I mean unnaturally hot, sick or sleepy.'

I spoke for Billy. 'Thank you doctor. I will ask Mrs Makepiece if we can take care of Billy until he is all healed.'

As we left the doctor's room he put a hand on my sleeve. 'This changes things completely Esther, I hope you will be vindicated in your story. Don't tell anyone about the stave and cradle until I have had time to speak to the constable. You are a very lucky girl to have such a good friend in Billy.'

We had started to leave when he called me back. 'There was one other thing Esther. Coad maintains he gave you nothing to care for the child as his story is that you stole her. Is there anything that can link him to the money you say you have – how much was it?'

'He said he was giving me fifty pounds but it was only thirty-five. I think he thought I couldn't count.'

'Even so, thirty-five pounds is a lot of money just to have in hand. Do you know if he might have been doing some business that day with anyone?'

'No, but the bag was stamped with the bank's name and his own brand.'

'Thank you, that might help. Can you remember how the money was made up – notes, coins etc.?'

'Aye, I can. I do not have that much money that I would get confused.'

I was able to tell him the exact denominations.

Chapter Twenty

Billy and I returned to Mrs Makepiece's house where we found Miss Wardle. She had been taking a drop of the brandy and was a little pink in the face.

'Billy,' she said. 'I wish you would come and look after my pigs and chickens with me. I am getting on in years and I know you would be able to do the work and Sally behaves much better for you than me. You could sleep in the outhouse, which I would make comfortable for you. It would be much better than living on the streets or in Sally's sty and you would get your bed and board.'

I thought Billy would be pleased at this offer but he hummed and haa-d before asking if he had to work all day, every day. Once he was reassured that his work would be in the mornings and evenings only, he agreed.

'I'll do it, ta Miss Wardle. I reckon old Sal will be made up with me being there, she's a rare good piggy, perhaps we could keep some more of her piglets to fatten up and sell.'

'That's the thing Billy, we'll make enough money to cover your wages and more.'

'Wages, will I get wages an' all?' Billy smiled gratefully.

We were all very chirpy that evening despite Billy's injuries – he stayed with us for the next few days until Miss Wardle was ready to welcome him to his new home – the first he had known since his family died. The outhouse would be a great improvement to the way he had been living.

The very next day he and I made our way to South Farm to tell the Elwoods all that had happened and for me to see and cuddle Beth. She had changed in just the few days that I had been gone and I wept a few little tears into her ear. Cecilia was delighted to be able to tell me that she had smiled her first real smile and spent most of her time cheerfully crowing and blowing bubbles.

Farmer Elwood came in whilst I was sitting with Cecilia and was very interested to hear about Billy's battle with the Coad boys and the finding of the sharpened stave and cradle. I told him that the money Coad gave me was in a bank bag and I thought that the coroner was particularly interested in that and thought it of use to the case. I explained that it was upstairs with the belongings that I hadn't taken to Mrs Makepiece's and he bade me retrieve it. I sped to my room and pulled it from the box, returning to lay it on the kitchen table where we all peered at it as if it would speak. Farmer Elwood suggested that we put the bag and money in a safer place in case it was requested as evidence by the coroner himself or the constable. He took it to his office and it was locked up.

Billy-alone and I returned to Keere Street that evening after he had spent most of the time in the farm kitchen making Cilla laugh. I couldn't resist commenting that Cilla seemed to like him and had all but fainted when she saw his poor battered self.

It was true and it cheered me that such a good cheeky lad was benefitting from his own generous actions. I would have been a lot poorer in spirit and fact without young Billy keeping me company throughout my troubles. For a moment I wished I could find someone like Billy to share my thoughts and feelings with but I knew that I was not a likely wife for anyone. My twisted leg and plain looks were not likely to find me a man. I sighed before remembering Beth and my many advantages in having good friends who cared for me. I thought myself lucky to be a free woman still despite the serious charges laid by Farmer Coad against me.

Chapter Twenty-One

White Gooseberry or Champagne Wine
Take cold soft water, four and a half gallons,
White gooseberries, five gallons.
Ferment. Now mix refined sugar, six pounds, honey, four pounds, white tartare, in fine powder, one oz. Put in orange and lemon peel, one oz dry or two ounces fresh and add white brandy, half a gallon. This will make nine gallons.
MacKenzie's Five Thousand Receipts in All the Useful and Domestic Arts

The days shortened into winter and I waited. I waited for release from the accusations that hung over me. I had no idea whether I was on the edge of freedom or the drop of the gallows or perhaps even transportation to the colonies. I spent as much time as I was able with Beth at South Farm where the Elwoods had continued with Mary-Jane's employment. She seemed to blossom in their kitchen; her own little tacker looked a lot cleaner and healthier too. She undertook much of the heavier work as well as feeding Beth. Cecilia had thrown off her weakness as if it were a cloak. She was cheerful and full of pleasure in having Beth in her household. I think, knowing that I was not Beth's natural mother, made it easier for her to take on her care when I was in Lewes. I will admit to feeling a little jealous but put such thoughts aside as mean-spirited, but it caused my heart to ache no matter what my head said.

My time at Mrs Makepiece's house also became easier. The townsfolk were not treating me as if I were a murderess. No one was overly friendly but neither did they cross the street when I walked by. I know I owed this to Becca's pa who took every opportunity to accompany me about town on any little errands I was undertaking. Not long after my release from the town tower, a gang of boys had followed me – taunting and throwing stones and I had hurried back to Keere Street greatly upset and bruised where the stones had hit me. After that terrifying experience, I found I always had company when I had to go about. Mrs Makepiece, Becca's pa and young Billy-alone all took turns to keep me company. Even Miss Wardle seemed to regard me as a personal friend despite my not being a pig or chicken.

Chapter Twenty-Two

Cowslip White Wine
Take of cold soft water, eighteen gallons Malaga raisins,
thirty-five pounds,
White tartar, in fine powder, two ounces.
Ferment: Mix cowslip-flowers, sixteen pounds, Add white
brandy one gallon, This will make eighteen gallons.
MacKenzie's Five Thousand Receipts in All the Useful
and Domestic Arts

Winter came early that year and there was much unrest with the price of basic foodstuffs and poor quality bread. The mood in the alehouses was mutinous with some shopkeepers boycotted for their light loaves and adulterated meal.

Bad weather came before Christmas and with it harsh biting winds that lifted the lying snow from one field to another. Many beasts died for want of feeding and I know Farmer Elwood was worried. His farm was larger than most and he was fortunate enough to be able to bring the sheep into calmer pastures where the shepherds could tend them without being frozen to the iron-hard ground.

I loved going to the farm, I learned so much about the cycles of growth and husbandry of the animals. I tried to help wherever I could and I think that my preserving and bottling added to the family table and store cupboards. My mother never let anything go to waste and I was able to teach Mrs Fisher a thing or two. She never quite thawed to me but I don't think she actively tried to put me down any more. I don't know what brought about her change of attitude; perhaps it was seeing so many good people defending me, including her mistress who she held in high esteem.

But I get in front of myself. I went to visit Billy-alone in his new home in November and what a cosy place it was. Miss Wardle had asked a jobbing carpenter to make a raised platform that was to serve as his bed. It was built down the length of one wall and was so long it quite dwarfed Billy. When I laughed at this great structure she pointed out that Billy wasn't done growing by any means and she was planning for the future. She was such a practical person and had thought about the draughts from the stable door and had nailed heavy pigskin pieces to drop over the open window and the bottom of the wooden door. The window could be strung open in the good weather but provided protection against the worst of weathers. Billy had cast good fresh reeds on the floor to keep the room clean and warm. He had no shoes so it was more comfortable to stand on grasses rather than cold stone. There was a bowl and pitcher for water at the side of his bed that didn't look as if it had been used recently so I deduced he was still averse to washing any more than was necessary. I did, however, suggest that he use the washing facilities when he came to the farm, particularly, if he wanted to impress young Cilla. He must have thought I was speaking sensibly because he looked a great deal cleaner after that conversation.

I was introduced to Sally the favourite pig and I thought her a lovely great creature. I tickled her back with a stiff brush that Billy kept especially for that purpose. She squirmed against my legs and nearly knocked me off my feet. I couldn't help thinking that she was a great deal cleaner than many of the men and women I saw about town – and fatter. I don't think Sally went short of food. There were a host of chickens scrabbling round underfoot and they too looked well fed and contented. I whispered to Billy that it must be good living at Miss Wardle's.

'Aye,' he said. 'She's a good sort, in a bad-tempered way. Mind you, I steers well clear of the owld man at the poor house – he don't take kindly to me change in fortune. I found him a new lad, someone who can defend hisself and if all else fails can run fast. He should be grateful.'

I laughed at the faces he pulled as he said this.

'Billy, have you heard any more about my case with the constable? I don't know what to think, whether to be happy that I have been left alone or whether this is the calm before the storm. I spend so much time in anxiety that my low spirits might overwhelm me.'

'No, I ain't 'eard nuffink. I can ask Pot, if you like?'

'I'd be obliged Billy. I would wish to have an idea if I am to be formally charged. At the moment I try to see every day as a bonus but, in truth, it is a hard position to maintain.'

Chapter Twenty-Three

The Bonfire Prayer
Remember, remember the Fifth of November
The Gunpowder, Treason and Plot
I see no reason why Gunpowder Treason
Should ever be forgot
Guy Fawkes, Guy Fawkes,
'twas his intent
To blow up the King and the Parliament
Three score barrels of powder below,
Poor old England to overthrow;
By God's providence he was catch'd
With a dark lantern and burning match.
Holloa boys, holloa boys make the bells ring.
Holloa boys, holloa boys, God Save the King
Traditional prayer still used by all the Lewes Bonfire Societies

And:
A penny loaf to feed old Pope,
A farthing cheese to choke him
A pint of beer to rinse it down,
A faggot of sticks to burn him
Burn him a tub of tar, burn him like a blazing star,
Burn his body from his head,

Then we'll know old Pope is dead.

Traditional and referring to papal plot to kill King of England.
Cliffe Bonfire Society of Lewes still carries 'No Popery' banner

The very next day was the Lewes celebration of Fawkes' night and I saw Pot myself.

He told me that everything 'was gone quiet' and perhaps it would all blow over. I couldn't quite believe that but I tried to take some comfort.

Mrs Makepiece, Billy, and I all went up into the town to see the burning of Guy Fawkes while Miss Wardle stayed at home to guard the animals. I didn't quite understand that at first but all became clear later. It was a dark crisp night and we wrapped up warm, and even before we got up into the town I could smell wood smoke. I was amazed to see a huge structure of faggots and tar barrels at the top of School Hill. The towering unlit bonfire stretched some seventeen feet and was protected by a rowdy and threatening crowd. Mrs Makepiece told me that the previous year the Justices had been roughly used and there had been a riot. This year, the law must have decided they had met their match in this patriotic revel and stood at the dark margins, though I noticed they were armed with staves and even blunderbusses. I was more than a little frightened by this heaving mob of humanity and my fear increased as I saw a large group of masked men forcing their way towards the bonfire. The leader carried a lantern in one hand, a lighted taper in the other and a bundle of shavings slung across his shoulders. The throng behind him all carried kindling torches and were lustily singing the kings anthem. As the bonfire was lit everyone around me took up the refrain and my fear disappeared as we all roared our approval and joined in the singing and chanting. We all marched down the hill toward the river; my lipsy leg didn't slow me up as I was fair carried along in the general surge and Mrs Makepiece was gripping my arm for all she was worth. When we got to the bottom of the hill and near the river we came to a standstill in the press of folk. I couldn't see what was happening but I felt part of it as I was forced into a wall with Mrs Makepiece alongside of me. Billy and Pot were in the thick of it and told me later that tar barrels were thrown into the river, with a few people too. The bonfire boys had been met at the centre of the bridge by a crowd from Cliffe. We were stuck there for quite some time as the singing and shouting got louder and more general, though every now and again a bonfire anthem struck up and the voices merged into something that sounded quite musical and heartfelt. Eventually, we managed to get out of our safe spot and made our way back up the street before we were again engulfed by revellers. We managed to dodge the squibbers and those throwing fireballs around and made our way towards the top of the town again.

The fire on School Hill had burned ferociously and one building had been scorched but no one in the crowd seemed to care. The power of the night was in the revellers and it would have taken an army to disperse so many people drunk on enthusiasm, as well as brandy and gin. I couldn't help thinking that the Justices must quake at this show of strength from the population and would do as much as they could to prevent it. I was assured by Mrs Makepiece that Lewes was a bonfire town and for one night a year the people ruled and woe betide anyone who got in their way. It was all very exciting and if I had been a man, I would have wanted to be in that group of firelighters though I didn't like the squibbers much.

The next day Billy and Mrs Makepiece both told me a bit about the revelry. It seemed that the Guy Fawkes' celebration was just a part of it and that the putting to death, by fire, of seventeen good protestant people on the very same spot where last night's bonfire was built was of equal importance. The martyrdom of these local men and women at the hand of Bloody Mary had become an important part of a celebration against the ruling class. Lewes, according to Mrs Makepiece was a hotbed of dissenters who on that one special night celebrated martyrdom and revolution with fervour. Mrs Makepiece called it letting go and where was the harm in that? She also said that the Trade were heavily involved in the night's events, and one group carried 'No Popery' banners which referred to a papist plot to the King's life, which was another reason why the Justices were unhappy at their loss of control of an entire town and many of the surrounding villages and hamlets.

I wasn't able to judge whether it was just as she said or an altogether more sinister show of force for its own sake with the reasoning blurred by history. Whatever it was, I had felt greatly excited by the press and power of the people.

Chapter Twenty-Four

I was summoned again to the coroner's office and once again Farmer Elwood accompanied me. We were shown into a different room and as well as the coroner there were a number of official looking people who had a very serious look about them. I sensed it was not good news for me and I felt my knees give way as I stumbled toward the bench they indicated. Farmer Elwood stood at my side and when I was requested to stand he held my elbow tightly at once supporting and comforting me.

I am afraid I don't recall the exact words that were used to charge me with murder.

I do remember that there was no mention of kidnap. I remember that there were angry voices spilling all around me and that I was allowed to sit through it all once the pronouncement had been made.

I was taken by the constable to a cell and was very distressed to be sick in front of this man who clearly believed that I was indeed a murderess. The next thing I remember is the gentle ministration of the coroner wearing his physician's hat. He had some burning herb held under my nose that brought me back into the present with a jolt.

Farmer Elwood was red-faced and angry by my side. He turned on the constable and demanded that he leave me to the doctor's care pointing out that I was in no fit state to attempt escape. The man spat on the floor in disgust and grumbled his way round the room before leaving – making a great show of locking us all in.

The nausea overwhelmed me as I quaked and quivered in a state of fear, and bubbling anger that anyone could think I would do such a wicked thing. I was unable to speak at all but I knew my innocence and it was agony not to be able to make others see it. I was robbed of my voice though it continued in my head. In due course the uproar surrounding me abated and I was left alone in the cold bare cell though not before Farmer Elwood put his arm around me. 'Don't fret Esther, we will resolve this monstrosity of injustice.' I huddled into a corner and shivered uncontrollably. I had not taken in details of the charge and what would happen next but I felt exhausted and without hope despite my friends goodwill.

I passed a fretful night and woke to a bleak cold light coming through a grill high on the wall, too high for me to see out of even if I climbed on the bucket set in the corner. I had to suffer the indignity of my bodily functions in full view of the guards who constantly passed by and looked in. I was given some cold meal for breakfast but it turned my stomach and I was unable to eat it. I asked the surly guard for some fresh water or small ale but received none.

Farmer Elwood returned that morning. He explained gently that he and other townsfolk had undertaken to seek my release and that it might take a few days and I must be patient and trust in the goodness of people. I wept. How could I trust in the goodness of folk when I was so unjustly accused by wicked people who were believed before me? Did it not show that power was in the hands of those who were strong rather than right? Who would take my part against such a powerful family? I poured this out to Farmer Elwood bitterly.

'Esther, they are not powerful, they are just a family the same as many others. We just have to present your case and evidence and justice will be done,' he said.

'You must believe in yourself and bring forward your spirit to fight this. You must not succumb to fear for it will act against you and give your opponents a victory that they should not be allowed to have. Fight, Esther. Fight for Beth. Fight for your good friend Becca who died for her baby. Fight.'

Once again, I was alone and I tried to pull my thoughts together in a rational manner.

Every time I found a positive thought, few though they were, the fear, the hurt swamped over me and I was thrown back again into a quivering and weepy state. I know Billy-alone came to see me but he was not allowed in. I heard him calling from the street.

Chapter Twenty-Five

I would like to say that my spirits recovered quickly and that I regained my belief in myself but it was not so. The length of time I spent in that grim cell worked into my bones and by the time the Elwoods, Mrs Makepiece and the coroner had achieved my release on surety of their good names I was but a ghost of my former self. I was taken by carriage to the farm but not before the constable took the opportunity to threaten me with the gallows. He smirked as he slammed the cell door emphasising his belief of my guilt and inevitable incarceration or death.

Cecilia stood at the front door with Beth in her arms and tears streaming down her face. 'Come in, come in, you must be frozen.' She turned and handed Beth to someone behind her and pulled me into her arms. 'Oh Esther, this has been too cruel, there is nothing left of you, come to the fireside and let me warm you. Mrs Fisher, the soup, some bread, some brandy. Hurry.'

I was ensconced in Farmer Elwood's big wing chair, carefully sipping the delicious meaty broth. I say carefully as my hands were shaking and I felt very light headed.

Cecilia was on her knees in front of me. 'Did they not feed you Esther?' she asked as she studied me.

'Aye, but I couldn't eat it – I was too upset and mostly it was just gruel and a rind of stale bread. You had to pay to get a proper meal and the constable didn't seem to want to help me. I asked him to get a message to Mrs Makepiece and ask her for some food – he said it wasn't his job to run round after me. I couldn't eat anyway, I felt sick.' I looked down at the bowl and felt my stomach turn.

'I'm sorry Mrs Fisher, it is lovely but I can't manage any more.'

I turned to Cecilia who was looking at me with great concern.

'How is Beth, has she been well, is she feeding properly?'

'Oh, she is bonny and very greedy. We think, that is I think, she might take some solids soon. She smiles and laughs and has us all wrapped round her little finger. Esther, if you want to change and have a bath, I have asked the girls to heat the water for you. I didn't think you would want to cuddle Beth with the dirt of the gaol all about you.'

'No, no, of course not. I'll go up then and perhaps I can see Beth as soon as I come down?' I asked, trying to ignore the jealousy that pinched my heart.

'Yes, of course,' she smiled gently. 'Don't worry Esther, Beth knows you are her mother and she will soon be back in your arms.'

'I'm sorry Cecilia, It is just so hard not to see her and I am so grateful to you for stepping in and loving her.'

'There is no need to thank me, we are happy to care for her and Esther, you must not think I am trying to usurp you. I am not.'

I struggled to compose myself: to control the jealousy, the mean-spiritedness that threatened to overwhelm me, when all these people had done was to help and protect us.

'I know, Cecilia.' Hot tears tracked down my cheeks. 'I just feel so unsure of myself now and thoughts come into my mind that shouldn't be there. I have tried to find my spirit, as Mr Elwood advised, but I just seem to be floundering in a pool of doubt. Please forgive me.'

She smiled and took me by the hand as we walked up the stairs to my room. 'Have your bath Esther, make yourself fresh and pretty and Beth will recognise you as her mother.'

Chapter Twenty-Six

To dry salt beef and pork
Lay the meat on a table or in a tub with a double bottom, that the brine may drain off as fast as it forms, rub the salt well in, and be careful to apply it to every niche; afterwards put it into either of the above utensils; when it must be frequently turned, after the brine has ceased running, it must be quite buried in salt, and kept closely packed. Meat which has had the bones taken out is the best for salting. In some places the salted meat is pressed by heavy weights or a screw to extract the moisture sooner.
MacKenzie's Five Thousand Receipts in All the Useful and Domestic Arts

Time moved on and I was feeling stronger when Farmer Elwood, Cecilia, Mrs Makepiece and I all agreed to put dark thoughts and deeds aside until after the Noel celebrations. My case would not be heard until the spring assizes and we were all in much need of some cheer.

Billy-alone came over one morning and Cecilia and I put our coats, hats and mittens on and walked though the orchard towards the fields. It was very cold and hoar frost crystallised the grasses and hedgerows. Lying snow had crisped up and our feet cracked the ice laying between the ruts in the trackway. Our breath sent little wisps of moisture in front of us as we marched briskly towards the coppice where, we had been assured, were evergreens and berries to decorate the drawing room and – for the first time – the kitchen.

Billy clambered up the bushes to pick the choicest boughs and we laughed when he fell right into the centre of a big fat laurel. We tied the branches into bundles and put them into trugs to carry home. Billy dragged the bigger ones that didn't have berries. I also cropped some old man's beard, which grew abundantly.

'We need to stop in the orchard, ma'am, I know where there be some mistletoe, a fine big sprouting,' said Billy.

'And who is the mistletoe for Billy, who wants to do the kissing?' laughed Cecilia.

'Why not me?' he declared stoutly. 'It's tradition ain't it? Some in the hall, some in the best room and…'

'…some in the kitchen,' we sang at him, laughing. For a brief moment my troubles lifted from my shoulders.

We had been out for several hours and were glad to get back into the warmth. Mrs Fisher and Cilla had made some mince pies and the kitchen smelled delicious with hot spices and sweet flavours all around. I still had not regained my appetite but I took one of the pies and enjoyed it very much. Billy took a piece of the mistletoe and with much prancing and laughing he clambered onto the big table and tied it to a beam. I glanced at Cilla who had gone quite pink. I didn't think it would be long before the evergreen symbol of romance would be put to use.

I couldn't help reminding everyone that the berries of the mistletoe were very poisonous and care must be taken that they did not fall into food or drinks.

I didn't want to break the joyous moment but I was seeing dark shadows everywhere and I couldn't help myself.

I needn't have worried, the good cheer and laughter soon took hold again as we started to decorate the entrance hall and the drawing room. Cilla and Billy undertook to do the kitchen and when we all progressed round the rooms to admire, we were very impressed with their joint effort.

Farmer Elwood returned to the house after dark and Cecilia, Beth and I were waiting in the hall to welcome him with mulled wine, warm ale and more mince pies. He pulled his lovely young wife into his arms and gave her a boisterous kiss right under the mistletoe. He tickled Beth with his whiskers and gave her a kiss too. I hung back, not sure where I belonged but he held out his hand to me and pecked me on the cheek. For the first time in weeks I felt happy. For me, it was all about belonging.

Chapter Twenty-Seven

Softening of skin and healing chaps
Take of prepared hogs lard 2lb
Rose-water 3 oz
Beat the lard with rose-water until they be mixt then melt the mixture with a slow fire, and set it apart that the water may subside; after which, pour off the lard from the water, constantly stirring until it be cold.
MacKenzie's Five Thousand Receipts in All the Useful and Domestic Arts

It was but a few days to Christmas and at last I began to feel normal again. The hardships of the gaol seemed far away as the house filled with wonderful smells and there was much giggling and secrecy as we all did our best to make little gifts for each other. I had bottled some fruit in brandy that Mrs Makepiece acquired for me from a source I didn't enquire into. I planned to give a bottle each to Farmer Elwood, Mr Franklin, and Mrs Makepiece. For Cecilia I was working on a sampler to decorate her bedroom. I struggled to think of anything for Billy but finally lit on some homemade slippers. I asked Miss Wardle for some small off-cuts of piggy leather and fashioned them into slippers using wool and leather thongs for bindings. Beth was easy – I made a little jerkin from some fragments of material from Cecilia's linen box. I had enough scraps left over to make a hat and mittens and socks. Miss Wardle entered into the spirit of giving and for her I made some ointment, according to a receipt of my mother's, to protect the skin from bad weather, though it had to be said it might be a bit late to help her old, wind-chapped hands. I did wonder if it would be right to give Dr Grieve a small gift. Cecilia and I discussed it and she said that I should bake some of my little pies and make up a parcel for him. It wasn't too personal and he liked his food.

Chapter Twenty-Eight

Bramble Wine
Of fresche picket black beries take a gallon measure; pour on an equal mesure of boyling water. Stand the Beries and Water till they be colde. Strain the liquid into an Hoggeshed; stir in of suchre three or foure Pounds. The Wyne may be dronck in one yeare or near.

Old English Recipe

The Elwoods would be 'at home' to visitors on Christmas Eve when the carol singers would come by and sing for the family. They invited their neighbours and local friends round for a drink and sweetmeats to celebrate the birth of Christ on the morrow. I didn't join the festivities as I felt myself still to be an object of gossip; Cecilia tried to reassure me that their guests would all have goodwill at heart but I couldn't quite bring myself to satisfy anyone's curiosity. However, I listened to the carols with enormous pleasure as they carried the message of hope.

The singers, lamp-bearers and musicians were all invited into the hall for mulled ale and biscuits after their boisterous singing of half a dozen festive songs. Beth and I sat on the stairway, out of sight, and watched them troop in. They seemed a bit uncomfortable but soon settled into themselves once refreshments were offered by Cilla, who had donned a maid's uniform for the occasion. Once tongues had been loosened by the ale there were good wishes and good health declarations which went on for some time – the first from the lead singer, a rather gruff looking elderly man who had a fine pitched voice, albeit a little tremulous on the higher notes. Farmer Elwood replied with his own hopes for the community at large and the health and wealth of all the people present. Everyone wanted to say something generous and all had to be given a courteous reply but last of all came expressions of goodwill for the Lady of the House. This was volunteered by one of the lamp bearers who was, perhaps, the most senior of the group. Cecilia blushed prettily and hoped that all the ladies in the group would benefit from a peaceful and bounteous Noel. After all the good wishes, the choir were offered gifts to take home (nuts and spiced preserves) and a jingly purse for the benefit of Southover Church Choir, with particular regard to cushions for the uncomfortable kneelers.

I went to bed with Beth tucked into my arms and thanked God for my good friends.

Christmas Day dawned frosty and clear and for the Elwood household began with a family visit to church – everyone went including the farm hands, their families and the household staff. I went too but with my head covered with one of Cecilia's hats with a lace veil. I knew everyone was looking at me but with Cecilia on one side and Farmer Elwood on the other I managed to hold my head up. The sermon was very long and people were shifting back and forth in their pews, no doubt thinking of the feast waiting at home. I remembered the sermons at Hamsey and the loud hectoring tone of hellfire and damnation and decided that Southover Church and its incumbent were much more to my liking.

The joy of spending Christmas with everyone I cared for and Beth's very first Noel almost overcame me but it was a wonderful day. We ate, we played, we sung, we laughed and exchanged our gifts. Billy-alone was in the kitchen, again, and he was made up with his new footwear. He presented, with a great flourish, a pretty little handkerchief for me. I didn't ask where it had come from and I am sure he was relieved that I didn't. I had given Miss Wardle her cream on Christmas Eve and I was touched when she gave me a quick hard hug and a pot of her bramble jelly.

'Now don't eat too much at once my dear, there is a good measure of brandy in it to give it some flavour.' I was amazed – did everyone in Lewes have a barrel of smuggled brandy in their cellars? I was quite sure my parents had never even tasted such strong liquor but wasn't I perpetuating this crime by making my own gifts from illegal alcohol? Who was I to criticise when I drunk the tea, ate the salt and spices and enjoyed a nip of brandy on occasions? I joined all the rest by turning a blind eye.

Cecilia and Farmer Elwood gave me a length of muslin to have made up into a blouse.

I thanked them, it was so pretty with sprigs of flowers in forget-me-not blue. I hoped they hadn't wasted their money in buying me something that might never be worn if I was taken to the gallows. I would leave the making up for a date in the future, if there was to be one.

Mrs Makepiece was invited to Christmas dinner and she was staying the night so we were able to spend a good while together with Beth on her knee. She was very pleased with my bottled fruit and handed me a little box with one of her own pieces of jewellery in it. I opened the box carefully and found a tiny brooch. It was a knot of silver with a little seed pearl at its heart.

'My dear husband gave it to me many years ago and I would rather you have it and wear it for me. My boys are far away and would not know what to do with such a delicate thing.'

I turned the beautiful brooch over in my hands, marvelling at the intricate silverwork.

'Where are your boys tonight?' I asked, hoping that they were enjoying their Noel as much as we were.

'I don't know,' she sighed. 'They are all in the navy, as was their father before them. They come home on occasions but it is not often enough. I worry about them in these troubled times what with the Frenchies and everyone fighting.'

I felt my eyes prickle. 'Thank you so much for this and everything you have done for me. I truly feel like you are my saviour – you have never doubted me and have stood up for me. No matter what happens…'

'Nothing is going to happen my dear,' she interrupted me. 'We will get rid of this silly man Coad and all get on with our lives, with Beth here growing up to be a lovely young woman and you making her a home here in Lewes.' I smiled at her belief and was comforted and said nothing more. Christmas night was upon us and we stood round Cecilia's piano and listened to her playing – her fingers traced the keys with delicacy as she sang a lullaby. Beth crowed in delight and tried to reach the source of this lovely sound. I put her next to Cecilia and she transformed the playing with her own version of thumpity-thump on the keys. We all went to bed laughing at her antics.

Chapter Twenty-Nine

A Poor Man's Soup: Pick a handful of parsley leaves, mince them fine, and strew over a little salt; shred six green onions, and put them with the parsley in a sauceboat. Add three tablespoons of oil and vinegar, with some pepper and salt.
A Cheap Rice and Meat Soup: Put a pound of rice and a little pepper and broth herbs into two quarts of water; cover them close and simmer very softly; put in a little cinnamon, two pounds of good ox-cheek, and boil the whole till the goodness is incorporated by the liquor.

MacKenzie's Five Thousand Receipts in All the Useful and Domestic Arts

Farmer Elwood

The New Year has arrived and I endeavour to keep the troubles of the world from my family but, in truth, I am concerned. There is much local disturbance with the price of grain and lack of basic foodstuffs. The harvest last year was poor and the early frozen ground yielded nothing. We are fortunate that women make the daily trek from Brighton with fresh fish. As South Farm is on their route over the downs we are lucky to get first choice. The one advantage of the heavy frost was that food did not spoil too soon. Mrs Fisher, though only a plain cook, makes the best of supplies and Esther is a great asset as she has skills with herbs and spices that improve our plain diet. The unrest in France is of great personal concern to me, my brother and uncle are both in the navy and I feel them to be at great risk. Piracy as well as smuggling is commonplace and the taking of boats, fully laden, by privateers is nearly as much a problem for the forces as is the smuggling. No one balks at the taking of Frenchies but many lawless men who have no allegiance to king or country roam our waterways.

When Esther came into our lives we were in great distress at the death of our first child. I feared for Cecilia's health and state of mind as she was distraught and has no close family nearby to help ease her pain. Esther's arrival came just in the nick of time and her gentle care of my fragile wife will stay with me. It was difficult to see and hear the child Beth in our own cradle and know that we might have had one such baby ourselves but for the cruelty of fate. As the weeks passed Beth wound herself round our fingers and hearts and Cecilia recovered. If I am honest, she did more than recover, she became stronger, happier and I had hopes that nature would take its course soon and we would be blessed with our own child. It is not unnatural to want sons to carry on our name, and work the good land that I am privileged to have inherited. But, a little girl is something different, something delicate and beauteous that needs protection and nurturing and I long for one such for Cecilia and me to cherish.

Since Noel, I have spent a number of evenings with my friend, Dr Grieve, who also happens to hold the office of coroner in Lewes. I am concerned as to why Esther is being charged with a murder when the coroner believes that young Becca, Beth's mother, died of drowning before the dreadful injuries were inflicted. The Coad family clearly had the motive to hurt both the girls. Becca because she could talk and Esther as a scapegoat for the wicked deeds inflicted by Farmer Coad.

I am deeply indebted to Esther and I believe her story so with the agreement of my dear wife I decided to fund the girl's defence. Dr Grieve has to appear impartial but I know him to believe in Esther and knew he would help with practical advice and his particular knowledge of the court's machinations which, I am grieved to say, did not always come down on the side of the innocent. Esther's simplicity could work for or against her and it was necessary to find a barrister who would present her case with clarity and be able to knock down the arrogance of the Coads. I relished the prospect of defeating this odious family who are a disgrace to civilised humanity.

It is February and I have a meeting with our chosen barrister, Mr Josiah Button.

'Tell me again, Mr Elwood, about the bag that the money was handed over in – you have it in your house?'

'Yes, it is kept safe in my study.'

'We need to fetch it – I will take it with me and make enquiries. I will also need to speak with the young woman before the case comes to court.'

'That is easily arranged. Tell me, do you think we have a good chance of acquittal?'

'Ah, that is indeed a question. We have a legal system that requires the jury to understand the evidence and act accordingly. Regretfully, in my learned opinion, juries are largely drawn from the less educated classes for the simple reason that there are more of them. Because of that we also need a judge who can see the wood for the trees and direct the jury to the proper conclusion. Alas, this does not always happen. A jury can be swayed by many things, not necessarily pertinent to the case.'

'Surely, the case depends on the evidence presented?' Mr Button laughed at my words and I was discomfited to hear him. I wasn't accustomed to people deriding my opinion.

'My dear sir, clearly you have not been in touch with the courts before now. I congratulate you but regretfully the jury is often the Achilles' heel of the system.

I banged my fist on the desk in frustration.

'Well, what are we to do then? Why am I employing you, at great expense I must say, if you cannot be certain to win our case?'

Mr Button raised his silver topped cane to his mouth and tapped it against his teeth.

My dear fellow, you are employing me because I can out-think and then outwit any jury and certainly the public prosecutor.'

I was uncomfortable with this declaration but Dr Grieve seemed to think that Josiah Button was the best we could hope for in the defence of Esther.

Later, at home, I confided in Cecilia that it wasn't as clear-cut as I had believed; that Esther's very innocence made her a 'sitting duck for the prosecution' according to Mr Josiah Button.

'But how can that be, my dear?' A crinkle of concern had knotted her brow.

'Her testimony can be manipulated by the prosecution because she hasn't the knowledge of mankind to appreciate how wicked some people are. In other words, she is gullible in her innocence.'

'Oh John, what are we to do?'

'We must hand over the evidence – the stake, the bag, the money and prepare Esther for a rough ride. Mr Button will arrange investigators to seek out the facts and he will, God willing, find enough facts to carry the jury without putting Esther on the stand.'

Cecilia grasped my hands and we sat in sad silence at the unfairness of it all.

Chapter Thirty

Esther

I am to meet the barrister that Farmer Elwood has employed for me at the inn near the court. He has arrived a few days early to question and prepare. He has been provided with a list of people who will give testimony on my behalf. I am frightened. I don't like this man. I worry that Farmer Elwood is spending money on me that should be going to his own family and farm. Times are very hard and no one can afford to waste money. I clutch Beth to me in fear and misery.

Cecilia

Esther is to be put on trial for murder tomorrow. Today, I am charged with preparing her for what will be a frightful miscarriage of justice if she is found guilty. We believe in her innocence, we don't even understand why she has been charged. That horrible man who will defend her has demoralised her, us, completely. He has tortured her with memories; he has browbeaten her with interpretations – false interpretations. He has bullied us all and we no longer know what it is we think. Today, my dear husband is to take Esther to the market tower where she will spend the night in a cell before being taken before the judge tomorrow. We have been told that the judge, his Honour George Pettigrew, is a stickler for procedures and, fortunately for us is considered a fair man.

This morning Esther rose and packed her little bag with some clean undergarments. She hesitated and then pulled a sweet comb from the bag and handed it to me saying, 'If, Cecilia, things go badly for me, then I ask you to save this comb and give it to Beth when she is older. It was her mother's and she loved it dearly. Please also give this brooch to Beth. Mrs Makepiece gave it to me for Christmas and I don't think it sensible to keep it by me.'

I dropped my eyes as I took the comb, I didn't want her to see my tears and believe that I had lost faith, not in her innocence, but in our ability to protect her.

I took Esther in the carriage to Mrs Makepiece who was all of a flutter and not much use in keeping either of us calm. We left Beth with her when my husband arrived to escort us all to the market tower. We were determined to show the town that this young woman was under our protection and as we are considered to be people of substance in this community our protection was a public declaration of her innocence.

I could not bring myself to enter the gaol but waited outside in the carriage as John escorted my dearest friend inside. I could hear a lot of noise and I gathered that the assizes were to try a very full list of cases. Later, John told me that Esther was incarcerated with some light women and several trampers. Mrs Fisher had prepared her a decent basket of refreshments and at the very least I can be assured she won't go hungry again. John had advised her to sew some coins into her hem in case of need. We went back to collect

Beth and returned home. I retired to my room once I had made sure that there was a good dinner being prepared for John and Dr Grieve who had accepted our invitation to dine. I spent my time playing with my poor motherless Beth and saying prayers for Esther's deliverance. It was a distressing day for all of us.

Chapter Thirty-One

Esther

The constable came and entered my name into a great book. He took my basket from me and searched it. I felt very uncomfortable when this uncouth man pulled my drawers and bits and bobs out for all to see. He then proceeded to unpack the food which Mrs Fisher had kindly put up for me. He smirked as he put the food and ale to one side. 'That'll make me a nice lunch today. Here, I'll leave you the apple.' I ignored his familiar looks and kept my eyes down. I felt beaten already. In some ways I hoped that I would be sent to the gallows rather than a long internment in a prison or a prison ship.

I felt I would not be able to adjust to incarceration no matter how brave I might become. I knew I should not be thinking like this – giving up hope. I should be full of my own innocence and people would see it and know me to be not guilty.

Somehow, I had lost hope that I would overcome the Coads. I was in such a low state that I considered pleading guilty just to get it over with. I had not told anyone my thoughts as they would be greatly shocked and distressed and I couldn't bear for them to suffer on my behalf.

We entered a cell that was already crowded with other women: coarse, dirty women who all stared at me. I cringed back and tried to stop but the constable put his hand on my back and gave me a great push. I fell into the squalid little room and grabbed at the nearest person to stop me from falling onto the dirty floor.

'Oi, gerr off… what d'ye think yer doin?'

'I'm so sorry, I didn't mean to…'

'Oh, I say, a bit lah di dah ain't we? Look loveys we got us a posh one 'ere – what you in for m'lady?'

'Murder,' I whispered.

This seemed to startle the woman who peered at me with interest.

'Landsakes, who did you top then, yer ol' man?'

'No, I am innocent of the charges. I didn't murder anyone. I am falsely accused by a man who wants to cover up his own wrongdoings.'

My voice had risen and grown stronger as I continued and in the end I told my fellow prisoners all about Farmer Coad and his wicked sons. It was the best thing I could have done because after that they seemed to have some sympathy for me and my night in their company was not so very bad. We were five in that cell and there were others all around waiting their turn for summary justice. There was only one pallet in the corner of the room and three of us sat on it side by side – the women decided I was entitled to a spot on the pallet because of my lipsy leg but in the end we all swapped round throughout the night.

No one could sleep because of the noise from the other cells. When daylight eventually filtered into our space I began to quiver with fear again. Sarah, one of my companions, told me that Justice Pettigrew was a sour but fair man and that I should put some faith in being honest.

'How do you know?' I asked.

'I've been up before his almighty-self many a time and he and I is on remarkably good terms,' she cackled through her broken teeth. 'I's expecting to go down for a whiles this time tho, maybe even transported. Suit me fine, getting out of this Godforsaken country, startin' afresh somewheres else, find me a man and a nice little cottage in a warm place.'

I listened to her dreams with pity, I had heard all about the conditions on the transport ships.

'I hope you are released,' I said, as optimistically as I could.

The constable came by with bowls of thin gruel and five crusts of bread, which Miss Wardle wouldn't even have given to her piggies. I handed my share to Sarah who tucked in without complaint dipping her bread in the gruel to soften it. I was called to the bars and told that I was up first and to prepare myself. A few minutes later the door clanged open and I was handcuffed and led up through a tunnel and into the heaving courtroom.

Chapter Thirty-Two

Balsamic and anti-putrid vinegar
Take rue, sage, mint, rosemary, and lavender, fresh gathered, of each a handful, cut them small, and put them into a stone jar, pour upon the herbs a pint of the best white-wine vinegar; cover the jar close, and let it stand eight days in the sun or near a fire; then strain it off and dissolve it in an ounce of camphor. The liquid sprinkled or fumigated will much revive and prevent attendants from receiving infection.
MacKenzie's Five Thousand Receipts in All the Useful and Domestic Arts

It was very noisy in the court and I couldn't make out where the judge was. I saw lots of beetley black men scurrying about in wigs and carrying files. A number of grandly-dressed women were sitting in the front pews waving fans under their noses for the smell was not pleasant. Clouds of dust rose as soon as anyone moved and there were a lot of people moving: coming and going – rising and sitting – moving along to allow others to squeeze onto the benches. At last it all settled down into a stillness of sorts and I was able to identify my friends in the crowd. Cecilia was separate; she sat upright and tense. I felt she should have stayed away: the court is not a suitable place for such a genteel person. I expect they were going to call her as a character witness. I gripped the rail in front of me as a loud voice shouted, 'All rise, for his Lordship Justice George Pettigrew…' I didn't hear the rest, my hearing seemed muffled. Everyone stood as a stooped man in a black gown and yellowing wig made his way to the bench. He sat. Everyone sat back down but not me. I was held up by the determined young man.

'M'Lord, this young woman is charged with the deliberate murder of her colleague and friend Miss Rebecca Franklin…' It all faded away from me as I swooned onto the hard chair behind me. I was aware of a lot of noise around me and the insistent banging of a gavel.

'Silence, silence! I will have silence in my court. Young lady, stand up and pay attention.'

The court was told of the finding of Becca's body, of the dreadful injuries inflicted on her, of the knowledge of a recent birthing and finally of the accusation from Farmer Coad that I had deliberately and wilfully held Becca under the water until she drowned and then had violated her poor limp body in a fit of temper. That I had stolen the child that Becca had borne just hours before. Not only had I done this dreadful deed but that I had boasted to the Coad family of my acts.

There was a lot of talk, back and forth, legal and plain speak. I lost track; I couldn't hear well and people seemed to be talking about someone other than me.

The judge finally addressed me personally, 'Young lady, how do you plead – guilty or not guilty?'

I gathered myself together and looked at him directly. 'I plead, your Honour, not guilty.' There, I had done it. I spoke aloud and clearly for all to hear. Not guilty.

If I was not on a charge of murder I would have soon got bored with the progress of the trial. I thought the judge looked as if he was falling asleep. It was very warm and sickly in the court and I struggled to keep my attention on the prosecutor who was outlining, at great length, the detail of Becca's death and recovery from the river. At one point he raised his arm and pointed to me with a stick saying, 'this wicked young woman, who sits before you, in a parody of innocence, deserves nothing less than to be hanged.'

He turned on his heels and addressed the jury of men. 'Don't let her innocent looks and good clothes distract you. This woman committed murder and stole a child and we will offer such facts that will prove it to you gentlemen of the jury.'

The judge sighed and held a nosegay of herbs beneath his nose as he said in a tone of utter weariness. 'Can we get on with it then? Haranguing the court proves nothing. Let us get to the point, and quickly,' he looked at his pocket watch.

The prosecution brought forth every little detail that could blacken mine and Becca's name. How we had made an exhibition of ourselves at the fair, how we had flaunted our feminine charms before God-fearing men and women. How Becca had given herself to an upstanding local man who had been tricked; tricked with a love potion into committing carnal sin. And, as a result of the one transgression of this honest fellow, a child was born. Born out of wedlock to this tramp of a girl.

And then he came to me. How I, as a dowdy, disabled creature, marked by the pox and unlikely to ever find herself a man was overtaken by jealousy and when everyone else on the farm was warm in their beds had sneaked out and held Becca under the water until she drowned. Not content with murder, I had then taken a sharpened weapon and had beaten the poor girl's body to a pulp.

'Mind, what I say, gentlemen of the jury. A pulp.'

According to the prosecution, with my dreadful deed completed, I had returned to the farmhouse and washed all traces of my wickedness away and had stolen the child. Farmer Coad and one of his sons, the eldest, were called to the stand and swore on the Holy Bible that the prosecutor's tale was God's honest truth.

This corrupt version of our tragedy was reiterated over and over again in one form of words or another until the judge called a halt for luncheon. I was returned to a holding cell in the passageway below the court while the judge and his retinue took their meal at the White Hart. It must have been a good meal as they were gone a long time.

Josiah Button appeared at the door of my cell, making me jump. 'How do, Miss Esther. Ready for the off? Now I want you to speak clearly, no mumbling or downcast eyes. Look at the judge and the jurymen and answer honestly or as I direct you *if* I call you to the stand.'

I was bewildered by that and just nodded. I would do my best. Beth needed me and I hated to see Becca spoken of as a light young woman who would sell her favours. These disgusting claims made me feel physically sick. I could only see the pitiful picture of a girl, barely out of childhood herself, who was wickedly violated over and over again. My poor Becca, how I missed her. Mr Button was bustling all around me, full of energy and conviction. If only I had just a small part of his demeanour perhaps people would believe me too.

I was served a small lunch and as I picked at it I reflected on the terrible things that had been said about Becca and me. How dare they? How dare they treat us like light women when all we had done was care for each other. By the time I was called back to the court I was beginning to feel a worm of anger; I would fight this. I would fight for Becca's reputation and my name. Back in the dock I could see Farmer Coad and his three sons in the room. They kept their eyes on me all the time and the eldest kept smirking at me. I wondered where Mrs Coad, their mother and my kinswoman, was.

Mr Josiah Button filled the court. He was everywhere – leaning on the jury box; walking the width of the courtroom; holding his arm out to the public as if each and every one of them were of the greatest importance to this trial. He addressed the judge in tones of respectful humility. He poured scorn on the prosecutor and made the public laugh at his wit. He tore the prosecutor's case to shreds. He called witnesses to declare me a paragon of virtue; he summoned Billy-alone to tell of the incident on the river and he humiliated the Coad sons.

He talked gently, almost caressingly, to Cecilia who whispered of my care and nursing in her hours of desperate need. He summoned the matriarchal Mrs Makepiece and talked to her as if she were the most respected inhabitant of Lewes, as indeed she was. Then, when I thought he was done he called the coroner who stated clearly that the unfortunate death of Becca was, indeed, a suicide as planned by a fourteen year old out of her mind with what had been forced upon her innocent young body. When he used the words 'repeated rape' there was an outburst of chatter in the court. Mr Josiah Button held Becca's fragile cradle aloft and took it to each jury member to touch; to smell the scent of newborn baby; to see the care of the mother in each bent and folded reed.

I cried silent tears as I beheld that tiny cradle again. I looked across to Cecilia. She was as white as a sheet and clearly suffering thoughts of her own child.

Mr Josiah Button used the courtroom as his own stage; he was an artist of imagery as he painted my story in its true colours. I felt blessed to have him speaking of me in such high regard. I felt that wonderful emotion. Hope.

Finally, and with great drama he called Mr Thomas James Paulter. I leaned forward to get a glimpse of a young man who I had never seen or heard of before.

'Mr Paulter, will you tell the jury and the good people in this courtroom where you were on the day before this dreadful happening?'

'I was at work, Sir'

'And where, Mr Paulter, is your work and what do you do therein?' Mr Josiah Button examined his nails while waiting for an answer.

'I am a bank clerk, sir and on the day before the poor girl was drowned I was at Lewes bank which is just a few steps away from the c…'

'Yes, yes my good man. I know where it is but what I want to know from you, is did anyone in this courtroom come into the bank on that day Mr Paulter? For example, did Miss Esther Coad come in and withdraw any money?'

'No sir, Miss Coad does not have an account at our bank. I am pleased to be able to tell you that I know all the account holders personally. Anyways, to answer your question there are one or two faces I recognise here but they did not come in on the day in question except that one sitting over there, with his three sons.'

'Can you tell me his name my good sir?'

'Yes, indeed, his name is Farmer Coad.'

'Did Farmer Coad withdraw any cash on that day?'

'He did, sir, he was intending to buy some new stock and he had particularly requested a substantial withdrawal from his account.'

'Are you able to tell us how much cash was withdrawn on that day and what form of notes and cash was paid?'

'Yes, Sir – I gave him thirty-five pounds in all and it was a mixture of notes and silver. Farmer Coad prefers notes on account of the lighter weight so I gave him three ten pound notes and five pounds in coin.'

'Was there anything unusual about the notes, young man?'

'Not unusual but the notes were all new. I drew them from the vaults that day and they were unused.'

'If I were to show you some notes might you be able to identify them?'

'I might. I make a small pencil mark as part of my counting procedure.'

Mr Josiah Button spun on his heels and went to his desk in the foot of the court and picked up the bag that Farmer Coad had given me. He withdrew the notes and cash from inside it.

'Young man, can you identify this bag?'

'Why yes sir. It is the bag that the bank uses to give customers their money. They, that is the customers, also use it to pay money into the bank. See here, he has marked the bag with his own brand CF as well. People do that in case the bag gets mislaid.'

'Look carefully at these notes, young fellow. Can you identify them?'

The young man peered closely at the notes and pointed to a faint pencil mark in the top right hand corner. These are the notes that I gave Farmer Coad. Here, you can see the mark CF.'

'Are you sure? Is there not a shadow of doubt?'

'No sir, there is no doubt whatsoever. I can't identify the silver but it is in the right denominations and adds up to the amount given to Farmer Coad.' The young man left the witness box and all was deathly silent in the court.

I looked across at the Coads as this detail was revealed and saw a look of fear cross the master's face, his sons, perhaps not realising the implications of the testimony, looked unconcerned.

Mr Josiah Button paraded from one tier of seating to the other on the opposite side of the court. He appeared to collect the inhabitants of the court in the sweep of his hand.

'Gentlemen of the Jury. M'Lord,' He bowed deeply to the judge.

'I can tell you that Miss Esther Coad, who sits here in the dock in trembling innocence, has been maligned and cruelly used by a family who have conspired to blacken her good name. This man,' he pointed at Mr Coad dramatically. 'This man, was the reason for a tragic suicide. His behaviour, lust and wilful disregard of the integrity of British law and order is the reason why one young woman, a mere child of fourteen tender years, died needlessly and then, and then, gentlemen of the jury, suffered the indignity of a brutal vindictive attack on her mortal remains. An innocent baby had been born in the midst of this tragedy. That baby is motherless and if it weren't for the actions and care of young Miss Esther Coad, that baby, yes that blessed tiny baby would be, in all probability, dead. Yes dead.'

'Gentlemen of the jury, my fine fellows, I beg that you acquit this young lady of murder. She never did it. That's a fact. She never did it. I rest my case, M'Lord.'

I held my breath. I believed him. I never did it, just as he said.

After a lot of arguing back and forth between the prosecutor and Mr Josiah Button the judge called the court to order and proceeded to sum up all that had been said, on one side and then the other. While he summed up the prosecution's case I felt they were in the ascendancy but then when he got to the defendant's side, my side, my spirits soared as it appeared so clear-cut. The story of Becca, the repeated rape, the cradle, the money and my rescuing Beth from the family was told in such a way as to convince the jury that I was innocent. No one spoke to me at all. I wasn't called to give evidence.

The jury were told to go and deliberate amongst themselves. They muttered together in a corner of the room and finally came back to the judge, asking to see the stave that was used to inflict the wounds on Becca's body and the stave that was thrown at Billy. They muttered again and everyone was getting restless. The aristocratic ladies yawned into their hankies and the public seating area shifted back and forth with people gossiping, discussing and wondering. I waited quietly, my hands shredding Billy-alone's handkerchief into little bits.

'Gentlemen, have you reached a verdict?'

'We have, M'Lord.'

'What is your verdict?'

'Not guilty, your Honour.'

There was a great shout and hammering of feet on the floor.

'Silence, silence! I will have silence in court!' bellowed the judge.

Everyone settled back down into their chairs and those that had left were scrambling back in. The judge looked at me.

'Please stand, Miss Coad.'

'Your peers, the men of the jury, have found you not guilty of Rebecca Franklin's murder and you may leave this court today with your reputation untarnished, but, before you do so I wish to say a few words. You may sit.'

I sat. The judge put his fingers together in the manner of a steeple. He looked round the courtroom his gaze finding every eye and silencing those who shifted or whispered, even the aristocratic ladies. He drew his cane towards his nose and inhaled deeply before speaking. 'I find this case to be very disturbing. Why the case was brought in the first place appears to me to have been an act of malice. Mr Josiah Button, whilst I congratulate you on your thorough and effective work, I do not like such grandstanding in my court. Had you called the coroner and the bank clerk to the stand early on we could have dispensed with this case in better time, not to say spared Miss Coad the ordeal of sitting and listening to the evidence, much of which was distressing. However, for investigative clarity I commend you. As to whether there was ever a case to answer I require the justice's clerk and the constable to come to my chambers to explain themselves on this matter once today's business is done. I will recommend to the clerk of the courts that a summons be issued to the family who are at the heart of this dreadful story. Perjury is a crime that will be taken seriously by this court and I will personally see that this matter is investigated and punished fully within the scope of the law.

Finally, I would like to be assured that the financial welfare of the child is undertaken by the father. I would also like to be assured that the child is cared for by Miss Franklin's father, the child's grandfather and, if that is not practicable, then by whomsoever he directs. Is the grandfather present? Let him address the court.'

Becca's pa rose from his seat. He looked very frail. He was alone; his wife had not accompanied him.

'Are you able to care for the child Sir?'

'No, M'lud. I am sorry to say that I have not the means and that my wife has not the inclination.'

The court erupted into a babble of voices.

'Silence.'

'Are you able to appoint someone to raise the child and who is willing?'

'Aye, your honour. Esther would have been Becca's choice and she has been a fine mother to my granddaughter. I would like for that to be legal and above board, if it pleases you.'

'A sensible option. Miss Coad do you agree to raise the child until she be of age? I will appoint a sum of money to be paid to you from the father's income until such time as she is an adult. Do you agree to the terms?'

'I do my Lord, and thank you.'

'I wish you well young lady, you have suffered a

despicable attack and you may be assured it will not go unpunished. Guard, remove the bindings. You are free to leave Miss Coad.'

As I held my hands out for the bindings to be removed he continued.

'Guard, arrest that family: all of them. Put them in the cells until such time as I have investigated their perjury and whatever other charges I can think of.'

I staggered towards my friends who all rushed forward to hug me. Farmer and Mrs Elwood had their carriage brought round to the door of the court and I was carried bodily into it. Hurried arrangements were made to meet at South Farm and there I was able to absorb all that had happened and thank my dear friends who had done so much to bring the evidence to court.

My thanks were also due of course, to Mr Josiah Button.

Chapter Thirty-Three

South Farm had become such a place of rescue to me I would like to tell you that I lived there forever and a day in peace and loving kindness. It was not to be, but I run ahead of myself and if I am to pick up the threads of my story I will return to the days following the court case.

When we returned to the farm Farmer Elwood and Cecilia broached a keg of their finest brandy to sup with all who came to offer their congratulations and friendship. I was quite taken aback with so many messages of support from people I thought had shunned me.

I clung to Mrs Makepiece and Beth who began to wail at all the noise and my ever-tightening grip. Billy-alone was welcomed into the drawing room with young Cilla and made to tell and retell his story over and over again. The young man from the bank was invited by Farmer Elwood to take a drink with the family and repeatedly thanked for his careful testimony. The jury – my peers the judge had called them – arrived singly and together during the course of the afternoon. All were thanked for their diligence in delivering such a welcome verdict. Mr Josiah Button did not call in but sent his clerk with his bill. I don't think a bill was ever paid with so much pleasure, and relief that the money wasn't wasted.

I was exhausted and felt myself drifting off into a haze of confusion. I felt unconnected to the clamour that surrounded me and I begged to be allowed to take to my room with just Beth for company. Once alone I discarded my outer clothes and sat at my dressing table. Cecila had placed Becca's comb on my table and I held it to my heart as I wept again for Becca and all that had happened. I began to pull the comb repeatedly through my hair, soothing myself with this repetition. Beth was dozing on my bed and gradually I calmed myself as I sought a sense of connection to Becca through her comb. As I touched my hair with her last gift to me I felt a presence and looked into the mirror and for just a moment I thought I saw a hazy form at my shoulder and a light touch. It is difficult to describe but it was there and it left me peaceful and comforted. I have never told anyone about this moment of otherworldliness but it is something I cling to: an understanding, love, belief in good over evil, belief in life after death, I don't know but I do know there was someone in my room with me that day and she comforted me.

Part Two

Chapter Thirty-Four

Things settled down fairly quickly after the trial and for the first time I felt I could walk freely about the town. Mrs Makepiece accompanied Beth and me or, quite often, she looked after her whilst I roamed the passages and twittens that make up Lewes. One of these trips took me into the church of St Michael's opposite Bull House.

Since my moment of connection to Becca I felt drawn to places of worship, in spite of my previous lack of religion. However, the churches I went to disappointed me somehow and I rarely returned. St Michael's, however, was different. It had a round tower instead of the normal square ones and though dark inside I soon found a little door that led outside into a peaceful burial ground and I felt immediately uplifted. It was a quaint place with flint walls and aged trees. Among the graves were wild flowers and green grassy hillocks nestling between the higgledy-piggledy stones. A lone bird trilled a piping melody and I sank down on the grass to breathe in the warm sunshine in a place that felt to be my secret. I could see the mound of the castle beyond the walls and I spent many minutes there imagining past peoples and their stories. Apart from birdsong it was very quiet in the garden – I couldn't hear the noise and bustle of the town even though the high street was just a stone's throw away nor was anyone visiting the church at that time. Whilst I sat in peace and harmony with my surroundings I noticed a tiny plant struggling to escape the confines of the old flat stones. I probed the crevices with my fingers and freed up the straggling growth. I was curious about the flower, I had never seen such a one before and it had a pungent aroma. I felt it to be an herb but I was not sure of what type. I plucked a leaf and flower to take home and compare with my father's diagrams and notes.

Chapter Thirty-Five

The days were growing longer and Beth was changing daily. She chortled and crowed as we played in the warmth of the spring sunshine, her little limbs kicking and stretching as she tried to reach to pull herself upright. She had the most beautiful hair, bright of colour and with tumbling waves that fell about her pretty, tender neck. I loved her as if she were of my body and I could not have loved her any more. She brought such pleasure into South Farm – the only greater pleasure would be if Cecilia had a child of her own as well. I prayed nightly that she would be blessed soon.

South Farm was a delight in springtime with lambs everywhere. Farmer Elwood was greatly preoccupied with his breeding plans for a flock of special sheep. He worked with other landowners nearby to develop a breed that would bring credit and profits. His friend and colleague John Ellman of Glynde had worked hard to create a new type of sheep and Farmer Elwood was part of the plan to bring the Southdown breed into general use. Both Cecilia and I became expert in the finer points of animal husbandry and the general excitement of seeing the flocks mature and breed onward to improve the stock. The advantages of our flock were in the good meat, the sturdy limbs and the ability to thrive on the chalk downs.

In those few idyllic months there was only one incident

locally that occasioned worry and that concerned Billy-alone whose ongoing courtship of Cilla was both funny and determined. He was so cheeky and chirpy that he had wormed his way into Cilla's heart, and in truth, mine as well. I never forgot that I owed him a huge debt.

One day, in the late spring, I was walking in the orchard when I saw Billy running towards the farm. He was dodging in and out of trees and bushes as if he were being pursued by the hounds of hell. I called out to him and he burst through a hedgerow to come up alongside me. Beth looked at him, startled and burst into tears. His face was red and he was gasping for breath.

'What is it Billy, what's wrong?'

'The press gang are in town and I saw them talking to the overseer at the poor house.' Billy gasped. 'He hates me since I moved in with Miss Wardle. He pointed to me and they started running after me. I can't go, I can't go to sea. I'd miss Sally too much and Cilla too!'

'Are they coming after you or did you get away from them?'

'I don't know,' he sobbed, collapsing in a heap at my feet. He was still terribly thin despite all the good food he now got at Miss Wardle's and here at South Farm. He was still just a child for all his bravado and my heart went out to him. 'Stay here Billy, I will go and see if anyone is coming. Hide under the bushes if it will make you feel safer.'

I hurried down to the farm entrance with Beth on my hip and looked towards Lewes. I couldn't see anyone but I had heard that these men were a terrible risk to anyone they caught and forced to accept the King's shilling. If the overseer of the poor house was being bribed to name names and, worse still, directions, then Billy was at huge risk. In my mind it was legalised kidnap. I hurried back to reassure him and found him in the kitchen gulping down a jug of small ale as if his life depended on it.

There was uproar round the table and we all talked over each other as we tried to come up with a plan to keep Billy from the gangers. Cecilia promised to speak to Farmer Elwood and Billy was persuaded to stay at South Farm overnight.

Farmer Elwood

I returned home after a difficult day in the lambing fields. So many of my young ewes were presenting with difficulties I resolved to speak to John Ellman for his advice. My mind was intent on this plan of action and I would have ridden out this very evening to Glynde to call on him but my household was in uproar. Cecilia and Esther were wringing their hands and young Billy-alone was all but hiding under the table. My friend Dr Grieve arrived in the middle of the bedlam and I used his arrival to help restore order in the kitchen before asking my wife to come quietly to the dining room, with Esther, to sit with me and Dr Grieve. I gave orders to Mrs Fisher that a meal should be served within the hour and that I was hungry and I had the satisfaction of seeing everyone jump to their allotted tasks.

I deemed it a good idea to pour some brandy and gradually peace was restored though both the women were a little dishevelled and had tracks of tears on their faces. It amazes me how involved my lady becomes with the lives and problems, even minor, of our servants. Cecilia's family were all out of the top drawer and I couldn't imagine for one minute her mother being aware of her staff other than if they failed in their daily tasks. I suppose in many ways this trait and her kindness in general was what endeared her to me so I resolved to be patient and generous as well, despite my wish to be elsewhere.

'I am so sorry John, I didn't realise the time, we were all so upset about Billy I forgot my duties.'

'It is Mrs Fisher who forgot her duties – here, take some brandy.'

'No, I don't believe I will, I am all of a quiver.'

I saw Esther look at Cecilia as she said this and wondered whether she knew something that I didn't. I suggested that while we waited for dinner we would determine what was to be done, if anything, about Billy. It was as if I had opened the floodgates, both women outstripping each other with their opinions and methods of saving Billy – all equally far-fetched and downright silly. Esther proposed covering him in grease from pig fat so he would slip out of the hands of his captors. My dear wife wanted to dress him as a girl whilst he moved about town. Knowing I was not to get any sense from either of them I asked Dr Grieve to tell us what he knew of press gangs and what were the chances of outwitting them.

He was of the opinion that there was nothing to be done now that the war with France was going badly. He said, 'The Royal Navy needs every man it can get. Once upon a time it was only seafaring men they took – usually as a merchant boat came into port they boarded and collared anyone who was youngish and fit as well as experienced. No matter that the men might have been away from their families for two years or more and unpaid like as not.'

'That's dreadful,' said Cecilia, wringing her hands with concern.

'Indeed, one local cargo boat was left with only one crew member and not the manpower to bring her in. The owners had to ferry a few old salts out to where she was drifting to capture and bring her in safely otherwise they would have lost the boat and her cargo.'

'But surely the sailors didn't *have* to go?' cried Esther.

'They did, unfortunately for them. What's more they had no recourse to the law and probably lost all their rights to the wages and rewards they had accrued with the Merchant Navy. Seafarers can often make large sums of money over and above their cargo value by capturing enemy boats or other craft and turning them into cash. Every sailor on board would get a share of the value whereas in the Royal Navy they earn a pittance, have rotten conditions and probably lose their lives into the bargain.'

Esther and Cecilia both protested that Billy was a landsman and had never even been in a craft larger than a rowing boat.

'The best thing Billy can do is hide out whenever the gangers are about and avoid going into public places and definitely not accept any hospitality from strangers. One trick they use is to drop a shilling into a beer jug and when the unlucky man drinks the beer he finds the shilling at the bottom. Apprentices used to be safe but even they are a target now. I am sorry ladies but if they catch him then he has no way of escaping his patriotic duty to fight the King's cause. His best legal hope is that they take lifers out of the prisons and make up their quotas that way. At least they get more or less willing men like that.'

'Surely there must be something that can be done?' pleaded Esther.

'Not much, my dear, but I will have a word with the scoundrel in the poor house and remind him that his duties do not include harassing local people. I will enquire if the press gang officer will take some prisoners in lieu of unsuitable urchins who get caught up in their net.'

As we drank our brandy he told us of some men so desperate to escape the clutches of the press gang they deliberately maimed themselves. 'It is not something I would recommend,' he said seriously.

I was very pleased to see Mrs Fisher and Cilla come in with our supper, which put an end to the discussion, though I did agree that Billy could stay with my shepherds for the time being in the hope that the gangers would forget him. I thought this very unlikely, but I didn't want Cecilia any more upset, particularly as she was already distressed.

By the time we had all eaten it was too late for me to ride to Glynde but I managed to have a few words with Esther before she retired to her room.

'Is Cecilia well?' I enquired, 'If there is anything amiss I would require that you tell me – regardless if she swears you to secrecy.'

'I am sure she is fine, I am not aware of any cause to worry you and she has not said anything to me. The first I knew about her queasiness was tonight as you heard. I will keep an eye on her, I promise, and let you know if there is any cause for… concern.'

I went to my study and remained there until the house was quiet before allowing myself to think that perhaps Cecilia might be expecting again. It had been many months since the death of our baby and we all prayed for another, or indeed, many children, to complete our family. Cecilia's brother had been a dear friend of mine before I had taken over the inheritance of South Farm, which had put paid to my social jaunts. He had invited me to his family home on many occasions and it was through his good offices that I was able to offer marriage to Cecilia. She accepted, despite our age difference, saying that if her brother thought so well of me then she could too. I don't think her mother was keen on the match – she was a cold, difficult woman and it was surprising to me that her children were so kind. I won her over in time and our marriage eventually went ahead. Cecilia worked on her mother because she was anxious to get away from the tight constrictions of her society family. She said as much to me when she accepted my proposal. She wanted her own home, her own family and a 'different' way of doing things. I consider our marriage a success and acknowledge that it was down to Cecilia's generous and loving nature – certainly not characteristics learnt at her mother's table. I have to confess though, I do not understand women. I wish they would speak plain and not make it so difficult to understand their wants all hidden by hints and artifice. In many ways Esther has helped us all with her good sense and lack of guile.

I made the rounds of the house as I do every evening, snuffing candles, locking doors and generally checking that all was well before retiring to our bedroom. I was very glad that my wife did not aspire to the society lady's need of a separate bedroom. As I climbed into bed and drew the bed curtains round us I could hear her gentle breathing. I settled down into the small of her back with great content. I would ride to Glynde first thing tomorrow.

Chapter Thirty-Six

Esther

A few days later I received a note from Dr Grieve, he must have delivered it very early.

'I have some news for you Esther – one of the women you befriended in gaol is still locked up in Lewes but she has received a sentence of transportation. I understand that she will be taken to the Port of London where she will be put on board a prison ship. I don't recommend that you try and see her as she is unrepentant and abusive to her guards.'

I would be abusive too if it is the same guards I had, I thought, resolving to visit Sarah as soon as possible.

I was in the kitchen as I read and heard Cilla say, as if in passing.

'Billy never came last night as 'e promised.'

I, who had been thinking only of my own predicament, said carelessly, 'Oh, I expect he has got caught up with Sally and the piglets, he do love them so.'

'No, he never turned up for to see the shepherd this day neither. He should 'ave been 'ere by dawn.'

A cold worm of worry turned over in my stomach. 'When did you last see him?'

'Day 'fore yes'day, he were going to Lewes to check up on piggies.'

'Did he put the disguise on?'

'No, he don't think it look right creeping round in lasses' dresses.'

'Mrs Fisher, can I leave Beth here while I go into the town and see if I can find him?'

'Aye, lass do that and don't come back 'til you've got good news otherwise I'll not get a day's work from Cilla here.'

I put my cloak on and some outdoor shoes before slipping out of the house and heading for Lewes.

'Miss Wardle, 'ave you seen young Billy?'

'No lass, I thought he was back with the shepherds. He were here yesterday, he left at dusk. I told him to use the twittens as I heard the press gang were abroad.'

I looked into his little room and found the clothes he should have disguised himself with. The place had a deserted feel about it and I felt something bad had happened.

Sally the pig was lying on her side with her little piglets clinging to her. She looked up at me reproachfully. I went back into the house and asked Miss Wardle to let me know if she heard from him then I decided to visit Dr Grieve who was most likely to know the news, good or bad.

I knocked on the door and it was opened by Mrs Jenkins who invited me into her kitchen.

''Ee you're up and about early lass. The doctor is away today, up in Lunnon, I do b'lieve. Is aught the matter?'

I explained that Billy had disappeared and I was worried he had been taken by the press gang.

'Aye, I heard they were about, they knocked up t'Castle public 'ouse yesterday and as the menfolk went in for their ale they pounced. There was panic round about and no one dared come out'f their 'ouses. Reckon, he might 'ave been caught up in it?'

'But Billy wouldn't have gone into the Castle, surely? It is such a rough place.' I tried to keep the panic from my voice.

'Maybe not, but when they put off in their boat this morning it were full and many the screaming women and bairns pleading with them. They be 'eartless them as do that job, even if it be in the King's name.'

'Do you know anyone who was on the boat?'

'Aye, Missus Arkwell's boy and husband were both took. She be left now with a parcel of little 'uns and none to feed them.'

'Where can I find her?'

'She'm down by the wharf trying to get t'men to go downriver and fetch 'em back. Some of the lads are all for rescuing them before they gets put to sea.'

I hurried down to the bridge and crossed over into Cliffe and was struck that this busy place was unusually quiet apart from a group of crying women.

'I'm looking for Billy-alone,' I shouted above their tears. 'Do anyone know if he was took?'

A respectable-looking woman looked up and called to me 'Aye, 'ee were one of they an' he took a powerful lot of 'suading to get in the boat. They cracked 'im over the 'ead and knocked 'im out'.

Another woman, not so respectably dressed and with three crying children clinging to her knees chipped in, 'Some lads 'ave gone after they, with pistols and what not. They be smugglers and knows their way round like. Is he yourn, lady?'

'No, he's a friend and I would dearly like to find him.'

''As he got babes to support?' A younger woman asked

before spitting into the river water swirling sulkily at her feet.

'No, he's the sweetheart of Cilla at South Farm and she is distressed not knowing where he is.'

'She be lucky she aint 'is wife then with a parcel of nippers to look to.'

I approached the woman who had seen Billy and said I would call back later and see if there was any news.

'Aye, lass you will find me in the public house down the way. We look after our own 'ere and that is where we meet.'

I gripped her thin hand. 'I am Esther of South Farm, I will come and find you later. God be with you and yours.'

'I put my faith in t'smugglers rather than God,' she replied and at that moment I had to agree.

Thirty-Seven

Certain groups were exempt from the impressment process, apprentices were exempt. Officially foreigners could not be impressed, although they could be persuaded to volunteer and there was an age limit of 18 to 55 years. But the rules were often ignored so that the press gang could earn their reward, they were paid by the head. Often men were knocked unconscious or threatened and often violent fights broke out as groups tried to prevent friends or workmates being impressed into the Royal Navy.

I hurried back to South Farm calling in again on Miss Wardle to give her the news. Lewes to South Farm is a good way and I was all but exhausted when I got back for all it was still only mid morning. I went straight to the kitchen and told them the gloomy news before seeking Cecilia. After I told her my discoveries and recovered my breath we sat and tried to decide what to do for the best.

'I think I must go to Newhaven and see if I can discover him,' I said.

'He'll be out of port by now, they won't keep the men on land for any longer than necessary,' she replied pensively.

'We don't know that, they might be holding them somewhere downriver.'

'Let me see if John's factor is still here, he looks after several properties at Southease and I think he was going down to Piddinghoe today to bring back some tools.'

Cecilia disappeared for a few minutes while I sat thinking how I could best help Billy. When she returned she was followed by a young man who she introduced as Wilf. He was dressed in working clothes and had a friendly smile. He held out his hand to me and I took it in mine.

'Wilf will take you to Piddinghoe, Esther. I have asked him to help you find Billy and providing he gets his work done his time is yours. I will tell John and I am sure there will be no problem. Now, make haste!'

Our journey began with little talk between us. I was preoccupied with worry for Billy and my companion was equally reticent. However as we jogged along in a farm cart pulled by a dappled grey of huge proportions we were much thrown together by the awkward terrain. Thankfully there had not been much rain recently so the ruts were dry and dusty but it was very uneven. Eventually, I asked Wilf why he was not making the journey by river.

'Engineers 'ave been working on t'river, straightening and deepening it in places as well as creating some drainage. It has been planned for some time so I knew it were not worth queuing on t'river.'

'So boats as left Lewes this morning would have been held up?'

'Aye, reckon so. You thinking about t'young lad?'

'Yes, I am so worried, he has been a good friend to me in the past. It be wrong to take him like that – he is just a boy and so thin.'

'You sound like you're his ma.'

I laughed and relaxed and at that moment a rut in the track threw us together so we both ended up giggling.

Wilf must have only been in his mid-twenties and despite

being similar in years I felt myself to be more mature. I felt comfortable with him though and relaxed as we travelled.

We rode on for some distance, chatting about the journey, the weather and nothing of reality but as we drew nearer to Piddinghoe I felt myself returning to a state of anxiety.

'What will you do? We are nearly there,' he said.

I looked at his open friendly face, his blue eyes crinkling in the corners as he looked quizzically at me.

'I don't know but I think first I must first find out whether the boat has got down t'river.'

'Let me get the tools sorted at Piddinghoe and I will ask around if they know anything.'

'Can I come with you?'

'Aye, but leave the talking to me.'

Piddinghoe was a small hamlet sitting right on the edge of the river. You could see where the river crept round the church when in full flow and, I was amazed to see another round tower like the one at St Michael's in Lewes. Wilf directed the horse to a small hard where some boats were moored. He jumped off the cart and came round to my side and lifted me off the seat down to firm ground. I gasped with surprise and felt the colour rising in my cheeks.

'Hey John, how be you this fine spring day?' he called to a wiry looking fellow.

'Not so brave boy, reckon this messing with the river be all wrong – there's been no trade today.' We all stood staring down into the water that was lapping fitfully at the banks.

'It'll be better when Mr Cater Rand has finished. He have rare vision and trade will only increase, don't you think?'

'I 'ope you're right lad. Anyways, I 'ave your tools 'ere and will help you load. Will your young lady take a sup yonder at the Crown? They have a parlour for t'ladies.

'No, no, I would like to help, if I may,' I said, anxious not to be left out.

Wilf laughed and told me to sit down on the grass while he and John went about their work.

I couldn't hear what they said to each other despite trying to creep nearer but there was much head scratching and lowered voices. I moved away into the churchyard and wandered among the gravestones. As I poked around I came across the same plant that was in St Michael's that I still hadn't managed to identify. I picked a few small leaves to take home. Finally, they finished and called out to me.

I met Wilf's gaze, and he indicated with a small shake of his head that I should not speak, so other than saying goodbye I was lifted back onto the cart and we were off towards Newhaven.

The sun was high in the sky and he pulled into a field and dropped the reins so Ida was able to graze. 'Here, 'ave a bite of me pasty,' he offered.

I refused, not wanting to take his meal from him but I accepted a drink from a leather bottle.

'Did he know anything?' I gasped as a draught of strong cider hit the back of my throat.

'Aye, he said that the press men came through not half an hour gone and were meeting up with others at Newhaven this night. They were mighty put out at having been held up.'

'When will they load onto their boat, did he know that?'

'There be a man o'war off Seaford Head and the men said they were to put about into Newhaven on tonight's tide.'

'Had he seen any men from Lewes who might have been giving chase?'

'He said there be a group of men riding down the smuggler's way and they is armed to the teeth and growing in number as they go along. They be mad as one of their number was spirited out of prison by the press gang before they could 'persuade' the justice to let him go.'

I felt a squirm of excitement that must have shown because Wilf suddenly turned serious.

'It is a dangerous business to mess with these men Esther. They don't leave anyone to talk and if there be fighting it will be dirty and men will get hurt, maybe even killed.'

'Oh, poor Billy, what should I do Wilf?'

'John did say that there be an unconscious lad in the boat and they were in two minds to put him off.'

'Oh, that must be Billy, the woman at the wharf said they cracked him over the head.'

'He must be in a bad way for them to talk about offloading him. He might be badly injured and you'd better prepare for the worst.'

We had been stopped for a while and I was impatient to get going. Wilf made Ida ready to move on.

Newhaven was a bustling port with lots of small fishing vessels as well as much bigger craft, bigger than could make it up the river, so there was unloading of provisions onto smaller boats which Wilf said were headed upriver for the Weald. I saw great piles of corn, barley and coal. The foodstuff all seemed to be under armed guard. 'Why are there so many soldiers around in a naval port?'

'Unrest. The poorer folk can't afford the prices for wheat and stuff to feed their families. There has been arguing with the merchants who want top prices paid and refuse to reduce their profits. Recently crowds have got physical and forced some to mark down the price. The soldiers have been brought in to restore order and see that men can go about their business, 'cept they are not all here yet. There is a whole battalion due to camp nearby. Didst thou not know that there was a bad harvest with many people starving?'

'No,' I whispered. 'But I did see such scenes of anguish and poverty at Lewes when they were unloading corn at the wharf.'

'Well, Lewes be just one place amongst many but there has been a collection and a fund to offer those with least to receive food from the parish. I 'eard they were doling out soup daily to women and children who had naught to eat. It be a difficult time and many are the families who are reduced to begging help from the poor fund. Some men try to profit but the mob will only be pushed so far before it all blows up into fighting. You mun stay near me Esther, this is not a place for a young lady on her own.'

I knew that I was one of those poorest of the poor but for my good-hearted friends who had rescued Beth and me from such troubles. Wilf didn't seem to see me like that and I was pleased that he saw me as a young lady to be looked after. I immediately felt guilty for thinking of myself when so many people were suffering the harshness of poverty and possibly starvation. I knew well from my father's writings that the youngest and eldest were vulnerable to lack of decent food, allowing terrible diseases to take hold.

We stabled the horse and cart at a public house nearest the port. Wilf tossed a penny to a young lad to look after his cargo even though it was securely stabled. 'You can never be too careful,' he muttered to me.

We walked around for some time before we saw a boat that could be the one we were seeking. It was drawn up at the far end of a wharf in a quiet area of the port. As we approached, another boat came in to berth, it was full of shackled, despondent men; there were naval men with guns at either end of the craft, which probably held twenty or more. We were still some distance from the dock when Wilf pushed me into the shade of a fishing smack that had been pulled up onto the hard. 'Wait, we'll see where they take them, they'll probably be put together, tho' I would consider it a bit risky if I had the charge of it.'

'Why?' I whispered.

'Desperate men all in together can be a formidable force if even one was to get free. Have 'ee never 'eard the saying: divide and rule? It looks like those men were all taken against their will and they'll do anything to escape.

I looked at Wilf in admiration, before noticing the glint of excitement in his eager face.

I tapped his arm. 'You must not get involved Wilf. I wouldn't wish you any hurt an' it not be for your own.'

He just grunted and pulled me down next to him. I couldn't help wincing as my lipsy leg pinched.

'What ails thee?'

'Nothing,' I replied. 'But I would tell you that I can't run.'

He looked round at me, his eyes troubled. 'If anything happens Esther just stay put and wait for it to pass you by, no one will hurt a woman. If we get split up make your way to the stable where Ida will kiss you welcome.'

I nodded, feeling that worm turning again in my stomach, not from excitement but outright fear.

We stayed put for what seemed hours with my leg becoming more and more painful with each passing minute.

At last Wilf rose, turned and pulled me up – he pushed back the way we had come and away from the military boats.

'Esther, quick, the boys are coming, I can hear the horses, they'll be on us in a minute. Hurry!'

We trotted as fast as I was able but before a few steps were under our feet I heard the crack of a pistol. Men bore down on us, some on horses and some on foot, bellowing and swearing terrible oaths. I caught the glint of weapons and slowed as the noise and anger engulfed us. My pace was a hindrance anyway but as the tumult surrounded us I became paralysed by fear so Wilf picked me up bodily and carried me away from the conflict into a shed where men were jostling at the door to see what was ado. The crowd parted for me and I was gently deposited on a chair before I lost sight of Wilf who had returned to the melee at the door.

''Ere lass, take thee a sup of this, thou looks all done in.' The kindly eyes that looked down on me were bright with interest. 'What be going on lass, were you in trouble like?'

'No, not me but a young lad, a friend, as was taken up by the press gang in Lewes and brought here.'

'Well, there be a right battle 'appening out there with the gentlemen engaging the navy men and the soldiers from the army not knowing who to fire on. There be no love lost 'tween soldiers and seamen and they all be outnumbered anyways.'

I began to weep at the thought of Wilf caught up in the fighting.

'Esther?' Suddenly he was at my side again, laughing at my fright.

'I thought you were gone and in the middle of it all,' I mumbled, feeling both feeble and foolish.

'No, not me, that's how my father got killed – getting in the middle of a smugglers' battle. We're safe here for now and when it dies down we'll go and look for your young friend. You might find him liberated along wi' the other Lewes men.'

'The smugglers have come for the Lewes men?'

'Aye, and they are in big numbers, a hundred or more – too many for the naval guards and the soldiers. It'll all be over soon and they'll disappear the way they came, ways not known to outsiders. The soldiers haven't got a hope of catching them.'

I hugged my knees praying that Billy would be spared any injury.

When we found our way out of the shed a half hour later it was all over, just as Wilf had predicted. A soldier was shouting at his men to return to guard the port business. There were a number of injured men being carted away – I saw at least three were bloodied – they were all navy men.

'What about the prisoners, the pressed men,' I cried in anguish.'

'They be spirited away,' he said. 'But I didna see a lad amongst them. Come, we'll go inside and take a look – see if he be hiding, wounded or both.'

Silence had returned to the wharf, the only sound was the mewling of gulls overhead; we were the only ones left and I shivered with fear that Billy had succumbed to his broken head or been shot in the fighting.

I clutched at Wilf's sleeve as we crept into the building where the men had been held. It was dark as night in there. As my eyes adjusted I saw the remains of rope bindings and chains. Further in I could see a shape under what looked like a blanket. Wilf stopped me. 'I'll go and look Esther, you stay put.' His voice sounded unnaturally loud in the gloomy place.

I ignored him and moved towards the shape on the floor, I tugged gently at the cloth, wanting to look but terrified of what I might see. It was Billy. He seemed to be unconscious – I looked more closely and saw one eye opening a slit. Was he winking at me?

'Esther?' The shape moved. 'Esther, is that you? Am I glad to see thee lass.'

In a matter of seconds the cloth flew upwards and I was engulfed by Billy.

'Billy, are you well, are you wounded? What happened to thee?' I was clutching at his thin hands and he cried out.

'Ow, let go Esther, I'm fine. Let go, you be 'urting me more'n they did!'

Wilf threw the blanket aside and looked at Billy long and hard before saying, 'Well, you don't seem to be hurtin' too much lad. Come on, we'll get you back to the horse and make our way home to Lewes. We've 'ad enough excitement for one day.'

We edged our way carefully back to Ida, sidetracking whenever we saw groups of men, be they navy, army or others. Wilf and I resumed our places and Billy sank deep into the cart and promptly fell asleep. There didn't seem to be any sign of a head wound but I hadn't had time to look properly.

We jogged on in silence for a while and as dusk fell around us it grew cold. Wilf put his jacket round me and we huddled close for warmth. Finally he spoke, quietly.

'There'll be a right to-do when the justices hear about

this: reprisals – more soldiers and meaner press gangs. Billy will have a care not to be recaptured. They will seek him out.'

'Nah, they won't do that – they thinks I be mazed,' came a small voice from the cart.

Startled, I turned, 'what d'you mean Billy?'

I got bashed on me 'ead and when I came round I pretended I was gone silly. They were goner let me go once the ship's quack had said I was no use to 'em. I just got to play loony whenever they turn up. Mebbe I'll do a turn round about town now and again so everyone do think I be oft me 'ead.

I heard Wilf chuckle as he pulled Ida up – he turned and said in the sternest voice, 'D'you mean to say we put ourselves to all that danger and they were just going to let you go?'

'I didna know you was goin' to come chasin' after me. But I was right glad to see you – if only to get a lift home.'

Wilf and I looked at each other, speechless, before collapsing in laughter while Billy looked on, bemused.

It was well after dark before we got back. Wilf dropped me and Billy at the stable before he headed out to his own home. He said, 'It were good to meet you Esther, I'll look out for you next time I come up to South Farm.'

I was sorry to see him go. It had been wonderful to be lifted out of the cart again, it made me feel warm and fluttery all at once. I had never felt like that before.

Billy rushed in to see Cilla and I asked her to tell Cecilia we were all safe before I too rushed up to see Beth asleep in her cot. I collapsed onto my bed, exhausted but happy.

Chapter Thirty-Eight

The following morning I rose early and despite being tired and not a little grubby I went straight to Cecilia and told her of our escapade to the coast and the successful gathering of Billy back to South Farm. She was amazed at our achievement until I reminded her that it was the smugglers who had brought about the release of probably thirty or so men and there had been bloodshed. Somehow, my story grew in the telling and it wasn't long before we were both laughing at Billy's clever ruse to escape and avoid future dealings with the press gang. We talked of Cilla's delight at the return of Billy before she went on to say in all seriousness, 'You are so lucky Esther, to have the freedom to just get up and go and be part of real life. That is one of the reasons I wanted to leave my mother's household: I felt trapped by values and ridiculous social constraints just because I was a girl and high born. My poor mother despairs of me, I fear I am a great disappointment to the family.'

I had never considered myself lucky compared to the daughter of an Earl before and thought that Cecilia was seeing my freedom and adventure in a rosy light rather than the reality of fear, danger and, for some as we learned later, death. However, I didn't want to spoil her enjoyment of our story so I said nothing.

It was a matter of just hours, before the whole district was talking about the smugglers' raid and Billy's method of escaping empressment. The other men who were released all melted into the background with some leaving for inland towns where they were less likely to be taken up again. Our part in the story was known to a few and gradually a few more until I became a figure of notoriety again. There were repercussions, as Wilf had predicted. A hardening of views against the methods used by the press gang; men became very cautious and a network of warnings established itself in and around the town. The justices, according to Farmer Elwood, huffed and puffed about the audacity of the smugglers in breaking out the men but as they were fathers and husbands and wage earners they soon realised that the cost to the town was less if the Lewes men were looking after their own families. This pragmatic view was not shared, however, by all and a large detachment of soldiers was soon seen parading along the coastline, impeding the smugglers in their efforts to bring the contraband in.

While waiting for the fuss to die down I made my visit to see Sarah, as much to take my mind off things as anything else.

The house of correction brought back terrible memories of my incarceration with Sarah and our fellow prisoners. I had been so frightened of the situation and of the women themselves but it was unwarranted. Once we got to speak to each other we found we were all women who were frightened and possibly misjudged, I certainly was. I didn't care what Sarah might or might not have done.

I borrowed a heavy cloak from Cecilia – it had deep pockets sewn into the inner lining and I took some little comforts for her. I rapped at the door and was admitted to the outer hallway where I was met by the very same guard.

He had not changed and when he tried to take my gifts of cheese and bread from me I resisted by telling him that Dr Grieve was aware that they were for Sarah and not him. He scowled but allowed me in, reluctantly, and with much swearing under his breath. He was a revolting man – slovenly and ill kempt – I averted my face from the disagreeable smells that accompanied him.

Sarah was in a cell on her own; her worn clothing did little to cover her sparse frame. How she would survive a long boat trip to Australia I couldn't imagine. I pulled her to me and whispered that there was a gift in my inner pocket.

'What is it?'

'A bar of soap.'

'Gor, love us, what do I want wi' a bar a soap?'

'It's got a secret,' I whispered before telling her that I had buried a coin inside it and tied a ribbon through it so she would not lose it.

She smiled, revealing a few blackened teeth. 'I knew you was a good-un, despite what them others thought.'

I laughed as I gave her the gift and some bread and cheese as well. It was a bit hard for her gums but she tucked in.

We spent some time talking before I left her, both of us shedding some tears. She was in good spirits despite our tears and didn't seem bothered by her upcoming trip halfway round the world. I gave her the warm jacket I was wearing under Cecilia's cloak for I would not be needing it until the autumn and by then who knew what would happen

Meeting Sarah again had unsettled me and I went to see Mrs Makepiece on my way home. I sat down and told her all that had passed between Sarah and me and about my parting gift; I had brought a bar of the soap for my friend as well.

'Oh, that smells lovely Esther, why don't you make some more and sell it?'

'Who would I sell it to? It's not like when my pa had the shop.'

'I'm sure we could find some way of getting it to people who have the money to buy. I'll think on it.'

I changed the subject. 'Cecilia's brother is coming to stay tomorrow. He is a friend of the Prince Regent and they are all to go to the races together.'

'I heard she were a proper lady but she don't put on any airs nor graces do she?'

'No, I can't wait to meet him. She adores him and speaks constantly about what he is doing, what he thinks and what he says. She must love Farmer Elwood very much to live such a quiet life away from the society that he moves in even though she says she doesn't like it for herself.'

'John Elwood was once quite the man about town but when his father died he had to take care of the family fortunes and he turned gentleman farmer overnight. He's a good man is he.' She nodded to herself.

'He asked me to tell him if Cecilia was with child. She isn't, but I feel sure she would want him to be the first to know. I pray daily that they might be blessed soon.'

'Aye, so do I. Will you take a drop of tea with me? I had a small delivery this week and it tastes so much better when shared.'

We laughed at the few leaves of guilty pleasure drunk at the expense of the government's revenue.

'I got a measure of salt too. The tax is so high I can't normally afford it but my tea supplier friend do know that I needed something to salt the meat.'

'Mrs Fisher never seems short of salt.'

'No, I don't suppose she is,' she nodded knowingly.

I decided not to comment further. Clearly, smuggling was not seen as a bad thing even amongst people who upheld the law. Who was I to judge?

I told Mrs Makepiece about Billy's near miss with the press gang and what Dr Grieve had said. She had heard the gossip around town and said she wasn't at all surprised and that her sons were merchant seamen and knew when to stay out of range. 'They take another passage from a foreign port rather than put into Britain and get caught up in the King's navy.'

'You must hardly ever see them,' I said.

'True, but they are safer on the merchant boats and get plenty of excitement without being shot at by the French as an act of war rather than just in passing and I am comforted that they are together.'

Strangely, I did not mention Wilf other than that he was my companion on our great adventure. I did not tell her how young and dashing he was nor how he had picked me up several times and how my heart had fluttered at his closeness.

Chapter Thirty-Nine

Accompanied by Mrs Makepiece I continued my exploration of Lewes. This time I ventured over the bridge into the village of Cliffe again. It was much noisier than my last visit and we stopped and looked along the river meadow and watched the boats that bustled to and fro. The tide was in spate and gulls screamed overhead. Mrs Makepiece discerned nothing of my memories of Becca dying in this very same river as she pointed out the little wherry's ferrying people and goods from the trading ships that had ventured upstream from Newhaven. It was all very busy with lots of shouting and calling from boat to shore and back again. There were a number of buildings that seemed to be storage places for goods that came upriver by ship. We saw grain being unloaded as well as coal and building materials. On the other side of the river wood was being loaded onto a big boat which looked very near ready to depart. The captain was in deep discussion with a uniformed official.

I asked Mrs Makepiece what was likely to be going on and she said the chap in the uniform was probably a preventative man who oversaw what came in and out so that the proper taxes could be paid and checked with what had come in at the port downstream. 'Are there smugglers here then?' I asked in all innocence. She snorted, saying, 'Smugglers don't come in daylight and they don't come into the port, unless they are rescuing their own. They be a bit secretive like and land their goods on the beaches or if they are shipping things out they have coves with nearby caves where goods are stashed and guarded until the time and tide be right.'

'I thought they only brought goods in?'

'Mostly they do, nowadays, but it wasn't long ago that they smuggled wool from the farms direct to the Frenchies and onwards. Southern wool is highly valued in Holland and such places so the smugglers make a profit both ways. Fact is Esther, smugglers deal in whatever is wanted or in short supply and they are not too bothered with the likes of law-abiding people. It don't pay to get in their way or talk too loudly and there's many a preventative man who has come to realise that, and turned a blind eye, otherwise he might find he hasn't got an eye with which to see any more!'

We hurried onwards over the hump bridge and following that gruesome warning I ventured no more questions about smugglers.

Cliffe village was a poor place; buildings were piled on top of each other with the highway running with mud and other foul-smelling slurry. The people were poorly clad and we saw scrawny urchins with misshapen limbs and open sores on their faces and skeletal bodies. It was a dirty street with very little to recommend it other than a few workmanlike buildings but even these couldn't match those of nearby Lewes. This place seemed all about work, hard labouring work. I shut my ears to the noise for it was overwhelming. Men, women and a few older children were scurrying about purposefully but for very little reward judging from their lack of decent clothing. We picked our way a few steps towards what seemed to be an open-fronted warehouse where men were naked to the waist heaving sacks of corn. There was much spillage and women and children darted in amongst the working men, scrabbling for the spoils. A man stood on a pile of sacks in the centre of the warehouse holding a lethal looking whip with a very long cord. I didn't see him hit anyone but he made full use of its threat, urging the men to greater endeavour. The corn was being loaded onto drays with two big horses to pull each one. As one pulled out of the yard, another took its place. I was quite disconcerted to see armed guards accompany each vehicle and remembered Wilf's tales of want and lawbreaking.

I watched the overseer scowl at a group of urchins as they urged each other further and further into the melee before he cracked his whip over their heads. They squealed and fled but while his attention was on them another group poked at a sack with a sharp blade. It spilled and then there was uproar as a horde of women and children charged into the centre grabbing dishfuls of the precious grain.

I couldn't bear to watch such scenes of desperation so we didn't tarry, instead turning and making our way back over the bridge. I was thankful to get away from such a dispiriting place.

Mrs Makepiece laughed at my shivers of dislike. ''Ee girl, you've come a long way since you turned up on my doorstep as a waif and stray. Think yourself lucky you were directed to me rather than to some goodbody down t'Cliffe.'

We walked in silence as I gave thanks to the truth in her words.

Chapter Forty

When children are about cutting their teeth they slaver much, are feverish, hot, and uneasy; their gums swell, and are very painful; they are sometimes loose in the bowels, and at other times costive; now and then convulsions come on. Leeches are often of use, applied behind the ears; also blisters.

MacKenzie's Five Thousand Receipts in All the Useful and Domestic Arts

Beth and I were so happy at South Farm, even when she was fractious with teething, and one of the nicest things for me was that I was included in the household. I wasn't treated as a servant but as Cecilia's friend and companion.

Having said that, I usually ate with the servants and Beth in the kitchen but occasionally, when there were friends visiting, I left Beth with Cilla and joined in the informal suppers. Farmer Elwood regularly invited other farmers to share his table and Cecilia and I would join them to make sure they didn't discuss work all of the time. After supper when the port was being handed round we would leave them to it and disappear into Cecilia's own little sitting room – a haven of femininity and comfort.

I was happiest when we all sat around discussing the local news and the doings of the farm and locality, in particular Lewes. Dr Grieve was often present and though I sat in awe of his skills and intelligence I felt myself to be of consequence. He often sought my comments when we were discussing general health issues and many times I was aware of him watching me. I did not imagine that he had a personal interest in me as a woman but I think he grew to respect what he called my good sense. Whatever it was he sought I felt valued by the household, and him. His visits to South Farm were regular and according to Cecilia more frequent than in the past.

When we were alone Cecilia giggled and said she thought Dr Grieve was coming to the farm to see me rather than them. I felt rather uncomfortable about this but couldn't resist asking if she really thought so. Later, when alone in my room with Beth I peered at myself in the mirror and wondered if a man, let alone an educated man, might find me attractive in character because I certainly wasn't in looks.

Chapter Forty-One

Lewes Race-course: In a most well-adapted spot, being moderately sloping and curved to these races do all the people of the country flock from every quarter, and there is much competition among the fashionable, both the lookers on and those looked at – at night balls for the dancers and other pleasures. That assemblage indeed is very famous for the number and splendour of the company, and principally because of the high-born Pelhams presiding there, who, as stewards, direct everything in the most sumptious manner.

Dr John Burton 1751 taken from *Lewes Past*
by Helen Poole

Cecilia was beside herself with excitement waiting for her brother. She was up and down all morning running to the windows, checking the kitchen and Mrs Fisher's arrangements for the family supper to be held that evening. It would be an intimate meal for just the three of them before an outing to Brighton tomorrow and the races on the following day. When he finally came he was riding a horse that filled me with awe as I watched from the window. It was a magnificent creature and looked the part to carry such a noble man. Two servants and a groomsman made up the group and there was much scurrying about as they clattered into the stable yard.

Cecilia and Farmer Elwood rushed out to meet their

relative in the yard rather than wait for him in the house. I could hear the laughing as he kissed his sister and slapped his friend on the back. I hung back behind the curtains as I watched this family reunion between brother and sister. For a brief moment I felt bereft having no family to call my own but I did have Beth I reminded myself and she was all the family I needed.

I hurried along to the scullery to check that everything was as Cecilia would wish and didn't venture back until it was time for me to retire. As I mounted the stairs Cecilia came out of the dining room. Her face glowed with happiness as she pulled her brother with her. 'Esther, Esther, come down and meet my brother, I have told him all about you and Beth. Come and meet him.'

Reluctantly I retraced my steps feeling very conscious of my shabby clothing and awkward gait. Lord Percival was tall and elegant and looked down at my prim little bob as I mumbled a greeting.

'Ah, Esther, is it? My sister sings your praises in all her letters – I can tell you that our mama is quite jealous of the amount of time you spend with Cecy.' He turned away and I was left there at the bottom of the stairs. I fled up to my room feeling very insignificant.

Lord Percy stayed for a week and he and Cecilia were taken up with visiting friends and enjoying the hospitality of the Prince Regent. Most evenings they were all invited out and I became aware of what a different life Cecilia had led before marrying Farmer Elwood. I wondered that she was content to live so quietly when her brother was not there but after he left she very quickly dropped back into her role as a gentleman farmer's wife. I had not taken supper with the family at all whilst he was staying but the night after he left Cecilia begged me to join them and discuss all the gossip she had enjoyed. I listened to her chatting and saw the sparkle in her eyes as she related a tale of intrigue at the Prince's court in nearby Brighton.

'You must miss your family so much Cecilia, how can you bear not to see them from one month to the next?'

She seemed surprised at my comment and said, 'It was good to see my brother but I do not want that kind of life as a matter of course – I will tell you that in my mother's household I had no time to myself, I was always to accompany her to this ball or that dinner with people who bored me. In marrying John I have my own household and I do not hanker for society. What I have here is everything I need to be happy. Another child would be a blessing and I hope that will occur in due course.

Oh, how she has matured I thought.

'Why don't we go and find the shrine to St Anne and see if she will intercede on your behalf? Mrs Makepiece was quite insistent that her church up on the hill is where the young women go to find a husband, and all that goes with that.'

'Oh, yes let's do that soon and we will also seek a husband for you Esther if that is her particular calling.'

'Oh Cecilia I don't think I'll find a husband but I think we should go.'

'Well, don't tell John – he would be quite put out.' We giggled conspiratorially.

We went into supper and enjoyed a pleasant evening together and I was glad that all had returned to normal.

Chapter Forty-Two

We made our visit to St Anne's the following week and stood in awe at the majesty of the ancient church. I was surprised that such an important church stood outside the walls of the town but according to the old man who showed us around this was because St Anne's was once a stopping point on the road to the old Cluniac Priory. I enquired about the anchoress reputed to be walled into the building, another of Mrs Makepiece's tales, but he was not inclined to tell me much, other than that she had existed and was thought to be buried there. Try as I might I could find no indication of where she had dwelled within the church. The old man accepted a small coin from Cecilia and left us to our own devices; we tiptoed towards the shrine where there were small offerings in the form of candles, ribbons and posies and both of us were quite overcome with the feeling that surrounded us as we prayed for our cause. I offered my prayer in thanks for the safe deliverance of Beth to me and for the wellbeing of her true mother who was hopefully united with her God in Heaven. I also prayed for a child to be born safely to Cecilia and her husband John. I told St Anne, in my prayers, what good people they were and how a child would bless their union.

As Cecilia rose from her knees she left her own token – a dried white rose. I had nothing to give but my thoughts. I hoped they were enough.

Chapter Forty-Three

Vaccination or prevention of smallpox
Could all parents be persuaded to inoculate their children with vaccine matter soon after birth, the smallpox might soon be entirely eradicated. Indeed, vaccination has penetrated to the remotest corners of the globe; and wherever it has been introduced, the increasing experience of every year has served to confirm a confidence in its efficacy. In vaccinating children and other persons, the following circumstances are carefully to be attended to: 1) The matter should not be taken from the pustule later than the ninth day of the disease. 2) The matter should be perfectly transparent, as it is not to be depended upon, if it has become in the least degree opaque. 3) The matter, if not used immediately should be allowed to dry gradually and thoroughly before it is laid aside for future use. 4) The punctures are to be made in each arm, the point of the lancet being previously dipped in the vaccine matter. 5) The punctures cannot be made too superficial, and on no account should more than one be made in each arm. 6) After vaccination, it will be necessary to repress, as soon as possible, any excess of inflammation that may happen to arise. This will be done best by cold applications etc.

MacKenzie's Five Thousand Receipts in All the Useful and Domestic Arts

I had been much frightened recently by Dr Grieve's insistence that Beth should be treated with what is called an inoculation against smallpox. I, who have suffered with the pox and survived might have given her immunity if I were her natural mother but, as I wasn't, Beth was in urgent need of this treatment as the disease was rife in the district. Some Lewes families from a very poor area had obstinately refused to go to the pest house and had consequently been imprisoned in their own homes with guards put at either end of their street to try to prevent the spread of the disease to the rest of us in the town.

I had recently seen notices in the local broadsheet advertising a visit from a physician who would undertake the treatment for a fee, a large one. But it was only when Cecilia told me that the Duchess of Devonshire – a friend of her brother and a confidant of the Prince Regent – was arranging for all her children to be treated that I decided to take Dr Grieve's advice. However, it was with great nervousness that I called at his house for him to make the scratch on Beth's tender little arm. I thought it risky to go to the man who advertised as he boasted about his 2,400 successes and did not mention the 49 or so who had died as a result.

We were admitted by the housekeeper, Mrs Jenkins, and as we sat and waited I was in two minds whether to run out and forget all about it. My heart fluttered with fear as I weighed up the balance of decision: death, or the scars of a terrible disease on my beautiful baby or the possibility of immunity or, again, death. At that time it didn't seem to be much of a choice but it was one I made only after the heated persuasion of the good doctor. Poor Beth cried bitterly at his ministrations.

'There there, little one, it's not so bad is it?' He offered her a tiny spoonful of strawberry jam to distract her before saying to me, 'Keep this clean Esther and don't fret if she has a slight fever: there is nothing to fear. It should be no worse than if she were teething.'

I mopped my own tears and clutched the hot and now sticky child to me.

'Esther, would you like to join me for a cup of tea? I have seen to all my patients and I know Mrs Jenkins has made a cake.'

'Oh,' I said, surprised. 'Yes, of course, I would like that.'

'Good, I will go and inform Mrs Jenkins, please go through into the parlour and I will be with you in a few minutes.'

I had never been into the doctor's private rooms and was very curious to see how he lived.

The room I entered overlooked a small garden that was being carefully attended by an elderly man. I looked for somewhere to sit and after moving a pile of papers to the desk I sat gingerly on a small spindly chair. The desk I faced was very untidy but after a few minutes I could see that the piles of papers were in some fashion quite organised and the pile I had just put on top did not belong. I leaned forward to move them before he came back and saw I had been interfering with his system.

Mrs Jenkins, the housekeeper arrived just in time to tell me to put them on the floor before asking, 'Shall I take the little one with me into the garden?'

'Thank you, yes, if it will not upset your gardener – he looks very busy.'

'Don't you worry about him none, that be my husband and he will enjoy seeing the child we have all heard so much about.'

I was quite taken aback when she said that but realised we had probably been the subject of discussion in most households in Lewes. Mrs Jenkins gathered Beth into her arms and left the room for the garden.

Dr Grieve reappeared a few minutes later rolling his shirtsleeves down and looking a little scrubbed.

'Well, Esther, I am glad we have a few minutes alone, there is something I wanted to discuss with you.'

I waited, nervously. I had thought there must be a reason that he would ask me to stay for tea.

'I have been very impressed with your manner, my dear. Clearly you have skills that would make you a sensible nurse. Would you like some cake?'

I was surprised by his words but I nodded to the offer of cake and balanced a tiny plate on my knee whilst a cup of tea wobbled precariously in my hand.

'Is the tea to your taste? Personally, I prefer some sweetener – a little honey perhaps?'

'No, no thank you. I like it without.'

'Good. Well, as I was saying. Mr and Mrs Jenkins have been with me a long time and I feel it is time that I had someone about the house to help me with my work. My patients would benefit if I were to train up a nurse to help me with day-to-day practical medicine: dressings, and preparation of my creams and medicaments. Mrs Jenkins used to help when I needed an extra pair of hands but she is getting on and I would like to prepare for the future. I wonder, Esther, if you would like to be part of that future?'

His eyes were fixed on me and I felt rather unsure what he meant. His offer of employment was a solution to my predicament of eventually finding a home for Beth and me but talk of being part of a future did not seem entirely relating to employment.

I stuttered my thanks for his interest and decided to buy myself some time by eating the cake.

'I can see, my dear, you are a little surprised by my offer, perhaps it would be a good idea to go back to South Farm and think it through. By all means discuss it with Cecilia and John. Let me just say that I would be very glad to welcome you and Beth into my home as a valued employee and friend.'

I breathed a sigh of relief at not having to make an immediate decision saying, 'Yes, I do need time to think, so will do as you suggest. Thank you for the tea and for looking after Beth so kindly.' I searched in my reticule for some payment for the treatment but it was waved away. I glanced out to the garden and saw Beth clutching at Mr Jenkins' leg as he led her in faltering steps from one clump of flowers to another. 'I am obliged for your confidence in me Dr Grieve, I just need a little time to absorb the implications.'

'I would expect nothing less from you Esther. Go back to the farm, keep Beth warm and clean and if a high fever develops then send for me immediately. I am sure that all will be well though.'

He was holding my hand as he reassured me and we seemed to be locked together. He only let go when I felt myself blushing – I pulled myself free and rushed to the waiting gig to make my way home.

Chapter Forty-Four

For Vomiting During Pregnancy
The morning sickness is one of the most painful feelings attendant on the pregnant state; and it is one of those which medicine commonly fails to relieve. A cup of chamomile, or peppermint tea, taken when first waking, and suffering the patient to be still for an hour, will sometimes alleviate the distressing sickness.
MacKenzie's Five Thousand Receipts in All the Useful and Domestic Arts

I didn't mention my news to Cecilia as she seemed preoccupied, so once Beth was settled for the night I sat at my window and tried to collect my thoughts, failing miserably. Despite sitting for some hours in the dark I was no nearer to a plan of action. I undressed and began my nightly ritual of combing my hair – it was the one thing I knew would calm me. I slipped between the cold sheets and fell into an exhausted and fretful sleep. Beth cried fitfully throughout the night but she was not overly warm so I did not worry.

The next morning was a picture of beauty with a wispy mist threading over the damp ground. A pale lemon sun rose tentatively beyond the orchard. I breathed deeply as I wondered how I could willingly leave this place that had become my refuge and latterly home.

I had risen early and Cecilia had not yet come down so after giving Beth her breakfast, which she ate as enthusiastically as ever, I settled her down in the care of Mrs Fisher and Cilla and went up to Cecilia's dressing room. I planned to tell her my news and ask her opinion. As I went in I could hear her retching and found her lying on her bed with a pitcher and bowl to hand.

'Cecilia, what is it?'

'I believe I am with child,' she said primly before collapsing into a fit of giggles mixed up with tears. 'Oh, God, I feel dreadful.'

'Does John know?' I questioned.

'No one knows, not even me.'

'Shall I call Dr Grieve?'

'Absolutely not. I will wait and see, but I am fairly certain. Don't tell anyone Esther, promise me, promise you won't.'

'John made me promise too – to tell him.'

'You mustn't, not yet, because he will be very upset when I tell him that my mother has insisted on me returning to Hadgwick Hall if and when I become enceinte.'

'You are going to leave? Why?' I was astonished.

'My mother insists that I must be cared for by her own staff and doctors so that the baby does not die.'

'But I would care for you, as would John and Dr Grieve.'

'She does not consider that good enough and blames John for the loss of her first grandchild.'

She was struggling to sit up so I put my arm behind her and lifted her into a comfortable position. She looked pale as she spoke. 'Esther, I am sorry but she won't hear of you coming with me. We have talked about it in our letters and I am afraid that she is a trifle jealous. When I tell her that I am with child again she will insist on sending the carriage immediately to carry me off to civilisation again.'

'But, surely, you don't have to go?'

'No, but I want to distance myself from the awful time I had here, before you came Esther. I want to do things differently and not live in the past as I am afraid I will do, endlessly comparing.'

'Let me get you some breakfast, it will make you feel better.'

'Don't be cross with me Esther, I must do this my way – this time.'

'Don't be a goose – why would I be cross? You must order your life as it suits you.' Or your mama I thought. Poor John, he would be bereft.

I didn't tell her my news as this new plan would clearly affect my position in the household. I had to think.

Chapter Forty-Five

The following morning I rose bright and early and despite being tired from a lack of sleep went straight to Cecilia's room to find her retching into a bowl again. We sat together with a light meal of oats and honey to settle her down. Gradually the sickness subsided and I promised, again, not to tell John until she was ready.

I was uncomfortable with this but after a few days of sickness Cecilia finally told Farmer Elwood of her pregnancy and persuaded him that her decision to return to her former home for the confinement was necessary. Cecilia only had to write to her mother and everything would change. I don't know if they discussed my situation in their household but now that Cecelia was definitely leaving I felt I had no choice but to leave the house although they never said. They were delighted for me when I told of Dr Grieve's offer of employment but I couldn't help thinking that I was going from one household of a man without his wife to another household where there had never been a wife, but rumour, according to Cecilia, of a mistress.

'If you are not happy Esther, you can return to South Farm as soon as I am back with our baby. I wish my mother was not so difficult and would let you come with me as my companion but she is adamant that my old governess holds that position. I do not feel strong enough to fight her on this.'

'Nor should you, Cecilia, your mother is entitled to have

who she likes in her own household and my being there would create difficulties for you when you don't need them.'

Later, when Beth and I were alone, I shed a few tears before writing a brief note to Dr Grieve, accepting his proposal, with thanks. I hoped I would be able to stay at the farm until Cecilia actually left in a month's time. I also hoped to meet up with Wilf again under more conventional circumstances. I became quite devious in trying to find out more about him.

My last month at South Farm was bitter sweet, with Beth and I constantly in Cecilia's company as she prepared for her journey. Beth was now weaned fully and was able to walk a few steps without falling down onto her plump little bottom. Her words were a joy to hear with everyone taking time to help her develop. She was a happy child and full of laughter. I often took her into Lewes to Mrs Makepiece's home where her grandfather would visit and play with her. His wife had never been reconciled to his dead daughter's child and I often wondered why people had such a large capacity for bitterness and jealousy. On occasion I had met Becca's stepmother in my trips round the town and she crossed the road rather than acknowledge me.

I spent many hours studying my father's journals in the hope that I would have the skills that Dr Grieve expected of me. As I read and reread his medical observations and my mother's receipts I was reminded of our happy household and wished that I could have a home and children to fill it. Such thoughts always seemed to lead to me thinking about Wilf. I had found out a little about his background and like me he had suffered great loss. His father had been factor of South Farm for many years and Wilf was brought up in his mould. Tragedy struck when he was about fifteen. His father had been set upon by a gang of local men when he tried to prevent them stealing from one of the properties he looked after. These men were after horses and weapons and were notorious locally for their callous wickedness. The poor man had been beaten to within an inch of his life and several months later had died of his wounds. He was able to identify some of his attackers who were taken up by the law and punished severely. One man was hanged and several others transported. Farmer Elwood's own father had arranged for young Wilf to be educated and adopted by one of his tenants in the hope that he would be able to work on the farm in the same capacity as his father when he grew into manhood and that was exactly what happened. Wilf was unmarried, though he had a sweetheart of long standing: a young woman who lived nearby in one of the farm's tied cottages. Cecilia thought that the relationship was not of the strongest otherwise they would have married. Wilf did not appear keen, she said, to tie himself to family life.

Chapter Forty-Six

Since my adventures with Wilf I had tried to understand the circumstances that were causing so much unrest. I had been quite stung by the way Wilf spoke to me of not being aware of the lives of the poorer people, of their hunger and deprived conditions.

I talked to Cecilia who told me that many local people contributed to the parish poor fund to enable families to keep together rather than be taken into the workhouse. Farmer Elwood had taken on extra workers whenever he was able but there were some families who just couldn't be helped – the lazy and the feckless for example. According to Cecilia the burden on the parish was great.

We talked much of bad harvests, severe winter weather and failed crops with famine stalking the South Downs. The weather was frequently the means of driving people down into the gutters. Some tradesmen tried to capitalise on the lack of supply with higher prices for their goods. Bread was often the touch paper for rioting; the light loaves that were sold produced less goodness with resulting ill health and weakness.

Some decent local people were so concerned with the hunger they took matters into their own hands and provided hot broth for upwards of 900 people in Lewes. Mrs Makepiece told me about many benefit occasions to raise money for the malnourished children. I volunteered to accompany her when she was called on to help prepare and serve food. Ladies of the town would make items of clothing from their own spinning and collections of scrap materials so occasionally you would see youngsters clad in the very best fabrics previously worn on the backs of the educated classes. Despite these attempts to help it never seemed to be enough.

A threat of violence built and Cecilia told me that some men had became sufficiently well organised to threaten those instrumental in keeping prices up; they promised an uprising of thousands of desperate men. Farmer Elwood was at the Star for the Saturday market when a letter was produced threatening violent destruction. The letter had been sent to the justices who promptly sent it to those who were deemed to be the cause of light loaves and profiteering. The writer of the letter claimed to have 18,000 men armed and ready to act, and, with such numbers no militia would be able to prevent a determined assault. Cecilia was greatly frightened by these threats and fretted constantly that she and her benevolent husband were being tarnished by the actions of profiteers.

Nowadays when I walked around town I saw Lewes in a new light. On the surface all seemed to be calm and prosperous with well-shod people smiling, talking and laughing with their neighbours but underneath in the dark alleyways and less popular areas of town I saw the grim evidence of hunger and want. Crying children with swollen bellies, mean housing, dirt and rampant disease; smallpox, consumption, scarlet fever, even malaria; women who were unable to cope resorting to gin and selling their bodies in order to feed the children. I was horrified to think that I had been enjoying the fruits of other people's labour with no thought for those who had nothing. I vowed to myself that I would do all that I could to alleviate the suffering of the sick when I began working for Dr Grieve though, in truth, I had never seen anyone poor at his house or the coroner's office except myself and Billy.

It was while Mrs Makepiece and I were on a trip to take eggs to a family she supported I had a dreadful shock. We turned a corner near the house of correction in North Street and came upon a small quarry being worked for chalk. As we approached some tiny cottages a young man appeared at the gate of the quarry: he was leading a horse that looked familiar. I clutched Mrs Makepiece's arm and dragged her back into the shade of a building. 'Wait,' I gasped.

'What is it lass? You look like death.'

'It's one of the Coad boys. The eldest. I can't go near him, please.' I pressed myself flat against the wall, my heart thumping.

Mrs Makepiece stood in front of me and shielded me from his eyes had he been looking in our direction which, thankfully, he wasn't.

'Esther you are going to have to prepare yourself to meet this family betimes. Lewes is a small place and there are a number of them.

'I know,' I groaned, but seeing him like that was a great shock. 'Since the trial I have done my best to erase all memory of those odious people.'

'Well come on, he's gone now, we'll go and deliver these eggs and see if the Higgins children are helping their poor ma. Now, turn your thoughts away from Coads and think about this decent family that is down on their luck.'

I tried, but it wasn't easy – that is until we got into their house, or what passed for a house.

Miss Wardle's piggies lived in better conditions than this family of ten. Everywhere I looked there was a grey face pierced by enormous staring eyes. The mother of all these children had a child to her breast and two more clutching her skirts. She looked drained of all colour and her dark and greasy hair straggled down her back.

As soon as Mrs Makepiece opened the door they fixed their eyes on her basket, which contained a small jug of milk, a dozen eggs and a twist of salt probably left over from the salting of the meat.

'Here Mary, m'dear, this will make a nice tea for everyone today and I've asked Miss Wardle to save you some lard. Have you heard from Samuel, word of mouth like?'

'Nay, not a dicky bird but I know he'll be trying his best to find some work inland, like.'

'P'raps he would be better occupied in staying put and doin' a bit of fishing,' she suggested.

'He's afeared of bein' taken up for poaching.'

'Aye. Anyways, my girl I brought you some soap so mayhap your eldest girls could offer to do a bit of washin'. P'raps some in the house of correction might employ them – they are not all vagabonds and thieves and some might pay to look clean afore their meeting with the justices. You tell that girl o' yours to give these childer a bit of a scrub like.'

Mrs Higgins thanked us for our visit and encouragement. She smiled as much as she was able through her blackened teeth. 'We be that grateful to you. I had naught to feed us tonight so a couple of these eggs will do just the job.'

As we left Mrs Makepiece turned to her and said sternly, 'You make sure you eat too, Mary. If aught happens to you these childer will be put in the workhouse. You need to keep your strength up until Samuel comes back.'

'Aye, I do know that.'

The conditions in that little home had taken all thought of the Coads from my mind and it wasn't until later that night as I was trying to sleep that they resurfaced.

Chapter Forty-Seven

Cecilia and Farmer Elwood have been invited to the wedding of His Royal Highness the Prince of Wales to Princess Caroline and afterwards Cecilia will go to her family home for the remainder of her confinement. They have asked me to stay until Farmer Elwood returns from Hadgwick Hall and I have agreed. Dr Grieve seems well pleased that I am taking up his offer and has offered to show me the accommodation that Beth and I will share in his home. Mrs Jenkins has been very friendly and her kitchen is large so I can prepare some of my receipts without interfering in her domain. I am beginning to relish the thought of earning my own money and being of value in the town. There are a number of physicians in Lewes and I am not aware that any of them have a resident nurse. I am rather nervous that my skills are limited to general work. I have no idea what I can offer in terms of birthing but hope to learn from the doctor. I do believe that most birthing takes place under the care of local women and that physicians' skills are limited to the wealthy. I understand that Dr Grieve has great experience and training in this most common of practices. It is an area of medicine that I am keen to learn.

The sun was shining when Beth and I arrived at the doctor's house to view our rooms. I felt quite nervous and I think he saw my unease and called Mrs Jenkins in to accompany us. The house was large and well furnished but not with delicate feminine pieces. The heavy oak dressers and bureaus were highly polished and dust free. Beth liked the shiny wood as she could see her face. She had a habit of licking anything she couldn't actually put in her mouth and I apologised to Mrs Jenkins for all the tongue prints as I gathered her up. We were shown into a sitting room on the second floor: it was large, airy and bright and my heart lifted. A bedroom with space for the two of us adjoined the sitting room. There was a good single bed and a little truckle bed for Beth. A little dresser with a mirror and four drawers for our bits and bobs stood against a wall. It was perfect.

Dr Grieve and I discussed the terms of my employment, my wages and when I would start. I explained about Cecilia and he agreed that I could start once she had left. I breathed a sigh of relief which I am afraid he accurately interpreted because he said 'Esther, this arrangement is important for both of us and if for some reason it is not acceptable then we will terminate it with no hard feelings. If, however, you enjoy your work with me then I hope we can move on to a permanent footing that will be satisfying for both of us.

I agreed wholeheartedly but as always when I was talking to him I had the feeling that I wasn't entirely sure I was interpreting his words accurately. I tried to tell myself that I, as a young and naive woman couldn't be expected to understand nuances of behaviour and language and if I made mistakes it wasn't my fault. I would go over his sentences in minute detail and couldn't fault what was said but always I felt I was missing something.

Both Mrs Makepiece and Miss Wardle seemed quite excited that I was moving and I do believe they were planning introductions and little entertainments that would include me. I pointed out that much as I would like to socialise with them and their friends I did not know when I would find time because of the work I would be expected to do.

Billy-alone was by now quite recovered from his terrible adventure; the only real effect was to make him more wary of life. Every now and again I would see him pretending to be mazed for the benefit of strangers. He spent his days with the shepherds and his evenings with Sally the pig and Miss Wardle. He benefited from the outdoor work and was looking much healthier. Being at the farm so often he would bump into Wilf and I would ask after him as discretely as I could. Then one fine day Beth and I were walking up to the mill above the farm and there he was. I felt a little shy as I approached him but Beth had no such worries and she trotted on her little legs right up to him holding her arms out wide expecting to be picked up. He didn't disappoint and swung her high in the air as she squealed her delight.

''Gain, 'gain' she demanded.

'Only if you tell me your name.'

'Beth I's Beth!'

'Are you sure?' he smiled down at her.

'I's Beth, I am!'

'Oh well, if you say so – here we go then – up, up and up again.'

We were all laughing and I forgot my shyness as I settled myself on one of the great stones near the mill door.

'How are you Wilf?'

'Grand, an' you? It's good to see you Esther.'

Suddenly I became aware of what a beautiful day it was and how pleasant it was to be high above the town with the skylarks singing above us. 'Yes, I am fine and you have just met Beth who has her own way of introducing herself. She'll be wanting more of the same every time she sees you,' I warned him, laughing.

'Billy tells me you are moving into town with the local quack.'

'He's not a quack, he's a physician and I'm only moving in there to work.' For some reason I thought it important to make that clear and I became all tongue-tied as I realised how could anyone think any different. I could feel myself reddening so I grabbed hold of Beth and started to tickle her.

'Will you be having days off then?'

'Aye, I am not expecting to be wanted all the time, the doctor has many calls on him that don't require a nurse.' I had just told Miss Wardle the opposite, shame on me.

'Well, then I will call round and invite you and trouble here to take a breath of air with me when I am in the area, like.'

'Oh that will be lovely, I am quite nervous about being there and it will be great to meet with someone I know so...' I hesitated.

'...well?' he offered.

I laughed, 'Yes, that is what I meant though I have promised Billy that I would go downriver a little ways with him soon, as I do believe I have family in one of the villages. He wants to help me find my mother's family.'

'Where do you think they live?'

'I think it maybe Southease, do you know it?'

A shadow had crossed his face as I named the village. 'Aye, I know it.' he said shortly.

'Is there a problem there?' I was curious as to what had caused his smile to fade.

'Some of the people there are wrong-uns. Make sure Billy is with you and go in the morning light. You don't want to be there at dusk. And don't take the little-un.'

'You sound very cautionary, in what way wrong-uns?'

He jumped up and shook his head before running and scooping Beth up in the air again causing her to shriek with pleasure. Once her giggles had subsided we carried on talking just as we had when rescuing Billy and we did not return to the subject of Southease and its inhabitants.

'Well I must be getting on otherwise Farmer Elwood will wonder why I am not back with the flour. Do you want a ride on the back o' the cart?'

I nodded, yes and he picked me up and then put Beth on my lap on the backboard and off we went down the hill by a more winding indirect route. He dropped us off by the stables and as I thanked him for the ride I said, 'Next time you are here, why don't you come in the kitchen and say hello – we can always offer a cold drink for those in need.' I was amazed at my forwardness but he replied with a smile, 'Aye, I will that, see you soon.'

Chapter Forty-Eight

Cecilia was still struggling with her early pregnancy and was in two minds as to whether she would be able to attend the Prince's wedding.

'You'll be fine, as long as it is not a dawn wedding and Farmer Elwood will take care of you in the crowds. You must try not to stand too long. What about your dress, what are you going to wear?'

'I don't know, that is a problem – what if I can't get into anything?'

'One month will make no difference to your shape and you are so small any gain would be tiny anyway,' I said confidently, knowing I had no basis of knowledge for thinking that. 'Let's go and look through your chests and see what is suitable and if anything needs altering, we still have time.'

'I have to look fashionable, I can't possibly go looking as if I am in last season's design.'

'We can choose something and then get it remade.'

'Oh, I don't know, my mother would die if she thought I was attending this wedding in old clothes that have been altered.'

'Is your mother going?'

'No. She is not invited, she is not part of the Prince's set.'

'Why don't we go and look and we can send into Lewes for your dressmaker to come and advise.'

'Yes, let's. I'll see if anyone is going in this morning. I'll write a note.'

We spent all morning rummaging through chests and eventually pulled two beautiful dresses out for trying on and perhaps an alteration to update. I had no idea what was fashionable but I could admire the materials, the workmanship and how beautiful Cecilia looked in both of them. They were both very grand and I can't imagine she had an occasion to wear them in Lewes so I think they must have come with her on her wedding.

Miss Simpson, Cecilia's dressmaker promised to call in during the afternoon and we were delighted to parade our two choices but she wasn't impressed and spent a lot of time tutting and sighing. She had brought some sketches of current styles with her and we pored over them before agreeing that one of the dresses was suitable for alteration. We decided that Cecilia would need a matching cloak and headpiece and Miss Simpson produced some sample materials in a range of colours. The design was settled as being empire line from under the bust, which would hide any development of pregnancy. We were all very pleased with ourselves and asked Mrs Fisher to bring some tea and dainties into Cecilia's sitting room. I presided over the brewing of the tea and having allowed the requisite brew time of five minutes I poured the hot amber liquid into three eggshell thin cups. Mrs Fisher had excelled herself with some delicious little fancy cakes. Cecilia declared that we were copying one of her mother's 'at home' occasions. I couldn't help thinking that her mother wouldn't be taking tea with a companion and a dressmaker but we all enjoyed ourselves and looked forward to the first fitting.

Chapter Forty-Nine

Later in the day I asked Cilla if Billy was likely to visit soon. She thought he would call in shortly, before going back to Miss Wardle's for the night and I asked her if she would call me when he arrived.

I wanted to talk to Billy about going to Southease so I could ask him what Wilf meant when he said there were wrong-uns there.

It was a lovely evening so I walked with Billy towards Lewes.

'What do you know about Southease Billy?'

'Nowt really – there's not much to it. A church, a few cottages, farms. Folk be a bit secretive down there, they don't welcome outsiders. The river floods a lot and you needs to know your way through the reeds as it be mighty wet. Some folks use the farm tracks rather than boats as finding your way through the marshes is a mite dangerous.'

'Wilf told me not to go there in the afternoon or evening and to be careful but he didn't say why.'

'Reckon that's 'cos of the smugglers – they're livin' all down the river and Southease and nearby Telscombe are known bases for they. But I'll come with you so there'll be no need to fret; we'll pitch up at the church and see if anyone knows about your ma.'

'When can we go then? I'll have to make arrangements for Beth.'

'I'll let thee know. I can get half a day, mayhaps next week, say Tuesday.'

We parted and I retraced my steps pondering what I knew about my mother's family, sadly concluding that it was not much. I was sure that her name, before she married, was Kempe but how I knew that I don't recall. She could not read or write until my father taught her but she was highly skilled with herbs and receipts, the knowledge of which was gleaned from her grandmother. I had a vague idea that she left her home when her grandmother died which seemed a bit strange but it was not unusual for whole families to be wiped out by disease or even hunger but my mother hadn't said that her family was dead. She had only said that they were no longer known to her and would purse her lips whenever I tried to open the subject. The memories were painful. I had a younger brother who had died first despite both my parents' care. My father went next and my dear mother within hours of him. At the time I wished I had died too. Now, with good friends and Beth I had much to be thankful for but it was always with me and I knew how Billy felt to be alone. If Billy was able to make next Tuesday then I would do my best to resolve any issues that had caused my mother to leave her family. My father's family were also closed to me – he had been, in some way, loosely related to the Coads, which was why I had been sent to them as a servant. Other than that connection I knew nothing and frankly I had no wish to locate any other Coads. Life for me and Billy had been bruising.

Tuesday arrived and Billy and I set off early to walk to Southease. We followed the track that Wilf had taken in the cart and no one else was about. It was a still day with curls of vapour rising from the damp ground and after a while a strong sun pierced its way through the mist and our spirits rose with the warmth. Wilf's comments were at the back of my mind and I had been rather anxious. I wished he had not said anything because I felt his opinion of Southease would colour my first impressions. I had been thinking about this visit all week and knew it was important to discover who I came from and if they knew about me or that my mother was dead.

We came to where we thought the village was and went off the track way, down towards the river and came upon a church. Another church with a round tower, my travels seemed to be punctuated by them. It sat low in the grasses and trees and its tower looked like it was sitting on shoulders. The proportions were unusual to my mind and I sensed that the building was ancient beyond any that Lewes had.

There was a small burial ground and I thought to walk round the stones and see if there were any Kempes. Billy had disappeared and I explored. There were a few stones with inscriptions but none that was of interest to me. I ventured towards the door and twisted the round ring handle. It was dark and damp inside but just as I thought to find the candles a streak of light came through the highest window and pierced the gloom but even with the ladder of sunshine it did not warm the interior or indicate a welcome. I heard a rustling and a movement in the shadows sent prickles of fear racing up my back. I fled.

There was a bench seat outside and I sank onto it waiting for my heart to stop pounding. I expect it was only a mouse but the inside of the church felt too ancient and eerie for me. I was relieved to hear voices and was truly thankful to see

Billy's cheerful face, he was accompanied by a small bent figure in clerical garb. The old man, for he was very old, peered up at me from under heavily-hooded eyes. 'Aye, I see the likeness. You be a Kempe girl. Come, I will point you in the right direction, may you be happy with what ye find.' He cackled in amusement. We were 'pointed' as he put it further down the hill toward the river where there was a row of low dwellings. I put a hand on Billy's arm and whispered 'perhaps we should go Billy, I have a bad feeling about this place.'

'Don't be daft, Esther, you shouldn't get afeared by now't. Come on, I'll go first.'

The dwellings were uncared for with rubbish strewn all around. A sullen dog, with his hackles rising, growled at our approach and broke into a high-pitched bark. The door was flung aside.

'Gor, love us, it be Sarah. No, hold on. Who are you, what do you want?' The woman kicked the dog into a whimpering silence.

Billy said, 'Are you the Kempes?'

'What's it to you?'

Billy looked at me.

'I am Esther, I d'believe my mother was Sarah Kempe.'

'You think, do you?'

'Yes… I do.'

'And what do you want with we, Esther'

'I am looking for my mother's family and I want to know if they live here.'

She sneered again. 'An' what if you find your mother's family, what do you want with they?'

'Nothing, I want nothing. I just want to know who they are and why she left them.'

'Well, Esther, daughter of Sarah Kempe, you had better come in and meet your family then.'

Her laugh was harsh as she stood aside and motioned us into the house.

My initial thought was not relief at finding I had a family but apprehension. We entered the kitchen; my eyes took seconds to focus and there was silence as I looked around me. There was a range with a cheerful fire burning which provided the warmth and light as not much was coming through the small dirty window. An elderly man sat in a rocking chair mumbling to himself. Another man, a young man, looked at us inquisitively and the woman who had opened the door spoke to him.

'Sam, meet yer cousin Esther.' He looked surprised before nodding to me.

'Hello.' My voice didn't seem like my own.

She continued. 'And this old fella will be your grandfather – your mother's father.

Me, I'm your Aunt Tilly, your mother were me sister. Yes, Sarah was me sister – the sister who left us. Left her mother and father, left me to care for they. Left us all in the lurch in fact.'

'Why?' I whispered. 'Why did she leave you?'

'She thought she were better than we and once she met that man, we didna stand a chance. He turned her aginst us.'

'My father?'

'Aye, him.'

'Ma,' said Sam with a warning note in his voice, 'Leave her be, t'were not the lassie's fault.'

I looked at him gratefully saying 'My name is Esther, Esther Coad.'

'Sh'm dead then?' my aunt asked with a curious note of satisfaction.

'They are all dead, my father, mother and younger brother, all taken by the great sickness.'

'So you be alone an' you thought you would come and look us up, maybe live with us, or would that be off of us?'

'No, not at all, I wanted to know if I still had a family, what you were like and why did she leave you. I want to be part of a family; I do not like to be all alone. Nothing more.'

Sam spoke again, 'Ma, leave the girl be. Will you take a drink Esther, you've walked aways?'

I nodded gratefully and at that moment the door swung open and a tall man strode in. He looked surprised and not a little grim. His hair was black and long and his face was pocked. He smiled but it looked more like a scowl as a deep scar distorted his mouth. 'Company, eh? And who be you?'

My aunt explained our presence but her tone of voice was altered, softened.

'Well, a cousin indeed, and one who wants to claim us as her own, now there's a surprise. Perhaps we should celebrate this, hey, Dad, what do you think?' he kicked the old man's chair.

I looked at him, wondering who he was.

He spoke to me with a mocking smile. So, Esther you've met my brother Sam and my father old Bill over there and my mother Tilly. Now, you've met me, Jeremiah and you be wondering be I a cousin or an uncle, eh?'

'No,' I denied, embarrassed to have been caught out. 'Jeremiah, I am pleased to meet you.'

'Well, Esther, that is a very pretty sentiment and we welcome you with open arms.' He laughed loudly. 'Fetch the jug, ma, we must drink on this.'

My aunt went to an inner room and returned with a jug and some little mugs. She poured a drop into each before handing them round.

Jeremiah raised his saying 'To the return of our dear cousin Esther and long may she be with us.'

We all tupped our mugs and downed the drink. Billy coughed and I choked on the fiery liquid. Jeremiah laughed loudly. 'So you weren't weaned on best brandy girl, not like your ma, she would have known how to down the grog without choking.'

Sam butted in, before I had a chance to interpret what it was he was saying.

'Tell us what happened to your ma and pa Esther and how you found us.' His voice was gentle and friendly and I warmed to him – unlike his brother.

Some stools were produced and I told them a little of my tale omitting the detail about the Coads. I explained that I was the adoptive mother of a little girl and that she and I resided at a farm near Lewes. I didn't go into any detail so my story took but a matter of minutes. For some reason I felt unable to talk about my friends and how I had come by them.

'And who is this young fellow who came with you today?'

'This is Billy-alone. He has been a good friend to me in all sorts of adventures.'

'Well, we look forward to hearing about those stories another time, Can we offer you some food, I am sure our ma could rustle up some cheese?'

I felt we had spent enough time with my newly-discovered family and I politely declined.

We all rose, except the man who was my grandfather who

looked at me with a flicker of interest in his vacant eyes before saying, 'Be you my Sarah?'

'No, but I am her daughter, my name is Esther.'

He lost interest and returned his weak gaze to the fire in the range.

We made our way out and it was an awkward moment as we took our leave. I looked back at the house: they were all standing in different attitudes. Sam waved, Aunt Tilly stood with her hands on her hips and Jeremiah doffed his cap, sweeping it to the ground.

Billy and I made our way up through the hamlet and past the brooding church with the round tower sitting on its shoulders, up until we found the Lewes track way and made our way home.

'Billy, did you understand the relationships between them?'

'Nah, but you don't need to know do you? It's not your concern. Now you have found them what do it mean to you?'

'I think it is just that I am no longer alone. I don't want anything from them and I have nothing that they would value but family is family. Their blood runs in me and we have common ancestors. I am happy to have found them.'

He looked at me strangely. 'Well if you be happy, how come you look so fearful?'

I searched my heart for an answer but could find none.

Chapter Fifty

Some days later, Cecilia, who was still struggling with her early day sickness, had arranged for the fitting of her dress to be in the afternoon. We drove into Lewes in the gig and Cecilia told the driver to wait for us.

Miss Simpson looked pleased with the compliments we were able to pay her after trying the dress on. It was absolutely exquisite and Cecelia's worries about the pregnancy showing were unfounded. While we were in Lewes we called on Mrs Makepiece and I was able to tell her and Cecilia about our trip to Southease.

'That is wonderful Esther; it is good to have family and roots nearby. Will you call on them again soon?'

'I didn't really feel welcomed,' I confessed. 'But perhaps that is not surprising, me turning up out of the blue and there had clearly been some bad feelings about my mother leaving them, as Aunt Tilly put it, in the lurch.'

'Aye, it must have been a bit of a shock to them.' Mrs Makepiece turned her attention to Cecilia and we talked on about the upcoming wedding and her departure from South Farm as we took tea.

In the gig as we returned home I asked her if she was excited about the wedding and returning to her mother's care.

'I am, but once I have been there a few weeks I know I will want to come back to South Farm but I must do what is best for my baby. You will call on John, won't you Esther? He will be quite lost without us all around him.'

'I will indeed – I am sure I will have time on my hands in the early days and I can walk over with Beth regularly. Perhaps I can accompany the doctor when he visits.'

'Will you write to me Esther? I will miss you and Beth so much and it would be good to know all the little things that are not noticed by John.' We giggled at her polite way of requesting the gossip.

The days were going by rapidly with Cecilia turning things out and selecting her travelling wardrobe. I was thrilled to be given two of her day dresses, a shawl and some underclothing, which I had never previously worn. She also gave me some bits and pieces to use as adornments if I went anywhere special. In the days leading up to her departure I was with her constantly and knew I would miss her terribly. Beth was constantly in her arms being kissed and cuddled. 'By the time you get back,' I said, 'she will be talking and walking properly and you won't recognise her.'

'Oh, don't say that, I would recognise her anywhere, she has been my dearest love. Excepting John and you of course. When I get back we will be together again and Beth will have a little one to play at being mother to.'

I laughed at the idea of Beth mothering a new baby but in truth I was dreading Cecilia's departure. I was very nervous of my new role as nurse and how Beth and I would fit into a bachelor's household. I truly liked the doctor and enjoyed our discussions but I was unsure of my place. Sometimes I thought him to be looking at me in a manner that wasn't quite as usual, I didn't know what it meant.

On the day before the wedding the household rose early

and everyone clustered around Cecilia as she stepped into the carriage. She looked absolutely beautiful and very dignified. I sensed her taking back her role as a peer's daughter and friend to the royal family. Our little world at South Farm was gently pushed into the background as she and Farmer Elwood took their place in the wider fashionable world.

After their departure the house fell silent and I went upstairs to pack up my small bag of belongings and Beth's clothes and toys, her little cloth dolly and blankets that she couldn't sleep without. The driver was to take us to the doctor's house in the afternoon and we must be all ready for him.

We had a light lunch with Mrs Fisher and Cilla in the kitchen before I gave them both a hug and promised to return shortly to hear all the news. I went to the stables and said goodbye to the gardeners and stable lads. I looked to see if Wilf was about and wondered at my sadness that he wasn't. Oh, how I would miss everyone. I gathered Beth in my arms and we waited patiently for Cecilia's driver to collect us.

Chapter Fifty-One

Garlic: Allium sativum – Garleac, a spear-shaped member of the leek and onion family was cultivated and eaten enthusiastically throughout the middle ages and was used for medicinal purposes from the time of the Egyptians. It had many uses, among them treating coughs and sore throats and 'it taketh away the morphew, tetters or ringworms and scabbed heads in children'.

The Physic Garden Booklet, Michelham Priory

I have been at the doctors for some days now and my world has changed completely. My day has a working purpose and I find I like it very much. The small household rises early and we all eat together in the panelled dining room. The doctor is frequently absent on calls: he is a very busy man and when he is away Mr and Mrs Jenkins sit with Beth and me to take a filling breakfast. Mrs Jenkins tells me about Dr Grieve's views on eating properly and very soon I fall into the habit of eating several courses comprising eggs and different meats or fish, whereas, at the farm, I barely managed more than a scrap of fresh bread and jam or honey. I am happy to see Beth tuck into her food so enthusiastically.

I start my working day in the doctor's study where he discusses the cases he expects to see and how I can help him either in the management of dressings, the preparation of treatments and making notes of his prescriptions and thoughts. I particularly like the preparation of medicaments to receipts that he has devised himself or received from colleagues. We see patients from nine in the morning, by appointment, and I am present for most of those. As soon as he has seen everyone he goes up to his office in the town and undertakes his coroner's duties. We take a small luncheon together with Mr and Mrs Jenkins and discuss the town news, of which there always seems to be a lot. The doctor sees the important folk and the Jenkins the small tradesmen and servants so between them they appear to know everything that is going on. It is very entertaining and with so much chatter Beth absorbs it all and does her best to repeat some of the words she hears. It thrills me that she will know words early on in her life that others might never know; I think I develop an ambition for her education.

One of the biggest changes for me personally is that I am always in company. I am rarely alone nowadays and at times I find that quite tiring. The doctor insists that I take time off to spend with Beth and others of my choosing. In reality there are not many who are of my choosing. With Cecilia gone nearly everyone that I mix with has a purpose for being in my company. I sometimes sit, in the evening, and think how I can make friends with people who seek my company for not what I do or am but for myself. In my heart I hoped that Wilf would fulfil that role or perhaps members of my new family but I couldn't force these desires forward – I had to hope that people would seek me out.

Whilst I worked with the doctor I left Beth in Mrs Jenkin's care and occasionally Mrs Makepiece or her grandfather would take her out into the town for a change of scene. She is developing rapidly and it is important to me that she learns from a number of people. Miss Wardle offered to look after her on occasions but I didn't think that a good idea as she was so preoccupied with Sally and the piglets Beth would probably end up in the stye with them.

So, despite being busy and excited by my new role in life I felt myself to be lonely without Cecilia and I hoped she would return soon.

One memorable day occurred about a month after moving to Lewes when I had not one, but two, visitors. Wilf called in at lunchtime and was invited into the kitchen to see how we were settled. He stood, ill at ease, and only found his tongue when Mrs Jenkins kindly suggested that I show him the garden. Beth was still munching her way through her food so he and I were able to walk round undisturbed. Still he didn't say much and I wondered why he had come if he had nothing to say to me. I tried several conversations to no avail until I mentioned that I had been to Southease, against his advice.

I saw him stiffen up. 'And what did you find, Esther, at Southease?'

'I found my family Wilf, I haven't seen them since but I am glad to know that I have some.'

'And their names?'

'I have an Aunt Tilly, my mother's sister. A grandfather and two cousins, Sam and…'

'…and Jeremiah,' he finished for me.

'Aye, do you know them?'

'I do that. They were with the men who killed my father. They beat him when he tried to stop them stealing from the farm. He took a long time to die, Esther and he told me that those two boys were part of the gang.'

'Stealing…?'

'Aye, stealing.'

But what…?'

'It's past history Esther. I put it behind me but that family destroyed mine and I can't see you any more if you are a Kempe.'

'But I am not one really,' I protested.

'You are, you're a Kempe. It's in your blood. even if you now have the name of Coad.

He left and I sunk to the floor, shocked beyond belief.

Chapter Fifty-Two

Mint: Mentha Spicata Spearmint and apple mint known as Monk's herb as, being milder, it was grown only by monastic infirmarers for use in cordials for indigestion. Fresh spearmint cured headaches, 'a sure remedie for children's sore heads'.

The Physic Garden Booklet, Michelham Priory

I had a lot of medications to make that afternoon which gave me no time to dwell on what had passed between us but I moved and thought as if in a trance. I fulfilled my duties before leaving the house and sat by myself in the nearby meadow. I had barely begun to pick over the angry words, the implications, before I was astonished to see my cousin Sam coming towards me. He called 'Esther, cousin. I was told by the old lady at the house that this is where you were.' He dropped to the grass beside me plucking a long stem and chewing on it as he looked me over.

I was never more flustered and was unable to get a word out before he invited me, at his mother's request, to the house at Southease for a bite on Sunday and to bring the little tacker with me. Sam would bring a cart over in the morning and collect us and deliver us back later that afternoon.

I blustered and hedged from giving a reply blaming my workload, Beth's health, the doctor's needs and anything that would prevent me from going until I had thought this all through.

'Nonsense,' he said. 'That old lady says that Sunday is your own to do with as you will. I will be here about noon.' I was mortified that I couldn't take control of the situation, only managing to blurt out that I had undertaken to spend time with Billy-alone, my friend.

'Well, bring him too, if you are worried about being with your family, the family that you sought out.'

I blustered some more saying, 'No, of course I'm not worried. It's just that I was surprised to see you. Of course I will come and I will bring Billy and Beth too. Please thank Aunt Tilly for thinking so kindly of me.' I rose from the grass and brushed myself down before wishing my cousin goodbye and hurrying back to the house. I looked back to see him standing, watching. I had the uncomfortable feeling that he was laughing at me and, despite the warm evening, I felt chilled.

Later in the week I made my way to see Mrs Makepiece. Beth and I sat in her tiny garden as I told her about my two visitors.

'Well,' she said, surprised. 'I remember when Wilf's father were attacked. Wilf was but a young-un then and it were never known all who done it. He were shot in the shoulder and despite being given the best care from his employers, the Elwoods, he took a fever and later died. Did Wilf say they did it definitely? I know some were punished but there was no mention of boys.'

'He did, with much bitterness. He said he couldn't see me because I was one of them.'

I am ashamed to say that I burst into tears. I had found my family and then tried to deny them, all in a matter of a few weeks, for the sake of a young man who had taken my fancy. Was that how it had happened with my mother?

''Ee lass, don't fret so. You must go on your visit and see what you can glean from them. Wilf will come round, he can't blame you for their deeds and it were over ten years ago. What I want to know is how he knows it were them. The two lads would have been too young though I s'pect they were up to all sorts. Your grandfather is suspicioned to be a smuggler but then so is everyone else who lives down the river.'

'How do you know that?' I asked defensively.

'I made it my business to find out who the Kempes are, and there is a deal of talk about they so you must keep your wits about you girl. Make sure Billy stays with you.'

'So what do they want with me then?' I wondered aloud.

'Perhaps they is not all bad. Perhaps your aunt be sick of menfolk with their fighting and drinking ways. Perhaps she hankers for some feminine company and a little one to coo over. She can't have had it easy with only an old man for company and more, and then, later when nature takes its course just getting two rough boys – both taught in the old ways.'

As we walked back to the doctor's I thought of what she had said, implied, and her advice. Aunt Tilly didn't strike me as a bullied, downtrodden creature just there for the needs of her menfolk. In truth I saw her as the kingpin of the household but perhaps it wasn't always that way. When my great-grandmother died and my mother left Southease, Aunt Tilly would have been alone with just my grandfather for company. No wonder she was bitter. I tried to clear my head of unsavoury thoughts but I went to bed that night with a headache and a curious dullness of spirit.

Chapter Fifty-Three

Sunday dawned bright and clear and after breakfast I put up a basket of biscuits and homemade jam. I also took a few eggs from Mrs Jenkins' well-stocked larder. For the menfolk I had purchased three different neckerchiefs and a pretty embroidered hankie for Aunt Tilly. I took pleasure in using part of my newly-earned wages on these little gifts. While I was at it I also bought two ounces of sweetmeats for Billy and Cilla to have later.

Billy arrived mid-morning and we all sat in the garden and played with Beth until I heard the cart arriving out at the front of the house. As we clattered off I looked up and saw the doctor watching from his bedroom window. There had been no medicaments to be made up today though I wished otherwise.

Beth was very excited at this venture out and her spirits lifted ours so by the time we got to Southease we were all very jolly. I had dressed her with care and she had a new sun bonnet to match her pretty dress – a parting gift from Cecilia, with a crisp white overskirt to help keep the dress clean. She was also wearing some tiny little slippers – a great novelty which she was constantly admiring. As we pulled up outside the cottage I was very thankful that we could focus on Beth rather than be forced to notice other things.

The kitchen had been tidied up and even the windows cleaned. The dog was banished to an outhouse from where he maintained a mournful howl. It was a little squashed as we mingled in the small room so I asked if we should walk down to the river and tire Beth's high spirits which could easily descend into tears. Everyone except grandfather thought that a good idea and off we went. After a few paces the trees thinned out and we could see the distant downs beyond the valley floor. The way was dry on a well trodden path but on either side were deep reed beds rising above our heads from which came the chirps of waterfowl and other mysterious but natural noises. In the distance I could see some cattle on the lower reaches of the hills. When we got near the river I looked backwards along the way we had come, it was very difficult to see the line of the path and I shivered at the thought of trying to find the way blind. The breeze licked the top of the reeds and there was an eerie whispering. I asked if many used the river paths and got an abrupt reply from Jeremiah.

'Only those as knows the way use it, all others disappears.'

We climbed up a small bank in order to look at the flat grey waters. I clutched Beth up in my arms, remembering our sad history with this river. 'Look,' I said, 'the sun is hiding, Beth.'

Sam, lifted her from my arms and she played with the bristles on his chin, laughing uproariously as he tickled her.

We returned to the cottage and settled down outside on a few blankets. I unloaded my basket and gave the gifts to my family. The biscuits were well received but I thought Aunt Tilly a bit ungracious when I presented the eggs.

'We have our own hens girl, we're not beggars, though we do not live in the style you do.'

'I am sure I never thought so Aunt, I just did not see any hens when I came last time – there was no harm intended.'

'Don't mind her,' grunted Sam, 'She is not used to polite society.'

Aunt Tilly returned to her kitchen before producing a small table laden with good plain food.

We all set to and demolished the savouries and cakes. My cousins helped themselves without any polite delays for the ladies. Beth copied them and grabbed handfuls of cake and in the end I didn't hold back either as there would have been nothing left for me and I was hungry.

It was a pleasant afternoon and my aunt went to great lengths to make us comfortable. My cousins were good company with lots of joshing and boisterous games involving both Billy and Beth. I did on one occasion catch a rather strange look exchanged between Tilly and her sons but put it down to their collective attempt to make us feel at home.

Just as we were talking about getting ready to leave, Jeremiah, who had wandered off behind the cottage, returned and exchanged a few quiet words with his brother. From that moment on I felt we were in the way and were hurried into the cart, our belongings pushed in around us.

They all called goodbye and disappeared immediately into the cottage as if they couldn't wait to be rid of us. Sam was to drive us back but suddenly he turned to Billy and suggested that he take the reins and he, Sam, would collect the cart from Lewes tomorrow. Then he was gone. I was dumbfounded and looking back was amazed to see both Sam and Jeremiah on horseback and heading in the opposite direction at great speed.

'What was all that about?' I asked Billy.

'Reckon they got a message.'

'What sort of message?'

'I dunno, but there was some comment about them cows on the hill, they said they was looking in the right direction and laughed.'

'How can that be a message?'

'Well, if they be facing the town it mean one thing and if they be facing the sea, it be meaning another. It is how messages are sent quickly from one area to another, they might light beacons but then others understand that so by changing the direction of tethered livestock the message is only understood by those in the know. See?'

I was not sure that I did see. 'What do you think the message is about?'

'Smugglers' business. They got lamps inside and all sorts of stuff used by the gentlemen and they ain't botherin' to hide it.'

'Billy, do you think them capable of killing people?'

'I dunno lass but I wouldn't want to be on t'wrong side of they and I don't reckon you should notice anything odd.'

'Do you remember what Wilf said about Southease Billy?'

'Aye.'

'Well it was to do with the Kempes. He blames them for his father's death and won't have anything to do with me now, Billy, because he says I come from the Kempe family and it was they.'

'Did you like him then Esther?'

'Aye, I did that.'

We travelled on in silence until we got to the doctor's house. The cart was unhitched and the horse stabled nearby as I went indoors to reflect on a very unusual day.

Chapter Fifty-Four

Knitbone: Conferva – to join together. Comfrey, the most important herb for treating fractures. Pound the root into a mass and spread like plaster around the broken limb where it set dry to hold the bone in place.

The Physic Garden Booklet, Michelham Priory

All aspects of my life had changed except one: my lipsy leg. It had been deformed since birth and I had no idea of cause, just effect. It had played a big part in my life – perhaps too big a part as it had limited my confidence. Lately, however it seemed just a part of me, it had become of less consequence and whenever I was with other people I didn't feel defined by it. One day I asked the doctor if he would advise me on how to improve my movement. At the time I asked (bravely I thought) I was finding that the unnatural pressures on areas of my foot were hurting me and creating sores that were difficult to heal despite my best efforts with lotions and dressings. I wanted more freedom of movement so I could keep up with Beth and perhaps be seen in a more positive and attractive light. Perhaps Mrs Makepiece was right, I should find a husband. Was it so improbable?

The doctor held my naked foot in his hand. His touch was gentle, almost caressing, but with Mrs Jenkins in the room it was all as it should be. On many occasions I was the chaperone when he examined single women. Married women didn't seem perturbed by the doctor's attention to their bodies; in some cases I think they positively flaunted themselves but he was always proper. I occasionally wondered if that is why he wanted me to work with him: protection from Lewes ladies.

He gently probed the reddened sore part of my heel and toes before examining and stretching out my feeble calf muscle.

'Esther, I think we could bring about a change to your leg if we break and reset it. This sounds alarming and it would be terribly painful with only laudanum to give you limited pain relief but I have much experience of setting bones and whilst it won't take the basic condition away it will improve it.' I gasped, horrified, before he went on. 'That is the most difficult option and is maybe one you won't want to entertain. Another option is that we can work to bring your muscles to a better condition by strengthening exercises. I can also make a block to bring your heel into line with your toes, which would improve your balance. I think these things would greatly improve your life and reduce the pain and broken skin where the foot blisters. This is something we should do now as the pressure sores will become worse. All three of us were peering at my poor little foot but I knew I could not face a deliberate breaking of my leg and then pulling it to put it into a better position. I wasn't that brave.

The doctor continued his examination above my knee but distracted me by telling me about a colleague, Thomas Bettany, who was experimenting with gases that would render people insensible while their surgeon wielded the knife. 'It is the future Esther, but regrettably I do not think he is quite there yet and I couldn't offer such a solution at this time.'

I sighed with relief that this Thomas Bettany's experiments weren't ready yet. I didn't want to be an experiment. I just wanted to be a little more comfortable in order to keep up with Beth.

Within days I was fitted with a carefully crafted wooden platform that was fixed into my boots. The top surface was covered with the softest sheepskin to cushion the pad of my heel. The doctor suggested that once I became used to the insert he would cover the sheepskin with very soft leather thus retaining the cushioning but the smoothness of the leather would be more practical to wear.

As he gave me the boot our hands touched and I was aware again of a peculiar tension between us.

'Esther, my dear, I hope this will help and if it is not quite right we will make adjustments. In the meantime, I have some exercises prepared for you that will strengthen your muscles.' We sat side by side with my skirts pulled up above my knee as I learned the movements. When I eventually returned to my room I sat and stared at my unfamiliar legs. I had always avoided looking at myself as I found it distressing to see the wasted muscle. I vowed to persevere with the movements no matter how painful it was.

Learning to walk on the insert was a revelation. Immediately there was the sensation of complete balance but I had been hopping about on my unbalanced feet for my entire life and it was not the matter of a few days to adjust. I worked at it every day, increasing wearing time by minutes until I was able to wear the boot most of the day. I did the exercises morning and evening and very gradually my body straightened along with my improved muscles. Sometimes it was all so painful that I whimpered as I rubbed soothing cream into the angry muscle and ligaments. Poor Beth became used to seeing me constantly working my legs and would sit beside me on the floor trying to copy the movements, thinking it a game. If I cried, she did too; if I smiled her little face lit up and I was lifted in spirit, which made it all worthwhile.

Chapter Fifty-Five

Life went on around me and I was happy in my role as nurse having seen no more of my cousins or Wilf. That is, until one momentous day in summer when Wilf appeared at our back door. Mrs Jenkins called me into the kitchen and I hurried in fully balanced and with my head held high. She disappeared into her scullery and I could hear her movements in the background.

Wilf looked surprised to see me so upright before he smiled his gentle smile. 'Esther, you look well. Living in Lewes clearly suits you.'

I replied as coolly as I was able, 'I am not sure if it is Lewes, or this household Wilf, but what can I do for you?'

'Naught lass. I did but come to ask you if you would walk out with me one day when you have the time, and Beth of course.'

I know I frowned, all the while thinking on our last bitter conversation.

'I was over hasty last time we met and I want to say sorry, like. My past history was never your concern and I should not have blamed you. I'm sorry Esther, I would like to make amends. Will you come with me to the Midsummer Fair?'

A lightness of spirit flooded over me and I was more than happy to say yes, Beth and I would love to go with him. We made the necessary arrangements and I all but skipped up the stairs to my workroom.

I bumped into Dr Grieve as I went and was surprised that he didn't seem to welcome my news about Wilf.

He said, rather stiffly, 'Well, you must spend time with other young people Esther but I hope you won't be neglectful of your work while you daydream about this young man.'

Daydream? That was unfair. 'I give everything to my work for you doctor, I would never let you down.'

'Hmph, yes well, see that you don't.' and he left me standing in the room aghast.

Later that evening I asked Mrs Jenkins why the doctor had never married.

She told me that he had been sweet on a young woman who had chosen another over him. Since then he had taken care not to become ensnared though, she added, many had tried.

I told her about our strange conversation and she laughed it off. 'Well, he will be worrying about losing your skills to a young man who might take you away from your work.'

Of course I thought, that explains it. I reassured Mrs Jenkins that nothing would take me away from my position of nurse in the doctor's household. She smiled at me and patting my hand told me to enjoy my leisure with that good looking young man who also had the reputation of having the lasses run round after him.

Wilf came for us early. It was a bittersweet day for me, remembering the occasion when Becca and I travelled downstream from Coad Farm enjoying our freedom from the chores. How many times had I wished we had been prevented from going; perhaps the chain of events would never have happened and Becca would still be here with me. I felt guilty for enjoying my life as a result of those events but there was nothing I could do and I wasn't such a killjoy as to allow the past to colour the present. Wilf was nattily dressed with a brightly coloured neckerchief bringing out the colour in his outdoor face. How I warmed to his company and Beth remembered his throwing skills and demanded the same before we had even entered the fairground.

We made our way round the stalls and tents enjoying the spectacle of travelling bands of actors and musicians. We purchased a few little bits and pieces from the tinkers and again I enjoyed spending my own money on some sweetmeats for my friends. I found a little piece of lace trim to make a collar for Mrs Makepiece and some pretty buttons for Beth. I even found a lovely ribbon for Billy-alone to give to either Cilla or Sally the piggy. I laughed up at Wilf as we wondered who would get it. We had a wonderful day sampling everything on offer and buying some little pies and biscuits for our lunch. Wilf was good company and I felt on top of the world as I walked evenly beside him. I was pleased to be able to introduce him to people we met and I saw the look of speculation in Mrs Makepiece's eyes as she summed the poor lad up.

'Guess we are setting the tongues wagging here Esther.'

'Aye.' I couldn't help blushing but the laughter was wiped from my face and heart as we walked straight into all three of the Coad brothers.

They blocked our way and I felt my confidence crumble as I faced their derision and sneers.

Wilf moved swiftly forward pushing the eldest and youngest aside but the middle boy held his ground. Wilf held his arm out for me and I managed to step boldly round him. I was gripping Beth tightly, so tightly she began to wail.

Her cries broke the threat that surrounded us and Wilf just hefted her up in his arms and holding me with his free hand pulled us away from their malevolence.

'You're alright Esther, just sit down here and I'll get you a drink, you've lost all your colour.'

'No, please Wilf, don't leave me.'

'Alright, I will stay with you but you showed them your mettle, my girl – you're stronger than you think.'

I burst into tears. He knelt beside me and pulled my face into his jerkin. I sniffed the rich leather underlaid by a masculine scent. It was overwhelming and my body buckled as I leaned into his, enjoying his protection. Beth broke the spell by patting at my hair as she reduced her cries to a mere gulp. Wilf pulled her into our midst and we all began to giggle in our tight, inclusive little circle. Amongst my anguish I felt a rush of joy.

Chapter Fifty-Six

Since residing with Dr Grieve I had searched his texts and books to try and identify the herb I had come across at Lewes and Piddinghoe. Finally, I found it, and was able to take a cutting from St Michael's and grow it in our herb garden. The entry in the text said:

Elecampane Inula helenium*: This is a very deep-rooted plant, a colony will outlast a house or garden.* Inula *may come from* hinnulus *meaning a young mule and it was used for centuries for treating horses. A magical Anglo-Saxon herb, all sorts of ailments require* Elecampane. *The root boiled very soft and mixed in a mortar with fresh butter and the pouder of ginger, maketh an excellent ointment against the itch, scabs, manginesse and such like.*

I was very satisfied with this discovery and it seemed to support my feeling that the round towered churches might be very old indeed.

Dr Grieve and I decided to use the herb and test its efficacy on anyone presenting with the itch.

'I have a number of patients who might be interested in it for their horses too.'

We laughed easily together before I hurried away to supervise Beth's breakfast.

Some days seem special and the joyous thing is that you don't know about them until they are finishing or gone.

Discovering the herb was but one of the good things that happened that day, the second was a letter from Cecilia.

'I am so frustrated being here, mama fusses continuously and I have a nurse, a governess (very old now) and every servant watching my every breath. I wish I was back with you all at South Farm. I am sure John is missing me dreadfully and I doubt Mrs Fisher is serving him his favourite meals. Have you been to see him Esther? Please go and cheer him up. Perhaps you could go with Dr Grieve and have dinner (and check on Mrs Fisher). I loved hearing about Beth's antics and reading between your sparse lines I gather you are quite taken with a certain young man.'

I smiled as I read this, I thought I had been quite circumspect. Dear Cecilia, I did miss her.

'Can you also send me some of that lovely ribbon we saw in Lewes? I hope to do some tapestry and I thought to use it for an edging. My brother is to be abroad for some months – he is to visit Venice and Florence – so envious. I have commissioned him to buy a present for John, which I can give him on my return. I thought a piece of glass, Venetian glass is very a la mode. *Do you think that too feminine? I could suggest a painting or a sculpture. What do you think? I finish now, mama insists I attend her! A million kisses for Beth and one for you my dearest friend.'*

I put Cecilia's letter aside and went to see the doctor. We had two patients waiting and one needed a dressing that was difficult to do without causing undue pain. Carefully, I prepared the ointment that the doctor had prescribed. I cleaned the instruments in the way he liked and laid out the dressing materials. Our patient was nervous and I felt it part of my duty to try and settle her. I made a tisane of chamomile and persuaded her to drink it thinking that it would help calm her. Together the doctor and I worked at releasing the old dressing before inspecting the wound, which had come about whilst hunting. The deep cut in the young lady's rib cage was worrying Dr Grieve and I saw him disappear behind the screen to sniff the discarded bandages I had handed to him. He nodded to me before reappearing with a broad smile on his face.

'We work well together, Esther,' he said later. 'Are you happy here?'

'Why yes, Dr Grieve, I love my work.'

'And when Cecilia returns will you want to leave me?'

I looked up at him trying to judge his meaning. Leave me, he said, as if I were a friend not an employee. I saw nothing but polite enquiry in his face so I replied that I was unable to predict the future. He laughed.

I mentioned Cecilia's plan that we should both visit Farmer Elwood, at South Farm and invite ourselves to dinner thus cheering and checking in one go.

'Capital idea, my dear, we will go tonight.' I shall look forward to escorting you and cheering my good friend.'

Wilf came by later and I told him I was to accompany Dr Grieve to the farm of his employer, he didn't seem to think it a good deed in the making, more an opportunity for Dr Grieve to take me out.

I was not at all put out by this interpretation for to my mind it indicated that Wilf was jealous. I never imagined that someone would be jealous over me. It was quite a heady feeling and one that I cushioned in a little box and drew out when I was ready to contemplate such a delicious thought. To be jealous one must care. Did Wilf care? I hoped so.

I dressed carefully for our visit to South Farm. I had a heavy dark skirt that I partnered with a pretty blouse made from the material Cecilia had given me for Christmas. As I looked at myself in the mirror I stood as tall as I could. With my improved posture and hair held in place with a clip purchased at the Midsummer Fair I felt quite acceptable. I went downstairs after giving Beth a kiss goodnight and waited for the doctor.

'Esther, you look very nice. How are your exercises going?'

'Very well Dr Grieve, I think you will be pleased when you see the range of movement.'

'Well, I will have a look tomorrow my dear and if your posture is anything to go by you have come a long way.'

Mrs Fisher was a bit flustered at our unexpected arrival but she rose to the occasion and produced three courses with only a short delay.

Farmer Elwood was so pleased to see us we promised to visit again in the near future. He was, as Cecilia predicted, lonely without his wife and Beth and me. He and Dr Grieve shared some jokey comments about me being settled with his household now. It was all a bit strange but I enjoyed the company of both men and whilst they took their port I went out to the kitchen to see how everyone was getting on.

The kitchen was looking a bit out of sorts – clearly Mrs Fisher had had to pull out all the stops to get three courses to the table. I offered to help clear up but once I had heard the local gossip I was shooed out. It was a little disconcerting for I didn't quite know where I belonged.

We settled down in front of the grand fire to talk about the farm when there was a knock to the front door. The doctor was called back to Lewes to help deliver a young woman expecting her first child. We hurried away and I accompanied him to the household for my first birth.

I was introduced as Nurse Esther Coad but the husband

was so thankful to see us he barely noticed an extra body in his wife's bedroom.

I busied myself with towels, hot water and soothing words as the doctor made his examination and talked calmly to the frightened mother. As it happened the birth was quite straightforward and most of the effort was needed for the anxious father. He and the doctor left the room while I attended to the mother's comfort. Later the doctor said to me that the first rule of birthing was to get rid of the father for they were a nuisance in the birthing chamber. I was pleased that the herbs I always carried were of use in sweetening the atmosphere as well as calming the patient. I was very proud to help deliver a healthy baby boy, my first. The young mother gripped my hand throughout and thanked me when I cleaned and dressed her in a pretty night rail. I brushed her hair and moistened her lips with salve. She looked positively blooming as we left her feeding her infant son. Her husband was a little befuddled with all the drink he had consumed to calm his nerves.

We returned to our house sometime during the morning, the very early hours and I was elated but exhausted. It had been a momentous day for all the right reasons.

Chapter Fifty-Seven

Fennel: Foeniculum vulgare – The use of wild or garden fennel dates back at least to the ancient Egyptians. The name comes from the Latin foenum meaning hay, the smell of which it resembles. Pliny lists its use in 22 remedies including curing hiccoughs and colic, and as well as flavouring salads 'the green leaves of Fennel eaten do fill womens brests with milk'.
The Physic Garden Booklet, Michelham Priory

The next morning, once I was fully awake, I thought through the events of the previous day and thought it was one of the best of my life. So many enjoyable things had happened and best of all I believed I had found my calling. I loved helping deliver the young woman of a healthy baby. I wanted to attend more births and I resolved to ask the doctor to help me train for this. Yes, it had been a good day.

I allowed my thoughts to wander from my work to the doctor and our rather strange relationship. Many times I had felt a connection to him and thought he felt that too. His choice of words was often misleading given the plain look on his face. He gave nothing away but I sensed a growing interest in me but was it as a person or as a nurse in whom he had a certain pride? Cecilia was convinced that he wished to become my beau. I thought her imaginative and deluded by her wish to see me well married and protected. Why would an older man who had the Lewes ladies flurrying around after him look at me? More to the point was I interested in him? I loved his inclusiveness, his wit and cleverness; he was quite inspirational and very kind, but he was twenty years older than me and didn't make me melt like Wilf did. Oh, it was all so confusing these emotions and strange sensations that came from my core without any help from my thoughts.

Once I thought of Wilf the good doctor was pushed aside. I acknowledged my delight in his company; he made me feel vibrant and fully alive. I wanted to touch him. I wanted to fall into his arms and hold him and most of all I wanted him to kiss me.

I pulled myself up and prepared for the day. Mrs Jenkins had let me sleep in and Beth was, no doubt, tucking into her breakfast. I felt so good about myself I took my time in dressing and doing my hair. I had been quite adventurous lately with pins and clips, taming my locks into a recognised style. I used Becca's comb every day and sometimes when doing Beth's hair I would tell her about the comb and that it had a direct connection to her mama who was watching over her. I truly believed that Becca was always with us. I smiled into the mirror and made my way downstairs.

Chapter Fifty-Eight

Salad Burnet: Sanguisorba Minor The Latin name means blood ball, after the appearance and the action of the flower and plant. A decoction of the roots or dried leaves stancheth bleeding and is a singular good herb for wounds.

The Physic Garden Booklet, Michelham Priory

Some weeks later I had another visit from my cousin Sam. He turned up at the back door and wanted to see me urgently. I was working in the doctor's study but once I had finished cleaning the instruments – a task I couldn't leave – I hurried down to see what was wrong.

Sam was clearly upset and begging me to return to Southease with him to look at my Aunt Tilly who was sickening. I suggested that we should ask the doctor to visit her but he was very agitated and said she would not see anyone except family and, as I was family, I must go with him.

I packed a bag with some herbs and things that might be needed and having arranged with Mrs Jenkins that she look after Beth until I got back, I clambered up behind Sam. We trotted off at a brisk pace and I tried not to notice the uncomfortable ride. The sense of urgency in Sam was affecting and I worried all the way to Southease that I would be unable to help. As we drew nearer the village I calmed down a bit, if I couldn't help I would send for Dr Grieve, come what may.

I hurried into the house which was back to its usual

dishevelled state and there sitting at the fire was Aunt Tilly. She seemed in fine health to me.

'What's wrong?'

She looked at me as if I had gone daft.

Sam chipped in. 'I had to tell her you were sick otherwise she wouldn't have come.'

'Of course I would have come. What's going on? Why did you tell me she was sick?'

'Jeremiah has been shot by the preventative men, girl, and we need you to put him right.' Her voice was cold and I knew immediately that I would not be allowed to leave until I had done what was necessary. Sam was leaning against the door; they both looked grim.

'Where is he?'

'In a barn nearby.'

'Can't you get him here where we can clean him up?'

'Don't be a fool girl, the constables will be looking for him. Take her Sam but blindfold her.'

I gasped, but Sam grabbed my arms and twisted them behind me before slipping a cord round my wrists, none too gently. A musty sack was thrown over my head and I was bundled onto the horse this time in front of him.

We rode for about fifteen minutes and I knew we were following the river as I could hear it nearby and the horse was picking its way carefully. When we stopped I had to wait for Sam to lift me down and untie the bindings as well as remove the sack. The light blinded me for a few seconds and I blinked furiously.

'Don't mind ma, her bark is worse than her bite.'

I didn't reply, I did mind, she was my aunt yet she was treating me horribly and so was he.

'Come,' he said. 'Follow me and mind where you walk, the wood be rotten.'

We went into a barn that looked to be derelict. Light filtered through broken slats and spars and beneath my feet I could feel the fragility of the wooden floor.

Sam helped me through a trapdoor and down a ladder. We were going into a black hole and I began to wonder if this was a trap.

At the bottom of the ladder I blinked the dust clear from my eyes, my mouth was dry. I heard a tinder strike and at last I could see that we were in an underground cellar where my cousin was lying on a pile of sacks. I could smell the sourness of blood and distress. I knelt down at his side and tried to ascertain what was wrong.

'We picked the bullet out,' said Sam.

'What with?' I was horrified.

'A knife. It weren't deep.'

'Did you sterilise the knife?'

'Aye, I held it to the flame.'

'Was he conscious?'

'No. It had to be done quick like afore he came round. Did I do right?'

'I don't know, this is beyond my knowledge Sam. When did he get the bullet?'

'Two days gone.'

'Has he come round?'

'Aye, but he seems to be raving now – can 'ee help?'

'I'll try. You will need to get me some things. I'll need my bag and some clean water, is there a spring nearby? I will need thread and a needle and a very sharp knife.'

I looked down at my cousin, he looked so much younger

than I had thought him to be. His skin was sallow and clammy to the touch. 'Sam, we really need the doctor, can you not fetch him?'

'No! It's as ma says, if they get their hands on him he'll be lost. We've lived life in the rough for too long and there would be no mercy from the excise. You must do it for us cousin.'

'Well, I'll try. Fetch me my bag and the things I need. Some clean cloth too. You might need to go and see Mrs Jenkins and ask her to get me a needle and thread for stitches. If you tell her it's for me and that your brother has cut his leg she might not question it. You will need to hurry Sam, we might not have long.'

He vanished silently, but taking the ladder up, I was left in the gloomy cellar with naught but a candle for comfort.

I tried to make Jeremiah comfortable and took his clothes off. There was clean water in a flask, which I used to sluice the wound. I surmised that Sam had to cut deep into the flesh to get the bullet out. The area round the cut was angry and infected. I searched his body for other wounds and found lots of scars from earlier injuries. My cousin had lived life hard. I also found strap marks where he looked as if he had been beaten. I wondered if that was how my grandfather had enforced his rules. What sort of man was he that would take his own daughter and get two children on her? She held my mother to be responsible for her downfall but surely the real culprit was the man that was their father.

Once Jeremiah seemed comfortable on my improvised bedding and I had got used to the dim light I looked round the cellar. It was clearly a hiding place with evidence of the smuggling trade all around: signal lamps, ropes, crates, staves, waterproof carriers and sacks and finally at the furthest point from the entry, barrels. There was also a locked crate, not big enough to hold drink but maybe a stash for tea, salt or baccy, which would need to be kept free of damp.

Sam had been gone a long time and I was getting cold and lonely. I hoped he would return before the candle guttered. I sat alongside my cousin and watched him closely. He was quiet and I thought it would be better to stitch him whilst he was unaware.

I held the flask to his mouth and he swallowed a little. I just prayed that he was strong enough to recover from what was obviously an infected wound.

It seemed hours before Sam returned with another man who seemed to know what was required. He built a small fire under a hole in the ceiling and put some water on to boil. I was able to clean the knife and needle in the boiling water. The thread had been supplied by Mrs Jenkins. I didn't ask what tale Sam had spun. Both men held lamps over my patient as I did my best to cut away the infected flesh and swill the wound with clean water. I boiled up some of my herbs to help with healing and impregnated some cloth with the mix.

Finally, I tried to draw some of the flesh together and stitch it. It wasn't possible at one end of the wound so I had to resort to tight bandaging. I made a tisane and got some between Jeremiahs lips, which were gripped tight together. He must have been conscious while I worked but he had not cried out.

I sighed, and shook my head at Sam. 'I don't know if that is good enough: he needs careful nursing and a change of dressings every day, the wound needs to be kept clean.'

'We're obliged to thee Esther; I will go and get you some blankets and food and more water. We'll stay here this night.'

'I can't stay here!' I gasped. 'I will be missed – I've done what you asked now I must go home to Beth.'

Sam smiled a slow almost lazy smile. 'You be one of us now girl, there'll be a price on your 'ead for 'elping such as we. I'll leave you now with Digger, who'll watch over you and my brother. Don't think about trying to escape – you'll never make it through the brooks alive.'

He turned to Digger, 'Don' 'ee touch 'er boy we got plans for she. I be back before dark.'

He was gone. Digger produced a flask and offered it to me. I shook my head, wanting nothing to do with him or my cousin. I huddled down and tried to put as much distance between me and my guard. He fixed his eyes on me and rarely looked away. I was petrified. Clearly these men had no moral standards and I could look for no help from them.

I tried to shut down my fears and focus instead on my patient. His recovery would be my best opportunity to escape. If he died I might become expendable. Clearly there was no loyalty for me from this cruel family. No wonder my mother had run away.

Jeremiah was groaning and I crawled over to him, my leg hurting at the hardness of the ground. His mind was wandering and I could hear fear in his delirium. He muttered constantly in dreams that seemed tortured. I hardened my heart and allowed no sympathy no matter what he had endured within his own family. He had forfeited my goodwill by the wickedness of his family's deeds. That they had spilled blood in the pursuit of coin and strong drink was reason enough to turn my back. I would only seek to help him in the interest of my escape.

Chapter Fifty-Nine

I must have dozed because when I woke the man Digger was closer to me. Still he watched, his deepset eyes only shifting from me when he took a swig from his flask. He saw I was awake and grinned at me – I thought he looked like a wolf with his unkempt hair and yellow teeth. Once again he offered the flask saying something indecipherable. I shook my head and attempted to move further from him but there was nowhere to go. He grinned again and crept even closer. I prayed for Sam to return before I had to fight this man off. Drink could overcome Sam's instruction to leave me alone and I felt very vulnerable. I was so frightened my throat started to swell and I could feel my heart pounding in my chest. Poor Beth, would she lose two mothers, who would care for her?

He was alongside me in a moment, I saw him raise an arm, I couldn't breathe but I could still smell him, I felt my senses distort and I collapsed into a whirling darkness.

Something cold was dripping on my face and I came round to find Digger sitting at my side and dripping cold brandy over my face.

'You have a drink girl. Jeremiah can't hurt anyone now.'

I took a few seconds to think this through before saying, 'does he hurt people then?'

'Aye, he do lash out when 'ee's cornered. It were only a matter o' time 'til he be knifed or shot.'

'What do you do in the gang?'

'I be lookout, look after people who need watching and getting rid of the stuff.'

'You don't hurt people then?'

'Nah, there's others to do that. I just look the part and frighten them.' He grinned at me.

'Digger, can you help me escape?'

'What d'you wanna escape for, these is your kin?'

'They don't behave like kin, I don't like them. they frighten me. Is my grandfather the ringleader?'

'Nah, it's her who holds all the keys.'

'Aunt Tilly?' I said in astonishment.

'Aye, she's real mean. Don't let her catch you messing up her gang, she'll have your guts for garters,' he smirked. ''Cept she don't wear none.'

'See lassie, if I lets you go you'll not get through the brooks an' I'll end up with a beating, or worse.' He grinned his wolfish smile and took another swig from the flask.

'But you won't hurt me?'

'Nah lass, you be safe with old Digger. It's the family you got to watch out for.'

'Are there many in this gang?'

'Aye, enuf to frighten the justices. If we get caught we bribe our way out and if they finds our stash we reform and ambush them 'n get it back. We be the free traders and everyone wants what we got, 'specially those old judges.'

'Does everyone know that it is Aunt Tilly who runs things?'

'Nah, she's too clever for they. Shh. Someone be there.'

I couldn't hear anything but a few minutes later Sam reappeared with blankets and some food as well as more water.

'How is he?' he asked.

‘Quiet,’ I replied. ‘I don’t think he is any worse.’

‘You’d best get some sleep cousin, you’ll need your wits about you tomorrow. Ma will come and see yous lookin’ after ’im, proper, like.’

‘And what if he dies?’ I asked.

He just shrugged and smiled that slow and sinister smile before handing me some bread and a slab of cheese. We all sat the long night through, dozing and waking, shifting and rolling on the hard floor. I kept forcing water into Jeremiah and feeling the heat of his bandage. Sam was sitting propped against the ladder and often I saw his eyes glinting. Like Digger he watched me but Digger was harmless – it was Sam and his mother who frightened me.

I was awoken with a kick. ‘He’s talking – wake up, you’ve got work to do.’

The tight bandage was cool to the touch but I poured cold spring water on it to make it easier to remove without tearing the fragile flesh underneath.

Everything came away easily and I sniffed. I couldn’t detect any putrefaction but that didn’t mean he was safe. Gently I bathed the edges with my mix of herbs and as I finished I became aware of his eyes on me. He smiled weakly before relaxing into a grimace as I replaced the bandage with clean material and wrapping it tightly. I did not know if I was doing this right, how could I know – I had no experience of such wounds. I prayed once again that he would live, if only for my self-preservation.

Sam had disappeared, taking the ladder up. Digger went with him for a few minutes. I needed to pass water and I didn’t want to creep into a corner and expose myself to them. I found my voice and shouted.

'Sam, I need to come up for a minute. I need some minutes alone, I promise I will not run.'

The ladder reappeared and I wobbled up it and came into the light of the barn. The sun was shining outside and the air smelled sweet and laden with fragrant flower. I breathed deeply as if it were my last.

'You can go behind those logs but don't think about running,' he warned.

I made myself comfortable but I was distressed at how dirty I had become so quickly.

I was sent back down and once again went to sit beside Jeremiah. He was sleeping, not exactly peacefully but quieter than he had been last night. His pallor had lessened and he was not so clammy. I had hope.

Chapter Sixty

Peony: Paeonia officinalis – *Peonies, one of the nine official medieval herbs, were grown in all infirmary and kitchen gardens as well as the pleasure garden. The seeds were used to flavour meat and 'fifteen taken in wine is a special remedie for those that are troubled with night mare'.*

White Dead-Nettle: Lamium album – *Possessing no sting and botanically unrelated to the stinging nettle, the dead-nettle was used to reduce inflammation. The candied flowers made a 'good colour in the face and vital spirits more fresh and lively'.*

The Physic Garden Booklet, Michelham Priory

I had some seeds of peony in my bag and asked Sam for some wine. He broke a bottle head from some stacked in the cellar and I was able to get Jeremiah to swallow them washed down with what was probably the most expensive of wines. I hoped they would calm his fears and would achieve some deep sleep that would be restorative.

Amongst my dried herbs, all individually wrapped in a square of paper, I sought some white dead-nettle. I had no flowers but the rest would do well to reduce the inflammation round the wound. I would use this herb when next I changed the bandage if indeed he was still alive.

It was late in the morning when I heard harsh voices above me. My Aunt Tilly appeared and came down the ladder. She was dressed as a man and her stony features gave no indication of feminine care.

'Well Esther, Sam says you have done well and Jeremiah is on the mend.'

'There is no certainty of that,' I said. 'He is quieter but could still succumb to infection inside the body. I have no way of dealing with that – you must just hope and perhaps pray.'

She snorted. 'We don't place no value on praying girl, we must look to ourselves for all that we do and achieve.'

She sat down beside her son and looking down on him I thought I saw a flicker of love but it was gone when next she fixed me with her cold gaze.

Sam be going to Lewes to fetch little Beth. When Jeremiah is better you can see her back at Southease. You will both settle with us now and be wed to Sam. As his wife you will be part of the family as your mother was before she ran away. See this as retribution for what she did in leaving me to fend for myself with the old man. Her mouth was fixed in a tight line as she studied my reaction to this wicked plan.

My mind barely took this monstrous idea in before I snapped, 'No! I won't wed Sam and Mrs Jenkins will not give Beth to him.'

She laughed coarsely fixing me with a hard stare. 'She will, my girl, and we will take a letter written and signed by you to that purpose. You be with us now and will earn your keep with your skills in the kitchen and herbs. You'll be our own medicine woman, there will be much for you to do.'

'Sam, bring some brandy we will drink to your new woman, soon to be your wife.'

Chapter Sixty-One

I was to remain in that cellar for five days, I think. Jeremiah took a turn for the worse and I had to try a different healing herb. I did not have an exhaustive supply in my bag but I did have some dried Herb Robert; Such a common little plant but with powerful properties in stemming blood flow and relieving inflammation. What I really wanted was some fresh Common Centaury but none was to be found so I made use of what I had and hoped for the best.

They forced me to write a letter to Mrs Jenkins asking that she give Beth to Sam and saying we would return to Lewes once my cousin was healed. Aunt Tilly watched over me as I wrote, she clearly knew her letters but I am not sure either of her sons did. I knew that I would not be allowed to leave as I told Mrs Jenkins but I hoped that somehow I would escape before the wedding service was conducted. I had tried to resist their demands but my aunt, after slapping me about the face, threatened me with abasement by members of the gang. I didn't doubt for one minute that she would see that through. I looked at Digger with appeal in my eyes but he just shrugged and passed me the quill.

I spent many hours of anguish suffering thoughts of my fate at the hands of these people. I wept and shivered with fear before I calmed myself and thought that I had been in dire straights before now and come through. I had to keep my wits about me and somehow, somewhere I would find a way of escaping. A little voice in my head kept saying that I had only achieved escape before because of others and that there were no others this time round.

Jeremiah and I were together in that dark dismal cavern permanently guarded by the amiable Digger who despite his friendship was no saviour for me. He had pitched his cap in with the gang many years before and there was no other safe future for him. I could look for no help in that quarter. I was glad, however, of his crooked smile and despite his frightening wolfish looks I knew I was safe in his company. It was a small comfort.

Sam had told me with a note of triumph in his voice that he had personally lifted Beth from the arms of Mrs Jenkins and she was now settled in the squalid conditions of the Southease cottage. Mrs Jenkins had taken my note on face value never suspecting that she was assisting in Beth's kidnap.

That was my lowest point. I wept and keened for my poor child as if she were dead.

Eventually, I was satisfied that Jeremiah would survive and recover fully despite some dreadful scarring and a hole the size of a guinea in his thigh. This realisation was a bittersweet moment for me. I had succeeded against the odds in saving his life but in so doing I was edging nearer to my miserable fate.

We were preparing to leave the cellar one still morning. I was carefully walking out of the barn with Jeremiah at my side on a makeshift stretcher when a body of men arrived singly and in pairs: they materialised soundlessly all about us. These were the men who carried the spoils inland and I heard the sounds of tethered donkeys and horses just beyond the clearing waiting patiently for their heavy loads. Loading would take place in the bright light of day because the smugglers were so confident of their hidden barn; travel across Sussex and Kent would be at nightfall. As I waited for a cart to take me and Jeremiah to Southease and Beth I noticed a boy staring at me. I looked back at him and saw that it was one of the Coad boys, the youngest. It all fitted; the mysterious wagons that purported to carry chalk and other goods that arrived at Coad Farm in the early hours of the morning and were hurried into the depths of the barns before we of the household could get nosy.

I moved over towards him, no one stopped me, they knew I was unable to escape.

'You?' he said.

'Aye it is me.'

'What are you doing here?'

'I have been kidnapped and so has Beth, your sister.'

His close-set eyes registered that strange thought – that he had a sister. His father's crime against Becca had obviously been seen as of the moment and he had not registered that the child who was the outcome was, in fact, his sister. I watched him turn the information over and saw a dawning understanding.

'Aye, she is your sister and she is in the greatest danger. You must know all there is to know about this family and how they treat women. I am to be forcibly married to Sam and what will then happen to Beth when she grows into womanhood? Will you let that happen to your sister? Never mind what you think about me – she needs protection from this family.'

He looked bewildered, he was never the quickest but he

was the gentlest and I often thought he could be different if he was not egged on by his older brothers.

'You must help me to save her. Please?'

'What can I do?' he muttered as he raised his hand acknowledging my cousin Sam.

'You must go to Dr Grieve's house and tell them we are in dire danger and I only have a few days left before I am force-put to Sam. I doubt they will bother with calling the bans but the result will be the same. I will be wed to all intents and purposes and unable to leave. Beth will become their stepdaughter and they will have power over us both. We will never get away and God knows what will happen to her.'

He walked away from me to sort his merchandise. As he went he turned and whispered

'Is she bonny?'

'Aye, as bonny as her mother was.'

He was gone and I had no idea if my appeal had fallen on deaf ears.

The cart we were awaiting pulled up at Jeremiah's side and I hurried over to ensure he was lifted carefully. He winced at every movement and I offered him some poppy seed tincture to help dull the pain. He refused but thanked me. I turned away and looked gloomily into the woodland that edged up from the brooks.

Chapter Sixty-Two

Field Poppy: Papaver rhoeas – *Fresh flowers were used as a sedative, also for coughs. Opium poppies: papaver somniferum were grown for their pain killing properties and an opium syrup was recommended for coughs by an 11th century Arabian physician. Field poppies also provided colour for wine and medicine*
The Physic Garden Booklet, Michelham Priory

Beth was excited beyond belief when I pulled her grubby little self into my arms. Oh, how I had missed her wet kisses and loving cuddles. I held her tightly to my chest and buried my face into her beautiful hair. Aunt Tilly had looked after her but not as I would and I itched to give her the care that only I could give. She had been sleeping in a tiny crib near the man who had forfeited the right to be treated as a decent human being. I snatched her little crib and removed it to one of the side rooms where there were cot like beds presumably used by my cousins. I looked to my aunt and said primly, 'Beth and I will sleep here together.'

She didn't respond other than shrugging her shoulders. But a little later she came towards me saying, 'You can make yourself useful and prepare a meal for tonight. You'll find grub in the scullery.'

It was not what I would call a kitchen but needs must so I did what I could with the meagre ingredients and prepared a hearty soup using the remains of a coney which I found in the meat safe. I cooked it long and hard as there were flies eggs and maggots embedded in the carcass. I used some of my precious herbs for flavour. There was some bread that I dipped in warm ale to make it more palatable and softer on the gums.

Jeremiah was made comfortable in one of the outhouses, which had been cleaned for the purpose. There was plenty of room for him and I spent time checking his wound and trying to get him to do some movements so he didn't stiffen up too much. He was a fit young man and had vigour on his side so I expected him to make a full recovery in due course. As I bathed him he grasped my hand and held it to his face. I pulled away: I wanted none of that, not even his thanks.

No one had come seeking him so Aunt Tilly had thought it safe for us to return from the underground cellar. I was soon to learn that there were safe areas all round the property and if anyone came calling Jeremiah could slide through a trap door into another cellar. The church itself was utilised as a hiding place though no one told me how.

Sam returned before twilight and made short work of my food. I had already given some to Jeremiah but left the others to help themselves. Beth and I ate in our little cubbyhole.

Chapter Sixty-Three

Ladies' Bedstraw: Gallium verum – Mixed with bracken and other anti-vermin herbs, bedstraw, which smells sweet when dried, was used to stuff mattresses in the medieval period. Dioscorides knew it as galion or milk plant as it was used throughout Europe as a substitute for rennet in cheesemaking to curdle milk.

The Physic Garden Booklet, Michelham Priory

I was delighted the next morning to find many herbs growing nearby and as it was a sunny day I did some harvesting. I remembered that my mother had learned her skills from her grandmother and it was only after she died that my ma had fled Southease.

My pleasure did not last long as there was much work to do in cleaning our sleeping area and distributing clean dry grasses to comfort us. Beth pottered around my feet and generally helped. At some point I put her down to sleep before tackling the food area.

I thought often of escape but every time I moved outside the dog accompanied me and barked continuously. I had no chance to run without everyone knowing in an instant. Aunt Tilly kept Beth near her as an inducement to keep me within range.

I had insisted that Sam go into Lewes and buy some fresh food. Jeremiah needed good vegetables and decent meat to build his strength. I also asked him to go to the doctor's house and tell Mrs Jenkins that we were well and hoped to return soon. He refused but I insisted that they would come looking for me if I didn't keep in touch.

Later, I found that he had visited and had behaved oddly enough to arouse Mrs Jenkins' suspicions but for now I felt I had no hope. All I could focus on was Beth, Jeremiah and cleaning. If I had to stay here then I would at least be comfortable and to be comfortable I had to be clean.

Jeremiah improved daily; he worked hard to reinvigorate his muscles. I anointed his scabs with oils to help clean healing. I shaved him and cut his hair. He seemed grateful and became more courteous. I wondered whether if he was shown kindness and generosity he would change his ways but with the old man's blood running through his veins it was unlikely. His was the only smile I received in that Godforsaken place.

Sam, for all his pretty looks, was as cold as his mother though he played with Beth in a boisterous fashion, which she loved. I was always nervous when she was with any of them. I listened shamelessly to his conversations with his mother when they thought I was asleep; he no more wanted to marry me than I him but he accepted his mother's view that I was better in the family than out. She pointed out the advantages – the healing, the cooking, and finally, the bedding. I heard him snort in disagreement and she replied 'all cats is grey in the night'.

God help me.

Eventually I gleaned knowledge of their plans and it appeared that my day in church would be three days hence. The old priest who would officiate did not ask questions of such a family and just to set the seal the entire gang would be present to witness me becoming a part of the smugglers' troupe.

There were no preparations other than broaching a barrel of best undiluted brandy. My last two days of freedom were spent in the same manner, cooking, cleaning and working with Jeremiah.

I was told on the morning that I was to be wed that day. Little Beth was to be my flower girl and Jeremiah was to give me away: cynical token civility.

I made a pretty garland for Beth but otherwise had no finery or pretty things to adorn myself with. I was instructed to make the bridal bed and was watched by my future mother-in-law – she had a vindictive glint in her eye as I spread the sweet smelling ladies' bedstraw. I had the thought to kill myself, I had the means in my bag, but I couldn't abandon Beth.

Chapter Sixty-Four

The hours passed slowly until I was marched towards Southease Church. Jeremiah haltingly led Beth who was prattling merrily all the way; together they had the same turn of speed.

The priest was dressed in black and the pews were filled with a motley band of smugglers who were all there under order from Tilly to see the fun.

My groom was at the altar waiting and joking with his friend who held the ring. There was a ring, a solid gold ring apparently torn from the finger of a dying woman – a wrecker's prize. I had learned so much about this family when I was supposedly asleep. I would discard it as soon as I could.

Jeremiah and I stood waiting for the church to quiet. He walked slowly and I was partly holding him up instead of the other way round. We arrived at the altar and the priest began.

He knew his service and intoned the phrases that are so familiar. My heart grew colder with each word but suddenly, when we got to the bit where he asked if anyone knew of a reason not to marry the couple before him there was a great shout from the rear of the church. I turned, stunned, as I saw Wilf, alone and unarmed in the centre of the aisle. Not a soul moved. It was as if we were all stupefied. He shouted again:

'Stop! This marriage is unlawful for she is married already.' My mouth dropped open in shock even as I saw

Beth tottering toward Wilf. There was uproar and I took the opportunity to run as best as I was able towards him scooping Beth up as I went. 'Don't listen!' It was Tilly standing on a pew. 'It's a trick, she b'aint married at all!' I looked back and saw her raise a pistol.

I wasn't going to stop – I kept running. A shot was fired and I still kept going. He grabbed us and together we flew out of the door as the gang realised we were escaping and fell over themselves trying to get out of the narrow pews to get to us. Wilf slammed the great oak door and twisted the handle putting a crook of metal into the ring. We turned sharp into the yew bush that was alongside the church and then he helped me climb into an open table top tomb. He dragged me down to the floor with Beth under us. The top was lowered onto us and it was only then I realised that people had come to rescue us. The slab was wedged open with a flint through which we could see what was happening outside. Later I was to realise that this very tomb was one of the hidey-holes that the gang used to stash their loot.

'Quiet,' he whispered urgently in my ear. I put my hand over Beth's mouth. 'The soldiers are waiting, the place is surrounded. We just need to lie low until they are rounded up.'

The oak door was sprung open as the combined might of so many ruthless men forced the hinges off the wood. They burst out, all reaching for what few weapons they had. Most had left their knives, cutlasses and guns behind at the house and with their horses for who needed weapons in a church at a wedding? It was a fatal error and cost many of the smugglers their lives. They were cut down in a hail of weaponry wielded by vengeful soldiers who had been made fools of too many times in the past. We were safe: clearly Wilf had indicated where we would hide and no one came near us.

It was all over in a matter of minutes. Jeremiah was shot in the back and died instantly. Sam was cut down by a sword wielded by a giant of a soldier who swung the blade round his head before bringing it down on Sam's. I covered Beth's eyes. I didn't see the taking of Tilly but she was taken and forced into a cart with her wrists tied to the side rail.

Of all the men in the church, probably nearing one hundred, thirty were killed, and forty five wounded, the remainder escaped, melting into the background. When we clambered out of our hiding place we were rushed by Farmer Elwood, Billy-alone and Dr Grieve; my friends who had once again come to my rescue. I collapsed to the ground weeping tears of fear, pain, joy, I don't know what.

Chapter Sixty-Five

Beth and I were taken back to South Farm where we had a bath and sank into our lovely beds. I slept the sleep of my life with Cilla coming to take Beth as soon as she awoke but before she started shouting for attention.

When I eventually made my way downstairs to the kitchen it was late morning and I was unprepared for the crowds who were there. Everyone I knew had come to greet me and before I knew it I had heard the whole story.

Mrs Jenkins had been disturbed by Sam's visit and told both Wilf and Dr Grieve that something was untoward. Billy-alone and Wilf had gone to Southease to spy on the household and on their way there they met the youngest Coad boy who warned them that Beth and I were being held against our will and that there was to be a forced marriage in a few days. Dr Grieve had extracted the date of the marriage from the terrified priest by threatening him with excommunication, prison, or stringing-up by a Lewes mob. He had given in quite quickly, perhaps glad to get rid of some of his troublesome parishioners. Farmer Elwood had enlisted the military through his contacts and got everyone down to Southease in total secrecy. Wilf's ruse about me being married was of course untrue but it had worked brilliantly shocking the congregation for long enough for us to escape.

I hugged everyone and was completely overcome with

the love that was showered upon us. Billy-alone was thoroughly enjoying his role in the rescue and Cilla's eyes shone with pride as she watched him. Farmer Elwood was thankful to see me safe, he had dreaded having to tell Cecilia that I had been kidnapped, married against my will or worse. Mrs Fisher and Cilla were feeding cakes and drinks to everyone who crowded in. Mrs Makepiece and Miss Wardle arrived mid-tale with Beth's grandpa and the story had to be told again. There were two people missing: Dr Grieve, who had his hands full with mending broken bones and cuts – injuries sustained in the attack, and Wilf.

I had to see him and so I went out of the door to look for him. Cilla caught me and said he was in the stable.

'Wilf.' He turned to look at me and I took in the strong arms that had pulled me from the nightmare at Southease, his broad frame and his kind eyes. 'How can I ever thank you Wilf?' I held out my arms and he came into them and put his arms round me. 'Well, I told everyone you were already married, perhaps you should be. To me.'

I reached up to kiss him. 'I never wanted anything more.'

Chapter Sixty-Six

We had to endure the trials of the gang members or free traders as they preferred to be called. Of my family only Aunt Tilly survived, her father having died whilst she was imprisoned at Lewes. Sam and Jeremiah were buried in paupers' graves though it was rumoured that great riches were buried in or around Southease. Tilly was undoubtedly the ringleader but there was little evidence and she had no previous counts against her. She certainly was the brains behind an extensive operation and it was her brains that had kept her from public notice. The court case was distressing as I had to give the evidence that would convict her.

Once again I sat in that court but this time I was called and led through my story by the public prosecutor. The room was packed as it had been for all those sent to trial. In general, sentences had been light as was often the case with smugglers who had links to sections of society who had the power to free them or arrange minor sentences. Aunt Tilly's position was worsened by her disreputable family history and mostly because of what she had tried to do to me, her sister's child. My own notoriety in Lewes lent me some sympathy but in the end it came down to my word against hers. On the last day of her trial the prosecutors produced a witness who supported my tale. In exchange for freedom from prosecution for this and earlier events, my companion in the cellar, Digger, stepped forward. Some effort had been made to tidy his wolfish looks up and when I saw him I smiled my thanks that he had finally turned away from the gang's crimes.

Aunt Tilly was sentenced to deportation and I hoped never to see her again. That she deserved such a lenient sentence I am far from sure but that was what was handed down.

The event that had saved me from marriage to Sam was never brought to light: the intervention of the youngest Coad. I do not suppose he told his family of his talk with Wilf and Billy-alone, nor do I suppose that he would have gone out of his way to call at the doctor's house so it was entirely fateful that they had crossed paths and he had felt able to act. That he had acted honourably by his half-sister was commendable in my eyes.

Chapter Sixty-Seven

It was a good many weeks since Aunt Tilly's sentence had been handed down for her part in the crimes of the smuggling gang, but still she was in Lewes prison, awaiting the boat that would transport her to the colonies. Her proximity to me was disturbing and I fretted constantly to be rid of what I felt to be a malign presence.

Every day began with the same thought: I won't let Aunt Tilly's presence spoil my day. Every day I failed in this desire. Somehow she was always in my mind, hiding behind thoughts, sneaking out when I least expected it, infecting me with her malice.

One day I woke particularly early. The dawn had barely begun its climb to dispel the darkness. I padded barefoot to the window and watched as fingers of opaque light threaded through night clouds; a pale shred of sunlight gently lifted the shadows until the light was full and vibrant. Gradually the birds began their songs and chirrups until the sky was full of exuberance and hectic activity. I might have been the only human on earth for nobody else stirred.

Beth turned in her truckle bed and I watched as she began to fidget: yawning, stretching and finally blinking rapidly before she opened her eyes fully. I motioned her to the window and she scrambled out of the pile of bedding and together we watched the morning arrive. It was going to be a lovely day and we held hands together to welcome it.

Our day proceeded as normal, breakfast, working in the doctor's study, seeing patients and preparing medicants. Today Dr Grieve was due to sit in the coroner's court and we started our lunch without him. His hours on such days were unpredictable so Mrs Jenkins plated up some cold meats, bread and cheese. I spent several hours with Beth who was learning her alphabet. We used some chalk to practice letters on a slate. Beth was two and a half, as she proudly declared to everyone she met, and she absorbed all the experiences of her daily life like Mrs Jenkins' mop.

I heard the door slam as the doctor arrived. Mrs Jenkins scurried to meet him and he shouted for me, 'Esther, Esther, come and join me.'

We sat at the dining table and he began eating, all the while looking at me with concerned eyes.

'What is it?' I whispered, suddenly afraid.

'It's your aunt, she has asked to see you. Can you face it? You are not obliged but it might help you to put this all behind you.'

'Have you heard about the boat?'

'Yes, she is to be taken to Tilbury tomorrow where she will be put upon a vessel bound for the Australias.'

'Tomorrow?'

'Aye, tomorrow. If you want to see her before she leaves you must go now, before dark. There will be no opportunity tomorrow. Esther, my dear, I know you are troubled by her and I think it might be an opportunity to lance the boil.'

I smiled at his use of a medical term but inside my heart was pounding at the thought of meeting her again. The last time we had met we were in court and she had watched me with anger in her eyes as I told the story of my abduction, imprisonment and almost marriage to her son, Sam, my cousin. During the trial I was asked, at great length, about my relationship to the Kempe family.

I tried to think why she would want to see me. It was my testimony that damned her.

In the end I decided to go, if only to satisfy myself, again, that she was indeed a very wicked woman and deserved no quarter from decent people.

Dr Grieve accompanied me to the doors of the house of correction but I declined his offer to escort me inside. I was admitted by a young man who was new to the job and much kinder to me than the gaoler who had previously incarcerated me in the very same cell as my aunt. I looked through the bars to see her crouched on a three legged stool looking very unkempt. 'You wanted to see me, aunt?'

Unkempt she might be but her eyes were as clear as ever and her look was withering.

'You asked us, girl, to be a family to you and you wanted to know about your mother. Well I am going to tell you. You might not wish to hear all that I say but it is your right to know.'

She spat into the corner of the room as she called for the gaoler. 'Bring the girl a stool, boy, can't you see she be crippled?'

I gasped. I didn't see myself as a cripple.

The lad brought a chair and I sat, waiting. I hid my hands in my cloak, I didn't want her to see that I was nervous.

'Your ma, Sarah, was my older sister and she were a bright spark. Our grandmother Meg took a liking to her and taught her everything she did know about her craft. She didn't bother with me.'

'Craft?'

'Aye, craft. Meg were known as a wise woman.' She looked up at me nastily. 'Or, in some circles, a witch. You be shocked girl, but there is not much difference 'tween the two. People think that a wise woman be for the good, and a witch for the bad; your great-grandmother Meg would be a bit of both, according to who she were treating. My mother was her daughter, and she were a weakly sort so it were a spell that bound our father to her, a spell cast by Meg.'

She paused in her tale before saying, 'Meddlin' in such things be dangerous and with all her knowledge and herbal skills she bound they two together as should never have been. Pa didn't want her but he sired Sarah then me, then ma died of the effort. It suited Meg to keep him tied to the family while she brought us up an' he took out his frustrations in smuggling. He led a gang of 'em, including many local lads who were looking to earn more than the few pennies they got legally. It weren't all about money – the drink and the excitement were heady payment and outwitting the law was part of the thrill.' She was looking into the distance as she said this and I could sense that she missed the life they had led, pitting their wits and cunning against authority.

'Our whole life revolved round the trade and your ma was as much a part of it as the rest of us. She were a bright girl and comely; our dad used her to deliver messages and keep the local constabulary sweet. She just crooked her little finger and sweet-talked them into befuddlement. She had learned well from Grandma Meg.'

'It were a bad day for us when Sarah met a young man, a stranger to our parts. She should have been acting as a lookout but she got flustered by this good-looking fella who stopped to ask the way. Because she took her eye off the game, two young lads were caught and one of they were later hanged; he were a bonny lad. Sarah were beaten as a punishment, as was the way with those that flouted our rules.'

'Who beat her?' I asked.

'Why, her dad, who do you think? He loved her, more an' me, but she nearly got us all caught.'

'Didn't her grandmother protect her?'

'You're not listenin' are you girl? We was all in it together and that was her punishment.'

Aunt Tilly spat on the ground again and continued.

'Some months later Meg took sick and died. 'T'were very sudden and with her death the spells broke. Our pa went looking for a new woman. Sarah, your mother, left us soon after, but not afore he had satisfied hisself.'

'No.'

'You'm not daft girl, your ma was useful in that way to your grandfather. He took her as he later took me. Who knows how many childer he got roundabouts.' She looked at me and laughed. 'D'you know how long it were before she got herself hitched to your dad?'

I felt sick and struggled for breath as I gasped, 'No, it's not true, you are just saying all this to get back at me. You're an evil woman and I wish you were hanged, just as you deserve.'

'Aye, maybe I do deserve hanging but you'm come from our seed girl and you'll never know whether the badness is in you. Your grandfather might be your father – he might not, but you'll never know and if you have childer they might be born idiots as some of mine were. They'm all dead now – two died after they was born, they were afflicted and one were a cripple–' she was looking at my lipsy leg '–and their dying was a blessed relief, but my two strong boys Sam and Jeremiah, there were now't wrong with they, but you got them killed.' She looked at me, accusing, accusing.

'Is this why you wanted to see me, just to tell lies? Well, I don't believe you and I won't let you destroy my memories of my parents. They were good people and they loved each other. I don't believe you. I don't believe you and I won't believe you. I won't!'

My cries had brought the guard running and I was let out of that hateful place. I ran, as best as I was able, all the way back to Dr Grieve's house and flung myself on my bed. Oh, how I cried.

Chapter Sixty-Eight

Everything she said was planted like a seed in my head and though I continued to live my life as before, the seed took root. I later learned that Aunt Tilly was delivered to the great hulking ship that would make its way to a different, unknown, world. Many times I thought of it, imagining the squalor, the disease and cruelty amongst those who had nothing to lose. I hoped she would succumb and die and with that her power over me would end. But it was too late, the seeds were putting out shoots.

Chapter Sixty-Nine

Cecilia had had enough of her mother and she was coming home to South Farm. We had a letter delivered by special messenger to say that she was arriving by carriage but two days hence. I hurried to the farm and met with Farmer Elwood who was in a considerable fluster. I didn't have time to ask the whys and wherefores, we just set to and spring-cleaned her rooms. The cradle that Beth had used was freshened up and I threaded pretty ribbons all through its woven structure. When the room was cleaned to my satisfaction I left some soaps, oils and herbs to make everything smell beautiful. By my reckoning, Cecilia would be about seven and half months gone in her pregnancy so to make such a journey was, to my mind, a mite reckless but I knew her mother would ensure that she was well cared for.

The morning of her arrival was a Saturday and Farmer Elwood, Dr Grieve and I were all waiting anxiously. The doctor and I had prepared some simple remedies for calming, just in case, but they were not needed as she arrived in a large coach, with a nurse, and in blooming health. She looked so happy as the coach drew up but Farmer Elwood was even happier. Carefully she was handed down from the carriage and she clung to her husband's arm as she made her way up the steps and into her home.

Dr Grieve and I returned to Lewes for Cecilia, though

blooming, was in need of rest after her long journey and she clearly wanted to spend time alone with her husband. We said our goodbyes with promises of visiting the very next day when I would take Beth, who was more than a little excited at the prospect.

We had so much to talk about: my adventures, Cecilia's escape from her domineering and over-protective mother, Beth's accomplishments and John Elwood's loneliness which had played a big part in bringing about Cecilia's early return.

'Tell me again how Wilf proposed to you and when you will be married,' she said.

I laughed, delighted to dwell on the wonderful moment when we had agreed to marry.

'What about the girl that he was supposed to be seeing?'

'I don't know, I didn't think they were actually together, perhaps you know more than me.'

'Oh, I am sure I don't – if nothing has been said then there must have been nothing in it.'

She changed the subject, enquiring about Mrs Makepiece and Miss Wardle.

It was only later that I wondered if I should ask Wilf about the young woman who Cecilia thought he had been seeing. I didn't want to tempt fate though so I put it uneasily to the back of my mind.

Some days later Cecilia asked if I would return to South Farm to help her and to be on hand if Dr Grieve was not available. At first I didn't know what to say – I was enjoying my life in Lewes where I was fully occupied and useful but I owed them so much. I wondered how I could stay at South Farm but continue working for the doctor during the day, and then what would I do with Beth?

I had been very involved in helping the doctor with his mothers-to-be and with the book learning I had done I felt that I could manage to deliver a baby on my own, providing there were no complications. Many times I thought back to Becca's experience of birth, alone and with no care or comforts. Locally, most women were delivered without a doctor present but they tended to be those who would prefer a local woman as midwife. Lewes had several such women and in the main they did very well but who was to say how many of their losses, mother, babe, or both, were down to lack of skill, poor conditions or complications. Losses in childbirth were accepted as part of everyday circumstance. The doctor and I discussed it many times and he said that he did not expect to have any losses, but his ladies were all well nourished and healthy unlike a lot of the townswomen, especially the ones who had babies year in, year out.

In the end, it was the doctor who proposed that I return to South Farm until after Cecilia's baby was born. He suggested that I be given a quiet little pony to make the trip back and forward to Lewes as needed. I said I was quite able to walk but he didn't seem to want me to do that, particularly, he said, if it was dark or the weather was bad. Billy-alone could accompany me at need and carry my bag.

'But, what about Beth?'

'She can be at South Farm with you and when you are occupied I am sure Cecilia can ask one of her servants to help. The wet nurse is still at the farm, is she not?'

'She is. When she stopped nursing she started work in the kitchens.'

'Well then, that's taken care of. We will drive over tomorrow and I will speak to John Elwood about a pony. In the meantime, you can use their gig or mine. That's agreed then.'

It all seemed so easy to him but I was in a flurry of concerns. Would I be able to manage a pony? Would Beth be unhappy without me? Would I be able to manage if Cecilia went into labour and the doctor was away?

Mrs Jenkins was sorry to see us go, she had become so attached to Beth and I reassured her that she would be back and forwards with me. Billy-alone was to be my escort on a daily basis and he would lead the pony whose name was Flossy. I went to the stables every day for a week to have lessons in how to ride properly. Wilf would come and pass comment on my 'seat' and we would be in fits of laughter as I tried to look elegant, ride comfortably and still maintain my seat. Finally I felt confident enough to take Flossy out, even if Billy was not available. Flossy was a lovely kind pony and once I got used to managing reins, feet and seat all together I found that the strain on my leg was greatly relieved.

Before I left Dr Grieve's I took tea with Mrs Makepiece, Miss Wardle and Beth's grandpa. We all met up at Keere Street where I explained the plans.

'Dr Grieve is going to miss you Esther. I saw Mrs Jenkins in town yesterday and she said he was going to be back to his old ways if you weren't there all of the time.' Mrs Makepiece said as she poured the tea.

'Well, I don't know what his old ways are. Did she tell you?'

'Aye, he gets very morose and slams the doors a lot. And, he goes out calling as he doesn't seem to like his own company.'

'Well, I've never seen him like that.'

'Exactly.'

Beth's grandpa suggested that he probably got lonely. I had the feeling that he was speaking from experience.

'Well I don't get lonely,' said Miss Wardle. 'Not now Billy-alone is there and I didn't much even before he came as I had all the piggies to keep me company.'

Mrs Makepiece gave her a strange look before looking up at me. 'Does he talk to you lass, apart from work talk?'

'Yes, he does, but we don't always see eye-to-eye and he is often grumpy with me too so I don't think you can read anything into his moods at all. Perhaps he is just getting old.'

'Old? He's not old. How old is he?'

'I think he is probably about forty. The same age as Farmer Elwood.'

'Cecilia is only twenty-one and I don't suppose she thinks her husband is old,' retorted Mrs Makepiece.

'I don't understand what you are saying.'

'Perhaps Dr Grieve is sweet on you Esther.'

'Nonsense, we just get on well together.'

'Hmm.'

I changed the subject and was quite glad when it was time to go. At supper that evening I studied my employer's face when he wasn't looking. I had to admit that he wasn't old, his face just looked a little lived in. He didn't always dress for supper when we were alone, in fact, he seemed to like being more comfortable in his clothes. I wondered if all the fine ladies who called on him would appreciate him if they saw him in his working shirt, waistcoat and slippers.

'What are you smiling at Esther?'

'I was just picturing Beth and I riding Flossy.'

'I will take you over to South Farm tomorrow in the gig,

so there will be plenty of room for all your bits and pieces. Your room will stay as you leave it, ready for when you return and if you want a nap during the day here. You will be spread thin, Esther, do you think you will manage?'

'Aye, I am sure I will, as long as you don't mind me coming and going at all hours.'

'I'm just glad you will be here during the day. I will miss you Esther, I have come to enjoy our suppers together.'

'I have too, Dr Grieve, and I am so grateful for all the opportunities you have given me.'

'Grateful? Ah well it has worked well for us both, and for Beth too.' He raised his wine glass and looked at me. I felt his eyes were reading mine so I dropped my glance in case he saw what Mrs Makepiece was suggesting. The very thought made me come over in a hot flush.

The next day, after lunch, we packed our clothes into the gig and set off at a smart pace for South Farm where Cecilia was waiting. Beth rushed up to our room and jumped up and down on my bed in her excitement. As soon as we had unpacked our few things we went down to the kitchen to say hello to Cilla and Mrs Fisher. Our first night back at South Farm was wonderful. I had supper with Cecilia and Farmer Elwood and I felt just like I had come home.

Chapter Seventy

We slipped back into South Farm life as easily as shelling peas and though I was busier than before I found life quite exhilarating. Flossy made all the difference. She gave me such freedom, and my attachment to her grew on a daily basis, until I said to Billy-alone that I could manage without him. He didn't think much of that idea but occasionally on fine days and when I could escape I would have Flossy saddled, climb onto her broad and steady back and away we would go. I felt free, and excited being able to trot and even canter. All my movement difficulties, better as they were, became as nothing: I was equal to anyone on a horse. Beth would sometimes sit in front of me and would stroke and tug at Flossy's ears. She was the gentlest, sweetest creature and Beth and I loved her, as did Billy-alone – when he got the chance.

Shortly after I returned to South Farm, Wilf arranged for me to accompany him on his work rounds. He visited a number of Farmer Elwood's tenants and overlooked some crops. We rode along farm tracks to out of the way cottages and hidden valleys. The South Downs were astonishingly beautiful with their great lifts, drops and folds. We rode up to Telscombe and pulled the horses to a halt in order to look back at Lewes. The sky was so large and clean I was able to breathe deeply and smell the good air.

We moved on towards the village where there were a few

cottages, a church and a large farm. Wilf asked me to wait while he had a word with the farm tenant and I sat on Flossy, as comfortable as anything and allowed her to drop her head and graze.

'You be Wilf's betrothed then?' I hadn't noticed the young woman approach me from the churchyard and she startled me. She was tall and of slim build but her stomach swelled in late pregnancy. Her eyes were hostile and I didn't know how to reply. We were betrothed, but there was no token or ring, just our agreement to marry in due course. Betrothed sounded very official.

'Well, yes, I suppose you could say that. I'm Esther – are you a friend of his?' I tried not to sound too curious.

'Aye, we were friends, good friends.' She caressed her bump before turning on her heel to leave.

When Wilf returned, she was nowhere in sight. 'A girl came and asked if I was your betrothed Wilf. She wasn't very friendly.'

'Oh, who was it?' He seemed preoccupied.

'She didn't say, but she was expecting, and probably very soon.'

'Was there a problem? Perhaps she knows you be a nurse.'

'No, I don't think so, otherwise she would have said.'

Wilf was much more interested in the tenant farmer's troubles with his milking cows and we returned to Lewes at a fair pace to consult Farmer Elwood's dairy manager. I didn't pursue the question of who the girl was until I saw Cecilia.

'Do you know what the girl who was going out with Wilf looks like?' I asked innocently.

'No, I don't but Cilla told me that her name is Molly and Wilf broke the relationship off when she was caught with a jobbing carpenter who was working at Telscombe Farm. The carpenter disappeared and she is going to be a mother soon. Why?'

'I think I saw her today, she seemed quite put out that I was with Wilf.'

'I expect she hoped to entice him back and make an honest woman of her and give the baby a father.'

'Wilf wasn't at all interested when I mentioned her.'

'Well that's good. I am sure Wilf is over her now otherwise he wouldn't have asked you to marry him. He is a steady and honourable man Esther and I know you will both be very happy together. Put her out of your mind.'

I did put her out of my mind until a week later when Cilla asked me to come down to the pot room where someone wanted to see me. It was her. I waited for her to speak while I studied the shape of her pregnancy trying to evaluate how long she had before her baby would be born. Not long, I decided.

'What yer lookin' at me like that fer?'

'I'm a nurse,' I said. 'I thought maybe you were in need of my help as your baby is near due. You asked to see me?'

'Aye, I wanted to ask you to speak to Wilf for me and see if he will get me a place where I can work and live.'

'Where do you work now? Can't you stay there? And why don't you ask Wilf yourself?'

'He don' speak to me nowadays and with you around there be no chance of me getting back with he.'

'What about the baby's da?'

'Gone. I don' need 'im.'

'Why can't you stay where you live now?'

'Missus says I 'ave to leave as soon as it comes and me ma

can't be doin' with young-uns any more.'

I felt slightly sick as I thought of Becca and her violation, now here was another young girl with a baby due and no means of support.

'I will speak to Wilf, but I don't know why he would be able to find you a place.'

'Wilf knows all the farms and their tenants. I'm a good worker an' he might help if you ask him.'

I nodded and told her to come back the next day. I wanted to be kind to her but she didn't make it easy with her anger – at me, at Wilf, the missing carpenter, who knew?

Wilf called in the next day and I told him about Molly's visit.

His face shut down, as it had when I told him who my family were. 'She needs help, Wilf, and you were her friend…'

'Aye, an' look how she treated me. She made her bed. 'sides, I don' know anyone who will take her in, and a babe too. She'll 'ave to go on the parish, like many afore 'er. The overseer will want her to name the father and they will serve a bastardy bond on him so the child is supported.'

'She said the father was long gone. Can you not think of any way to help her?'

'Why do you always want to sort everyone out, Esther? You have enough on your own plate without adding her to it, and she won't thank you, she is not like you.'

He was clearly irritated by the conversation so I dropped the subject and asked Cilla to tell her that we would let her know if we thought of anyone who could help her.

Chapter Seventy-One

Cecilia and I had fallen into our old ways except that Farmer Elwood was almost beside himself with anxiety, which made things nerve-wracking at times. I made a pot of chamomile tea for him, hoping it would calm him down, but he wasn't too keen on drinking herbal tea no matter how much I explained its qualities. In the end he seemed to calm knowing that I was physically taking care of Cecilia. She would get up late and I would make her comfortable in her sitting room before setting off on Flossy to Lewes for just a couple of hours. During the afternoon we would sew for the new baby. I would examine her bump to see where the baby was lying and whether the head was descending. Everything seemed as it should be and the baby was of good size so I had no hesitation in offering reassurance to Cecilia and John Elwood.

We had one moment of fright when Cecilia had a letter from her mother saying that she thought to come and stay until the birth, I don't know who was the more horrified, Cecilia, John Elwood or me. Fortunately for us, a more interesting social engagement got in the way and she didn't come, but it felt like a close call.

We spent a great many days in restful calm, the weather was benign, there was no great turbulence in the town and the spectre of hunger had receded as the crops were gathered in. When I was able I did some bottling and preserving, activities that I really enjoyed, they appealed to my need to store up food in a time of plenty for the cold winter days when there was no fruit to be had for love nor money. Wilf would call almost every day and I was happy.

A new week dawned and I went to Lewes to help Dr Grieve run his surgery. Mrs Fisher was looking after Cecilia with Farmer Elwood working on the farm. I took lunch together with Mr and Mrs Jenkins and listened to all the town gossip from the housekeeper and news from the doctor. On my way home I called in to see Mrs Makepiece and told her all the news from both households.

Keere Street was too steep for me to ride Flossy so Billy-alone stayed waiting with her at the bottom of the hill and when I got back to him he said that I was needed urgently. 'Well, why didn't you come and get me? Where am I to go?'

'The poor house.'

'Why?'

'The guv'nor there says you have to come as there is a girl askin' for you. It be that Molly I reckon.'

I clambered onto Flossy's back and we set off at a smart pace. The overseer was waiting, his woman too. Billy hung back.

'Where is she?' I asked.

'Her be not right,' was all he said, nodding towards a room just inside the door.

There was very little natural light and I shouted for them to bring me candles or rushes. A young girl obliged and I was able to see that it was Molly lying on a pallet. The stench of human misery surrounded her, blood, sweat and soiling. She was clearly dead and the baby still within her. I sank to my knees in the dirt and made her decent, she was pretty now the anger had gone from her face and she looked at peace as I pulled her bedraggled dark hair down to frame her face. I wished I could say some words but nothing would come and, what for? She wouldn't hear them and sometimes I couldn't believe there was a God to listen.

I called for Billy, he was at the door looking shamefaced. 'I's sorry, I just didna' want to come back here. Was it my fault she died?'

'Help me up Billy, please, no it wasn't your fault. I don't think anyone could have saved her, but I would have tried if that fool outside had called me much earlier.' I brushed the mess from my clothes and used my hanky to wipe the stains from my hands. 'Do you know how long she has been here?'

The overseer had come in and replied in a sullen manner.

'She came in two days since when her pains started. We did our best and put her in here on 'er own, nice and peaceful, like.'

I looked at him and felt a rising anger.

'Did you not think to call a doctor or a woman experienced in childbirth?'

'No doctor gonna come to the likes of she and nobody else was about.' His eyes were bloodshot and I could smell drink over and above the odours of his body.

'Did you not even try to help her?'

'Course I did, I brought her water and bread but she never wanted nuffink.'

'You are disgusting and I will speak to Dr Grieve about the way you run this place.'

'Don't you come 'ere and nag at me. 'Oo do you think you are, just because you be the doctor's bit of skirt, you're no better than the rest of us.' He spat at my feet before stomping off.

'Don't listen to him Esther, 'ee be a nasty old bugger and he'll say anything to get a rise.'

I was so shocked by his comment but it was as nothing compared to my anger at this waste of a life, nay, two lives. I was sickened by the lack of humanity.

Billy and I returned to Dr Grieve's as he was the coroner. Fortunately he was in and listened to my furious account of the cruel deaths. God, how she must have suffered.

'Esther, your sentiments do you justice but you shouldn't put yourself and Cecilia at risk by going into these places.'

I was aghast, 'Risk, what risk?'

'These people live in the depths of dirt and disease and you could carry such on your hands and clothes into the houses of good people who should not be contaminated.'

'That girl was as clean as you and me not a few days since, it was having to go into that filthy place, that this town pays for and supports, that brought her so low and no one, no one thought to get her help until it was too late. If they had called you, Dr Grieve, would you have gone to her aid?' I challenged.

'That is not the point.'

'It is the point. Because she was poor, and an inconvenience, you and all others turn your backs.' I gasped, a sob in my throat, I turned and left the house. Billy and I returned to South Farm in silence.

When we got to the stable I asked one of the stable boys to fetch Cilla for me. She brought me a change of clothes to replace those that might have been contaminated as Dr

Grieve put it. I used one of the tack rooms to change after I had washed my hands thoroughly in some cold water with saddle soap. I don't know why Molly died and I supposed, on reflection, that the doctor had a point, but realistically it was probably because she had too long a labour and became weakened to the point of death. I had to get up to my room and complete my toilet with my own soaps, after that, I would try and think through what had happened and what the overseer had meant by his crude barb.

Cilla helped me get to my room without meeting anyone and brought me hot water and a drink. I stripped myself and washed thoroughly, I scrubbed my hands and nails until they bled, and I was satisfied that I couldn't possibly harbour any disease. Cilla was going to put my clothes into the boiler. I couldn't afford to throw them away, I had very little and perhaps I should use some of my wages to buy a working dress and stout pinafore that could be washed easily.

When I finished I sat on my bed and allowed Cilla to bring Beth in, she had been wailing in the kitchen because I had not been able to pick her up. 'Ssh, ssh, mummy is here now,' I cuddled and kissed her wet little face and wiped her nose. As I clutched her to me I thought how lucky we had both been that Becca had managed to give birth with no complications.

Later, after supper, I told Cecilia what had happened and what the overseer had said to me. I got angry again as I described the poor girl's fate and that of the unborn baby.

Cecilia was shocked and upset and perhaps I shouldn't have told her about it when she was due to give birth within a month and remembering her firstborn had died. I apologised for burdening her but she said she was no lily liver and knew the facts of most people's existence and the hardship they bore. John Elwood came in and we changed the subject as he would likely have the same attitude as Dr Grieve. I believe it was that night that I had the beginning of an idea to create a safe place for women, high or low born, where they could give birth with proper care.

As for the overseer's comment about my relationship with Dr Grieve, she just laughed it off and said that people like him looked for muck to spread and no normal, decent, person was likely to think there was any impropriety.

The next day I told Wilf about his former sweetheart's tragic death and he was a bit shamefaced at the hard words we had had about her. He was, however, in agreement with Dr Grieve, that I should take care if going into unclean places. I resolved to take a change of clothing with me in future should I be called to help anyone. Farmer Elwood must have heard about it all from someone because he reminded me that I was at South Farm to help his wife, and no one else.

Once it had all blown over Dr Grieve told me that Molly's baby was in the wrong position in the womb and that would have explained the protracted labour. The poor girl was buried in a pauper's grave with her babe still inside her. I did not go to the funeral but I did go and see her mother at Telscombe. Wilf came with me. I only stayed a few minutes just long enough to see that the mother was hard and bitter that her daughter would no longer provide for her. There was clearly no love between them and the mother's concerns were entirely selfish. Just as I was about to leave she hissed at me that if I had not come along and taken Wilf from her daughter all would have been well. Wilf had been standing just outside the door and overheard her. He pushed up to the woman and told her in no uncertain terms that the girl's condition was brought on by her own actions and he would never have married her, even if the carpenter had not arrived to turn her head. We rode home to South Farm and agreed to put this unhappy story behind us.

It was not long after this awful incident that I heard of another death, one more closely linked to me. My smuggling guard, Digger, had been found with his throat cut. I mourned briefly for him because, at the very end of the trial when my aunt was declaring that it was just my word against hers, with no collaborating evidence, he had come forward and supported the accuracy of my story. It was my testimony that had damned my aunt to transportation and without Digger I felt sure she would still be in the country to hound me. Digger, more than most, knew what the smugglers were capable of, and was probably expecting some sort of retribution. Nonetheless, he had been kind to me when I was absolutely terrified for my life. Poor Digger, I shed tears for him.

When I heard of his murder I wondered how long the ramifications of that awful time were to go on. I also wondered fearfully who my father was. Could it be possible that my mother and father had hidden her shame at being taken by her own father? I wished I could talk to someone about this but it was so shameful I didn't know who to talk to. If Wilf and I had children would they be of normal physique and intelligence or showing the mark of incest? My only solution so far was to go to where I had been born, a small village in Kent, and see if my parents' marriage was registered in the parish church ledger and the date. My birthday had been celebrated in our house, as was my younger brother's, but who is to say that the birthday I was told was accurate. Again, the solution might be in the register at our church.

Chapter Seventy-Two

I wouldn't want anyone to think I lived in permanent crisis because I didn't, mostly my days were active and fulfilling especially when I helped Dr Grieve with his patients. Increasingly, he trusted me to do things properly, without him having to look over my shoulder. He was a good teacher and explained the purpose of every action. My nature was always to be clean but he took cleanliness to what others might consider extreme levels. It was so exhilarating to be party to his knowledge and observe his skills in real situations. Recently, I had begun to copy his notes with a fair hand and I was of real help to him in transcribing his spidery writing and annotations into detailed records for each patient.

We never discussed the moment when I had criticised his choice of clients in favour of those who paid. But, I think I must have pricked his conscience as he occasionally agreed to see those who had no money. Usually, he passed them on to me for practical treatment, but it was a start.

Cecilia was almost at her term and she looked very healthy though a trifle ungainly. We had agreed on a gentle plan of exercise – we walked as far as the orchard and back when the weather was fine. I was fast asleep one chilly morning when I was awoken by John, it was still dark with no sign of the coming dawn and I was cold even under my blankets. Autumn was well under way and the first frosts tinged the grass with sugarlike trails.

'Esther, wake up, Cecilia needs you.' It had begun.

Once I had worked out that the birth was not going to happen for a while yet I went back and dressed myself in the work dress I had recently purchased. I asked John to send a message to Dr Grieve that the contractions were well spaced at the moment and would he please come after his breakfast, then we all sat around waiting. We tried to allay Cecilia's fears and did everything possible to keep her calm, even playing cards. The baby was perfectly positioned for birth and Cecilia was young and healthy so it was all in her head that there might be problems. I told them both that every birth was very different and what happened last time need have no relation this time and so it proved because once the doctor arrived things moved on quite quickly. John Elwood went downstairs and left us to it and within just a few hours of full labour we were able to deliver a big strong boy, as healthy as you could wish for. We were all very emotional and many joyful tears were shed by the entire household. John was thrilled – his pride in his son was immeasurable and Cecilia was his clever girl, as she was mine.

The next two days were a whirr of congratulatory visitors and tenants who all came to pay their respects to the Elwoods. A message had been despatched to Cecilia's mother who thankfully, was unwell with a bronchial condition, and couldn't therefore descend on the household.

Gradually, we all settled into a routine that revolved round young Master Frederic Elwood, who was named for his late paternal grandpapa. Cecilia blossomed into motherhood and it did not take long for her to regain her strength despite Farmer Elwood trying to mollycoddle her. Beth loved her little man and whenever possible tried to supervise his bathing. I think Cecilia's mama was disapproving that she fed the baby herself but I thought it the best thing and I know it gave her great joy. We talked about it a lot and felt very sorry for the society ladies who employed a wet-nurse. Dr Grieve said that some women would prefer to keep their figures than feed their babies.

Chapter Seventy-Three

Five months later

Wilf and I planned to marry on Midsummer's Day and fears about my parentage were of increasing concern to me. It was springtime and the last few weeks had been fairly dry: good travelling weather. I told everyone that I wanted to return to the village where my ma and pa had lived in order to see that a stone be set on their grave. I had saved some money to pay for this acknowledgment of their, and my brother's existence. I asked Billy-alone to accompany me as he was the only person available for the length of time we would be away. This was a good thing – I didn't want Wilf to know about the real reason for my journey.

Mrs Jenkins was going to look after Beth, as Cecilia would find it difficult to manage two young children. She would be helped by Mrs Makepiece and Beth's grandfather. Billy-alone was released from looking after Sally's new litter of piggies, provided he hurried back as soon as our mission was accomplished. Everyone seemed to be looking forward to our journey except me.

We set off, Billy, Flossy and me on a bright spring morning. The sun was just warming the ground but the air was still cool. It was a perfect day for travelling; Farmer Elwood had written us directions to Kent and then to the village of Tenterden where I used to live. We made good progress on the first day and arrived at a coaching inn where we would spend the night before entering Tenterden towards the end of the next day.

I remember Tenterden well but cannot remember leaving after my parents' deaths. We both walked alongside Flossy as we made our way up the wide main street with its pretty cottages. Before I sought the place where we had lived we booked ourselves into the Star. Billy was to stay with Flossy in the stable and I took a room for myself.

I decided it was time to tell Billy my real reason for being in Tenterden. He just nodded and said he thought there was more to it than buying a headstone as I could have done that by post. Once I started on my admission I couldn't stop and poured out my worries that I might be the product of an unnatural union between father and daughter. He didn't try to reassure me but said that it was likely Aunt Tilly was just spitting venom out of spite. I told him that I couldn't marry Wilf if it was likely true. He was shocked by that and said he thought Wilf would have something to say about it. I swore him to secrecy before we set off to find my old home. We left our belongings and Flossy at the inn.

The house where we had lived was not much different to how I remembered it but the outside looked shabby and the garden was overrun with weeds. I had asked at the inn and the wife of the publican told me that the pharmacist had moved away to spend his retirement with his daughter in Pluckley, another Kent village. She told me, however, that the vicar was still the incumbent in the church and would likely be able to help me regarding parish records. I had told her that I simply needed to confirm my date of birth for a legal document. I needn't have told her anything at all but once I had opened my heart to Billy I seemed unable to stop talking.

Billy-alone and I approached the church, me with trepidation in my heart, and he as chirpy as ever.

'Don't let me talk too much Billy, I must keep things to myself.'

'Aye, lass I'll look after thee. Come on.'

The building was ancient but not imposing. I did not remember being in there before, which did not bode well for my enquiries, perhaps we were not registered. A sexton was cleaning some brass tablets in the wall and as I approached him I felt my resolve weaken but it was too late he had seen me and put down his rags and polish.

'Can I help thee?'

'Aye,' I said, my voice rising to a squeak. 'I wonder if I might see your parish records. I am looking for the date of my parents' marriage: they used to live in this parish.'

He looked closely at me before asking my name.

'Coad, their names were Benjamin and Sarah Coad.'

Billy chirped in, 'And your brother's birth date, Esther, you wanted to know that too – as well as your own.'

'Aye, that's right. I need to know all the dates for my family – they died here, of the great sickness.'

Thankfully, he didn't seem curious as to why I needed all these dates and it was a good idea of Billy's to bring my brother into the enquiry to detract from me and my nerves.

The sexton seemed a kindly man and lifting a great bunch of keys from his waist he went to a locked cupboard. Inside there were several large volumes bound in leather.

'I am sorry for your loss young lady, it is a common story

– whole families wiped out. What year did your parents marry – do you know?'

I was prepared for that and we selected a ten year period to search. The sexton left me and Billy with a candle and continued with his work.

The pages were dry and not at all damp; the ink was as good at the beginning as at the end despite being fifty years apart but the writing was spidery and cramped, and difficult to read. Luckily, Coad was an unusual name otherwise we might have been there for days. There were many Fullers and Prentices and we even saw a Makepiece. Eventually, I found what I was looking for. My parents had married in July 1770. I continued looking forwards for my own birth but was pulled up short when I came across a Coad in January 1771 – a mere six months after their marriage. My heart was in my mouth and I felt my knees buckle beneath me; I sank to the cold stone floor as bile rose in my throat, I retched. I looked at Billy, aghast. What was I to do? I could never marry Wilf or bear him a child and I knew he wanted children, we had even discussed how many. Billy dropped to the floor putting his skinny arms around me, as I sobbed bitterly on his shoulder. How long we sat there I do not know but it must have been awhile as I was frozen to the marrow when I tried to get up. The sexton was watching us and clearly wanted to know the cause of my misery but I turned my back to discourage him. 'Shall we still look for your brother Esther, we've come all this way.' I nodded, and returned to the hateful page. Billy was leaning over me and he asked what letter started my name, he couldn't read much but knew a few of his letters. 'I don't think this have enough sideways branches for E,' he said. 'It looks a bit different.'

I focused my eyes and read the line out loud, pointing to each word so he could follow.

'Billy, Billy, do you see, it's not me, the child's name is Helen. Oh, Billy what would I do without you – you're right, it doesn't have enough branches because it's an H. It isn't me. It isn't me. There was a girl child, and her name was given as Helen, but she died on the same date as her birth.'

I looked up and saw the sexton still watching curiously. I said aloud so he could hear, though my voice cracked with the effort of moving from horror to joy in less than a few moments. 'Now we need to find William, my brother, and me, of course. I trembled as we continued turning the thick pages and found my birth date as being June 1773, two years after my parents married. William was more difficult to find but eventually he was listed as being five years younger than me. We closed the book with relief and sat a few minutes, holding hands and quietly rejoicing.

I went back to the sexton and asked if I would be able to locate my family's graves. He shook his head sadly and said he didn't think so as with the great numbers of deaths in the parish there had been many communal graves. However, he pointed out where they might be in the churchyard and Billy and I stepped over many mossy stones and headed for an area where there were no monuments but lots of lush green grass. The open spaces were alongside a wall and it was a peaceful, pretty sort of place with climbing plants working their tendrils into the old stone. We sat on the ground and I pressed my fingers into the damp green grass as I thought about my parents, my mother's trauma, and eventual happiness when she found a good man who loved her despite bearing a child by her own father. I had had a sister, which was a great surprise to me, but clearly she had never quickened with full life after her birth. For a few minutes I sorrowed for her and her beginning and end. Finally, I thought of William, cut down as so many were before he reached maturity. Gradually, my sorrow at the loss of my family dimmed and I allowed the relief to flood through me, I wanted to be happy and a mother with a child or children who would be brothers or sisters to little Beth. I could marry Wilf in all honesty, and with no stain on my history. I was my parents' truly gotten child. I cried a few tears and Billy-alone patted my hand gently as he sniffed alongside me.

We went back to the inn and packed our belongings so we could leave at first light. I had a great deal to look forward to and both Billy and I could face our futures with our friends and new families. We had so much to look forward to.

Afterword

Three Round Towers is a work of fiction, however on occasion, I have peopled my tale with characters that already hold a notable place in history. Their story is the work of others but it would be remiss of me not to mention such people. One is Cater Rand, whose engineering works on the River Ouse made a material difference to workers, travellers, sailors – and smugglers. Another, John Ellman, created and developed the Southdown breed of sheep, which became the most successful breed of that time and for many years to come. His work would have been of particular interest to other farmers and stockmen of that time and later, just as it was to my fictional character, Farmer Elwood.

The use of currency, both coin and paper, is integral to my story and I have taken the liberty of bringing the common usage of paper money forward in time in the interest of a good tale.

Esther's story could be that of any bright young woman of that period. The intelligence and ambition to rise above the difficulties of time and place and carve a position for herself in a solidly male world where the poor and friendless suffered a hard existence with starvation, deprivation and rampant disease never far away make her unusual but not unique.

The three round towered churches at Lewes, (St Michael's) Southease, (St Peter's) and Piddinghoe, (St John's) speak to me of an older history before the Normans came and put their own stamp on the style of building. The ambience of each of them is, to me, palpable and I hope I have managed to convey that in my tale.

Old Hamsey Church, where my story begins is now largely unused (though I have been to a candlelit Christmas Carol service there) and it is wonderfully evocative and it was whilst sitting in amongst the gravestones on a beautiful sunny day that I felt the germ of my story take root.

St Anne's Church where Cecilia and Esther went to pray at the shrine would, at that time, have been outside the walls of the Lewes town and was known as a pilgrimage church. The anchoress who took up residence inside the church would probably have had a decent space to occupy and perhaps a small garden. Her remains were treated respectfully when alterations were made in that they were uncovered and reinterred within the main body of the church. All of the churches I have mentioned have their own points of interest and are worth visiting though I would suggest that to truly understand the character of these places of worship and social gathering a guide or parishioner who knows their stuff is worth seeking.

I would like to add a note of thanks to the Sussex Archaeological Society, owners and guardians of Michelham Priory whose little pamphlet *The Physic Garden* provided details of herbal usage – the pleasure of visits to the current herb garden was all mine.

Finally, I am not an historian and I would like to thank the many local writers and historians whose work I read and, in some cases, used to provide background knowledge. Their names and works are all listed at the end of this book and to whom I commend further reading.

Bibliography

Books

Brent, Colin, E., *Georgian Lewes, 1714-1830: The Heyday of a County Town*, Colin Brent Books, 1993.

Chapman, Brigid, *Southease Through the Centuries, AD 966-2009*, CGB Books, 2009.

Davey, L.S., Clark, K., *The Street Names of Lewes,* Pomegranate Press 2010.

Poole, Helen, *Lewes Past*, Phillimore & Co Ltd, 2000.

MacKenzie, Colin, *MacKenzie's Five Thousand Receipts in All the Useful and Domestic Arts*, James Kay, 1830.

The Jerusalem Bible, various editions.

Walker Horsfield, Thomas, *The History and Antiquities of Lewes and Its Vicinity, Sussex Press*, 1824.

Walker Horsfield, Thomas, *The History, Antiquities, and Topography of the County of Sussex*, Sussex Press, 1835.

Waugh, Mary, *Smuggling in Kent and Sussex, 1700-1840*, Countryside Books, 1985.

Booklets

Sussex Past Michelham Priory Sussex Archaeological Society.

The Physic Garden Michelham Priory Sussex Archaeological Society.

Various programmes for the Lewes Bonfire Societies

Borough Bonfire Society.

Cliff Bonfire Society.
Waterloo Bonfire Society.
South Street Bonfire Society.
Southover Bonfire Society.
Commercial Square Bonfire Society.
Nevill Juniors Bonfire Society.

Lightning Source UK Ltd.
Milton Keynes UK
UKHW011118250319
339732UK00001B/25/P